Jowls q
Meredith no
who spent a
out a better version of himself into the virtual world. His eyes were anxious and beseeching at her as though she should have a clear understanding of him and his life. Somehow, over the past hour and a half they'd been sitting next to each other—him playing video games and sharing his life story and her ignoring him the best she could—she had become his confessor and friend.

Meredith gave him what she hoped was an impartial-though-quasi-friendly smile. She reached for her purse and papers and rose from her chair. "Well. Nice talking with you."

The man was lost in his own train of thought and seemed only slightly aware that Meredith was leaving. He shook his head, morose.

"To make a long story short," he summed up, "I think my wife is trying to kill me."

Praise for Julie Howard

"It is a pleasure to read Julie Howard's clear, precise descriptions, natural dialogue and compelling story lines. Her characters are finely etched and well used. Julie is a wordsmith well worth reading."
~Frederick Foote, Author
"For the Sake of Soul" and "Crossroads Encounters"

"The cast of characters that populate Hay City are warm and inviting, but be careful. There's danger in the Idaho air that might just keep you up turning pages."
~Greta Boris, Amazon best selling author
"A Margin of Lust", book one of "The 7 Deadly Sins"

"This book grabs you from the start and you can't let go until the end. Add Julie Howard to your must-read list!"
~Sylissa Franklin, Author of the Sierra Scott mysteries

Crime Times Two
by

Julie Howard

Wild Crime, Book Two

This is a work of fiction. Names, characters, places, and incidents are either the product of the author's imagination or are used fictitiously, and any resemblance to actual persons living or dead, business establishments, events, or locales, is entirely coincidental.

Crime Times Two

COPYRIGHT © 2018 by Julie Howard

All rights reserved. No part of this book may be used or reproduced in any manner whatsoever without written permission of the author or The Wild Rose Press, Inc. except in the case of brief quotations embodied in critical articles or reviews.
Contact Information: info@thewildrosepress.com

Cover Art by *RJ Morris*

The Wild Rose Press, Inc.
PO Box 708
Adams Basin, NY 14410-0708
Visit us at www.thewildrosepress.com

Publishing History
First Mainstream Mystery Edition, 2018
Print ISBN 978-1-5092-2189-9
Digital ISBN 978-1-5092-2190-5

Wild Crime, Book Two
Published in the United States of America

Dedication

To all the wonderful people at my writing groups who inspire me to keep writing 'one hour at a time.'

Part One

The heart is a wild thing. It hunts and hungers all through one's life.

Don't ever take another's devotion for granted. As easily as love comes, it goes.

Sometimes it strikes out.

Chapter One

The computer screen blinked and faded to black. A half second later, the lights in the small library flickered off. Meredith Lowe stared at the dark screen and groaned. "Oh hell." She didn't have time for this.

The man sitting at the computer station next to hers gave a loud sigh. "Second time this week," he muttered. "Power company's doing some work on the road behind here; the men keep hitting the lines."

Meredith stared at the dark screen in the dim light coming through the lone front window. She hadn't saved her homework and it was due before midnight tonight. Only, she didn't have until midnight. Her five-year-old daughter, Jamie, needed to be picked up from kindergarten in a couple of hours, and there was no computer or Internet access at home. A couple of her Hay City friends offered to let her use their personal PCs which would save her the trip to the Twin Lakes library, but she'd relied on others too often in recent months. It was time she stood on her own two feet.

"How long until the lights come back on?"

She glanced at the man, but his head was now on his chest, eyes closed and breathing deeply. All that role-game playing must have tired him out, she thought.

Meredith peered around the small community library. Forty minutes from her home in Hay City, the place was situated in a decaying strip mall, sandwiched between a former gift shop—now boarded-up—and an insurance office. The place consisted of one reasonably sized room, with two walls of books, a corner dedicated to movies and three computers, and a solitary librarian who continued reading her book by flashlight. Aside from the napping man and the librarian, the only other patron was a sour-faced, middle-aged woman checking out the supply of romance paperbacks.

Twin Lakes, a small town within the vast area covering High County, was up a steep, winding road tucked in a notch of the Sawtooth Mountains and possessed the county's only library. The town also housed the region's only doctor's office, which was strange because the high mountain location with deep snows at least three months of the year made it accessible only by snowmobile during winter months. Anyone throughout the vast county unlucky enough to break a leg on a ski slope or from slipping on ice would have to drive much farther than Twin Lakes to find a doctor.

What is a chemical bond?

Meredith forced herself to think about the question she'd been answering on her homework before the screen went blank. She'd written the answer twice already, deleting the response once before getting the words right, then seeing the text pop into darkness when the power failed.

Here's a better question, she thought: Why is a twenty-four-year-old mother of two, living in the middle of nowhere, taking an online college chemistry course?

It's because I'm a mother of two, she answered herself. *I can't keep on like this, struggling to make a living. My kids deserve a better childhood than mine.* After a childhood filled with poverty and speckled with homelessness, she vowed she'd do anything to prevent her children from repeating that same life. At one point, she even considered murder...

She still didn't know what her ultimate goal would be with college, but her friend Honey advised her to start with a class or two while she was making up her mind. Idaho's state college offered online classes in nearly everything, so Meredith took a deep breath and enrolled in Chemistry 101. Even though she'd taken a part time job at the hardware store, her small pool of money ebbed away as each month passed. The money she'd tucked away in her savings account once seemed like a fortune. Unfortunately, the bills rolled in as reality came calling. The pay at the hardware store was only minimum wage, which took care of the utilities and a few groceries. If she didn't find other options for the future, she and her kids were going to starve. As it was now, they'd had to resort to meatless Mondays, Wednesdays, and Fridays to make the funds last.

The man next to her opened his eyes. He turned toward her, tilting his head to one side, and examined her with interest. "You sigh a lot."

She didn't turn her head. "You snore."

"My wife tells me the same thing," he admitted. "But tell me, if my snoring's so loud, why wouldn't the noise wake me up, too?"

She kept her gaze glued to her dark computer monitor, willing the machine back to life. If she didn't respond, maybe he would leave her alone.

"Still dead." His tone was glum.

The words seemed to spur a separate train of

thought; his gaze wandered to a corner of the room which he gave a blank stare. The words also flickered a memory in her mind. Her husband Brian. Her no-good, cheating, dead husband. Murdered by his girlfriend's grandfather. The situation still sounded too bizarre to be true and that was just the start. There was an illegitimate child too, tethering her and her own two to Brian's secret life. Someday, her kids would learn the truth about their father, and their half-brother. She hoped that day could be delayed as long as possible.

The months since Brian's death had been busy and staying in motion kept her from going crazy. For a time during the investigation, when she'd been the prime suspect, she operated one step below full-out panic. With the real murderer now in prison, she had a chance to focus on her children and their future. Atticus was a toddler, learning new words every day and busy getting into everything. Jamie started kindergarten and returned home filled with excitement about new songs, ideas and friends. Meredith spent hours in her garden, staking up tomatoes, plucking weeds, planting marigolds, and harvesting zucchini. Her skin was bronzed, the former peeked look to her face disappeared, and working in the sun intensified the golden highlights in her ash brown hair. Long evening walks down the path toward the mountains tightened her calf muscles and filled her with a feeling of serenity she'd never experienced before. Idaho had grown on her, in a way she hadn't expected when Brian moved them there in the spring.

It was Honey Stohler, the older woman who befriended her early on, who pushed her into taking a college class. Like a mother hen clucking around a wayward chick, the woman showed up at the house at unexpected moments with food, advice and a sympathetic ear. Two months earlier, she bustled in, carrying five jars of homemade applesauce and an online course catalog.

****

"Can't hurt to browse the classes that are offered," Honey had told her, tucking the jars away in a cupboard in Meredith's kitchen.

Nothing stopped Honey; her large, comfortable figure shouldered its way wherever she traveled. She popped in, often without notice, explaining that only strangers called before a visit. Soon after Meredith first moved to Hay City, the nosy woman's sharp eyes spotted the bruises on her shoulders and recognized the trouble she was in. Friendless and frightened at where her life was headed, she welcomed the friendship and they'd bonded over a common past with bad men.

The older woman was a pure force of nature. She tsk-tsked after she examined the inside of Meredith's cabinets, then got to work tidying and organizing. She rearranged cans of corn and beets, lining them up in an orderly fashion, then stacked ramen and dried pasta in a different cupboard altogether. Plastic cups disappeared into a lower cabinet where Jamie and Atticus could access them; the hodgepodge of water glasses and chipped coffee mugs were put next to the sink.

At first, Honey's forward manner took Meredith aback, but she now took the woman's non-stop interference and brassy demeanor in stride. In any case, the cupboards had needed a good tidying and if someone else wanted to do it, she didn't mind. The fact was a long time ago, this had been the other woman's house so …

At the time, Meredith pursed her lips at the idea of re-enrolling in college. It didn't work out well the first time. She'd met Brian, gotten pregnant, dropped out and headed down a rabbit hole that ended in betrayal, abuse, and murder.

"I don't have the money, a computer or Internet access," she protested. "Strikes one, two and three."

"Problem solved." Honey raised a hand, counting off solutions on each finger. "One, sell Brian's truck. That's money for the classes. Two and three, you can use the computer over at the county library where the Internet is free." A broad grin crossed her face. "I'd call that a home run."

Meredith thumbed through the catalog, still uncertain. "I wouldn't know where to start. I don't know what I want to do. Or be."

"Doing nothing always gets you nowhere," Honey answered in a brisk tone.

The multitude of classes and options in the thick catalog made Meredith's head swim. A world of opportunity jumped off the pages in front of her. She could ignore them or...

"Someone called wanting to buy the truck last week," she murmured out loud. "I just couldn't deal with it then and said I'd think about his offer."

"What's to think about? You're not keeping it, are you?"

Meredith shook her head. She wanted absolutely nothing to do with the truck. Brian was shot in the vehicle, after which it was taken away as evidence. For months, it sat in a police lot in Mountain Home, the next large town over, waiting for her to move it. Every couple of weeks, someone from the station would call and ask when she was picking it up. After a while, their sympathy for her situation reached its limit. In the last call, they warned if she didn't have it removed, they would auction it off at a fraction of its value.

The previous week, a man offered to buy it, saying he would deduct the cost of cleaning from his offer. He'd added it didn't bother him about what happened inside; but he also deducted a hefty sum from the price, considering a murder took place in the truck. He assured her few would make so generous an offer.

"It's settled then." Honey closed the cabinets one by one and picked up the phone. "What's this guy's number?"

****

The truck money bolstered her bank account considerably, giving her little reason not to take a class. Meredith had flipped back and forth through the thick catalog, chewing her lips raw, until she finally settled on Chemistry 101. The class fulfilled requirements for nearly every major and she always did reasonably well in high school science classes.

The next hurdle, of course, was the forty-minute drive three times a week to use the computers at the Twin Lakes library. Between getting Jamie to and from school, taking care of seventeen-month-old Atticus, and juggling a part-time job, she found herself breathless most of the time. Two months into the class, however, she was grateful that she'd been pushed into it. Staying busy kept her mind off the events of the previous year.

It didn't hurt that the trip up the long mountain road from Hay City was both breathtaking as well as calming, just what she needed at this point in her life. Views of towering peaks above and the green valley below flickered in her line of sight as she wound her way higher and higher up the mountain.

Meredith was disappointed but unfazed by the fact there were no lakes in Twin Lakes. In her short time in Idaho, she'd learned that nothing could be taken at face value. If her own town of Hay City had no hay and the town of Mountain Home wasn't in the mountains, why would anyone expect lakes to be in a place called Twin Lakes? There were several theories about why the founders thought the name was appropriate for a lake-less area, but there was no recorded history so no one knew for sure. She arrived at the conclusion town names in Idaho were picked based on wishful thinking, although she didn't know what this said about the people who'd named their towns Slickpoo, Dickshooter or Malady.

All of a sudden the overhead lights flickered, buzzed and then popped back on. The computers began the process of restarting and she squared her shoulders. She needed to bang out her homework and start back down the hill to get Jamie. She dragged her thoughts back to her homework.

What is a chemical bond?

She tried to recall what she'd written before. It'd been so perfect. Something about glue that holds atoms together. Or was it molecules? Or both?

A chemical bond is the glue that...

The man next to her shifted his chair a fraction closer and made no motion to leave. The odor of corn chips and perspiration drifted her way as he mumbled, "Guess I should head back home."

She ignored him, trying to stay focused.

...holds atoms and molecules together. This

bonding creates more complex...

"My wife's at work and I've been doing all the cooking lately," he complained. "She says she's tired of hamburgers and spaghetti, but what else is there to do with hamburger? I try to get creative, but she just complains, then complains some more until my head's about to explode."

Voices echoed from the counter; Meredith heard the romance fan talking to the librarian. "I keep mine in my backpack." She spoke with authority on the subject, with the confidence of someone who knew they were right about whatever they thought, said or did. "All the necessities of life. My book, my wallet…my gun."

Eyes wide, Meredith swiveled in her chair. Guns made her nervous. Only a few months earlier, she'd held one in her hands, pondering whether she could kill her husband. She'd been desperate to get out of the disintegrating marriage, one that surely would have led to murder—hers or his. The cold steel of the weapon in her hand made her realize she couldn't commit murder. But she'd considered it, hadn't she? Guns were all around her in this rural part of the state: hanging on racks in trucks, tied to the back of ATVs and now apparently, in backpacks, too.

The librarian, short and round with a head full of dark curls threaded with gray, emerged from behind the counter to talk to the romance reader. The librarian wore a holster, a detail Meredith somehow missed earlier. A gun was in her hands, being admired by the customer. Meredith realized she was holding her breath.

"Open carry state." The man beside her spoke matter-of-factly. "The second amendment ranks right up there for importance in these parts."

"She's wearing a holster." Her voice was tight, nervous. "Holding a gun. In the library."

"You only get one shot at returning your books on time." The man chuckled at his own joke. "And ever since her divorce, our librarian has a short fuse."

The romance reader glanced their way; her gaze settled for a long moment on the man next to her. The women's voices dropped to whispers; both turned to stare. Embarrassed to be caught watching, Meredith ducked her head. The man continued to eye the two women and seemed about to say something, but fell silent again, disappearing back into his own musings.

The librarian returned the gun to her holster and shuffled back around the counter. Meredith turned her attention to the computer screen. Knowing there was a gun-packing lady protecting this small town's cache of books was just one more unusual element among many in her life.

I have to focus, she thought. Chemistry.

The man went back to talking about his wife, vacillating between grievances and praising how hard she worked. "Burns the midnight oil, for sure," he continued. "I hardly see the woman anymore."

A heaviness filled her chest, anxiety building over the need to finish her homework quickly now. She leaned forward, her nose a foot away from the computer screen to concentrate. The conversation between the two women at the counter dropped to a murmur. The man's voice faded into the background as she continued on to another question and then another. Chemistry was mostly common sense when you came to think of it, she thought. You can't force attraction; there were internal forces at work, laws of nature ruling over everything.

Figure out the right combination and, voila, a complex relationship was born.

Her attention drifted to the county sheriff. Curtis, with his broad shoulders and easy smile, had been her champion in more ways than one. Her feelings toward him had run the gamut, from admiration to fear to attraction to…something solid and substantial that she couldn't define. There wasn't a week that elapsed that he didn't stop by for a visit and, bit by bit, they shared the narratives of their lives.

She opened up to him about her homeless childhood, alcoholic mother, and missing father. He told her about summers filled with fishing for steel head trout and his determination to be respected even though he was the youngest sheriff in the state. Meredith loved watching him talk, the way his eyes crinkled in humor and his earnest straightforwardness. To Curtis, the world was easy to navigate and people were intrinsically good. In less than a year he'd become an essential part of her life.

She wrenched her thoughts away from the sheriff. Why would he enter her head just then? Annoyed, she blinked and refocused on her chemistry homework. She answered the last question and breathed a sigh of relief.

At her side, the man continued to chatter, seemingly oblivious that she hadn't responded in a while. "…good woman, loves hiking nature trails, goes to church faithfully. Almost obsessive, if you ask me."

She logged off the computer, packed up her papers, and then turned to him, wondering if she should at least say goodbye. She didn't know him and tried to ignore him as well as she could, but it would be rude to leave without saying something. This was Idaho, after all.

Every interaction came with a choice: hostility or friendliness, with no middle ground. She didn't want to come across as hostile to this stranger, someone she might meet in the grocery store someday.

Jowls quivered under his weak chin. He wore the stained and frayed shirt of someone detached from reality who spent his time alone in dark rooms playing online games. His expression was anxious and beseeching as though she should have a clear understanding of him and his life. Somehow, over the past hour and a half they'd been sitting next to each other, him playing video games and sharing his life story and her ignoring him the best she could, she had become his confessor and friend.

Meredith gave him what she hoped was an impartial-though-quasi-friendly smile. She reached for her purse and papers and rose from her chair. "Well. Nice talking with you."

The man was lost in his own train of thought and seemed only slightly aware that she was leaving. He shook his head. "To make a long story short," he said, "I think my wife is trying to kill me."

Chapter Two

Legs weak, Meredith sank back into her chair. "Why would you think that?"

The memory of Brian's murder and the struggle to prove her innocence was still fresh and painful. Shock waves from the previous spring's events still rippled through her at times, catching her unawares.

He answered quickly. "I have no idea. I haven't done anything to her. I haven't done anything wrong, I mean."

She heard a saying about a chill going up one's spine, but it wasn't until now that she realized such a thing could really happen. It was more of a prickling sensation, uneasiness rousing her body to a heightened state, and nothing really to do with being cold at all. "No, I mean, why do you think she's trying to kill you? Has something happened? Has she done something specific?"

His eyes appeared almost haunted, frightened even. The man previously seemed more or less normal, maybe a bit chattier than usual, but she wondered if this was just one more strange country person. It seemed as though quirky people were drawn to remote locations, or maybe living in isolated areas drew out people's latent peculiarities. Perhaps he ran around, starting conversations with strangers by telling them his wife was trying to murder him. It was certainly an attention getter. She tried to recall all that he said about his wife while she did her chemistry homework. As far as she remembered, all he talked about was that she worked a lot, liked to walk in the woods, didn't care for his cooking and was religious. You don't kill someone because of spaghetti and prayers.

He gave her a knowing look and brushed back a lock of greasy hair dangling into his face. "I catch her staring at me sometimes, in a way that tells me everything. When you've been married as long as us, you can just about read the other person's mind. I know everything there is to know about this woman and I can tell you, she wants me gone. Dead."

Meredith felt bad for him. But wishing wasn't doing. She knew that well enough. Having a stranger tell her these things was disconcerting. The thought crossed her mind that this guy knew exactly who she was, and her history with a murdered spouse. Hadn't she wanted Brian dead? Hadn't he ended up murdered?

Anyway, the man never answered her question. *The* question. Had his wife attempted something specific? Meredith felt a sense of responsibility and resentment. After all, he behaved as though he were frightened. He'd mentioned the word murder. She couldn't just get up and leave, even if she was pressed for time. In a situation like this, you couldn't just say goodbye, nice talking with you, hope your wife doesn't want to kill you. After all, a person was required to ask a few follow-up questions.

She tried to keep her voice steady. "You said she's trying to kill you. What, exactly, has she done?"

He lifted his chin. She noted his salt-and-pepper hair, grown shaggy over his ears, and deep lines at the corners of his mouth. He exhibited the unhealthy, pallid complexion of someone who stayed inside all day and night. She wondered what kind of woman would be married to him, a middle-aged man who spent his time playing computer games. Wouldn't that lead to a few arguments, a little frustration on the part of a wife, a wish for something different? It was more likely divorce, not murder, that was in his wife's mind.

"She was supposed to fix the brakes on my car." His speech sounded breathy, urgent. "They're down to nothing. She drives to Blissful for work every day, so one day she takes my car, says she'll take it to our mechanic there for fixing. I asked her, 'Did it get fixed?' She says it's done; she had to stay late that day too, waiting on the car." He paused and gave her another one of his knowing looks.

"Okay," she responded, seeing that he wanted an acknowledgment. It seemed to her that he must have plenty of time to get his own car fixed but didn't mention this.

"The next day the brakes are still slipping on me, squeaking too," he said. "I took the car to a friend who knows about these things and he took a gander. Told me I got robbed. The brakes hadn't been touched."

"I'm sorry," Meredith interrupted. "How does this prove—"

"See, I know the mechanic in Blissful wouldn't cheat us," he said. "My family's known his family for years. I'm telling you, it's my wife. She never took the car in at all. She's hoping I'll go off the road next time I have to drive down the hill."

Red streaks cracked through the whites of his eyes. He really didn't appear healthy at all. She wondered if there was something wrong with him and whether she should suggest he see a doctor.

He stared at her intently, like he was waiting for her to say something. She didn't how to respond. He seemed to have a point, but it wasn't evidence of attempted murder. She would know, wouldn't she? There were other reasons why a person would lie about fixing a car. Perhaps the wife was busy with her job or forgot. It didn't warrant the paranoia this man was suffering.

"I'm not sure..." she started, but was interrupted by a burst of laughter from the two women at the counter. They leaned on the counter, heads close together, clearly settled in for a long afternoon chat. Meredith's eye caught the clock and she startled. "Oh," she said, rising quickly. "I have to get to my daughter's school. I can't be late."

"What should I do?" the man pleaded, his face turned up to her.

She shook her head. A nut job, she decided. There probably wasn't even a wife. Hostility was probably the best choice here. "I'm sorry. I can't help you."

She grabbed her things and dashed out of the library, passing by the counter without a glance. Her focus on the man and his problems were replaced with worries of Jamie waiting for her in front of the school. Her five-year-old could hold a grudge as neatly as a moody teenager. Meredith calculated that if she pushed the speed limit down the mountain just a bit, there was a chance she'd get there by the time the bell rang.

****

In the end, she arrived a full minute before the final bell and was able to meet Jamie at the classroom door.

"Hey, Mom." Her daughter struck a casual pose, hand on one hip and her head cocked to one side. Her face glowed with happiness and she seemed in no hurry to leave. "Want to meet my friends?"

School had been good for both of them, giving each a needed outlet. For Jamie, especially. Her daughter was too smart for her own good, and ready to absorb everything around her.

"This is Karin," Jamie said as a giggling girl ran up and wrapped her arms around Jamie. "She's my best friend."

"Hi, Karin," Meredith said, sparking another round of giggles.

"Come see my art," Jamie beckoned, releasing Karin and tugging at Meredith's hand. "My teacher said it's very good. Bye, Karin."

Karin ran off and immediately became absorbed into a circle of children milling near the bus stop. The shrill blare of a whistle sounded as teachers attempted to control the excited students. Inside the building, the kindergarten classroom was still and empty, with walls decorated with students' drawings. Meredith spent the next fifteen minutes wandering the room while her daughter chattered about her day. She gave Jamie her full attention and expressed enthusiastic appreciation for her five-year-old's crayon art of bunnies and chicks, colored a rainbow of green, red, and purple.

The elementary school in Blissful, despite its old buildings and weedy exterior, was cheerful enough on the inside. With fewer than a hundred students in the school, teachers knew the names of children in all grades. Supplies were often donated by former students, now grown and doing well in the world, who remembered the nurturing environment of their former school. Jamie called the principal a "princi-pess because she's beautiful and kind like a princess." Meredith was curious to meet the woman who so impressed her daughter but she hadn't yet seen the busy principal around the school.

She didn't remember her own kindergarten days. There was always a chance she'd never gone to kindergarten at all, what with her nomadic alcoholic mother and an absent father. She desperately wanted her children to have a stable life; one with a home, yard, and a tree swing. She'd fought hard to stay in this community and keep her house. It meant everything to her to give her children a home they would remember as they grew up. As difficult as it was to afford living in this isolated place, it was worth fighting for.

Someday her children would be able to answer the question, "What's your hometown?" Meredith didn't have an answer to that one, having relocated from place to place her entire life.

"We have to get Atticus now," she said gently, and Jamie skipped toward the door. Honey insisted on taking care of seventeen-month-old Atticus on the days Meredith traveled to Twin Lakes. She was grateful, although she still harbored doubts about her friendship with Honey. There were still unanswered questions there. Regardless, it was best to stay on the older woman's good side; being her friend was far better than being her enemy. One way or another, the woman was determined to have her own way.

"I'm hungry," Jamie announced. "Can we have cereal for dinner?"

This sounded like a great suggestion. Cereal was

her idea of the perfect meal. Nothing to prepare or cook. Just take it out of the cabinet and pour milk on top. It wasn't the most nutritious meal to serve two growing children, but after working part-time, driving to the library and back, then picking up and tending to both kids, the days mostly disappeared. Soon, it would be bath time with the long process of getting her children tucked into bed. Who could blame her for wanting something easy to serve for dinner?

Meredith smiled. "Sure. Cereal for dinner tonight."

****

Later, with the kids tucked into bed, she filled the small bathtub with hot water and sank gratefully and completely below the surface. She stayed under as long as she could, feeling the heat seep all the way to her bones, and then emerged gasping, hair dripping. She lay back in the water, her head propped on the rim of the tub, knees poking up from the surface, and let her thoughts drift.

She had lived in Hay City for almost nine months and in that short period of time her life had changed abruptly and completely. Brian swept them away from their life in Oakland—that noisy, crowded, busy, wonderful city—to this tiny place in the middle of nowhere. At first, Meredith hated it wholeheartedly. The house, the weather, the smallness of the town, and what she interpreted as the meanness of the people. The unfamiliar silence at night, its profound darkness, the wicked, forbidding peaks of the Sawtooths range looming over their valley. All of it, in every way, was foreign to her.

Sure, there was Curtis, the sheriff who'd become a friend, maybe even something more. There was also

Honey. But both relationships were... complicated. Crusty Connery, the jovial owner of the bar and hardware store where she worked, had been open and friendly from the very start.

The worst was how Brian's true nature came roaring out after they arrived. Emboldened by the isolation of Hay City, her husband's menacing behaviors became more loathsome every day. She wondered why she failed to recognize the abuse he'd doled out all through their marriage. It crept up slowly until one day she didn't recognize herself anymore: a spineless woman trapped in a malignant marriage. Realizing she'd never really known Brian, she began to hate him. Somehow, being in Hay City put her marriage into sharp focus, and she saw how ugly and dangerous it was. Fleeing wasn't an option; Brian let her know he'd never let her leave.

Meredith touched her throat as she recalled his hands circling her neck, his breath hot at her ear, when she threatened to take the kids and go. She'd been trapped, unable to leave and terrified to stay. It was only a matter of time before one of them ended up dead.

It was him that ended up murdered. Because I wasn't the only one he was mean to.

Her thoughts returned to the man in the library. That was a peculiar, unsettling conversation. He seemed honestly upset and afraid of what his wife might do. Who would confide such a thing to a stranger? He must be a local kook, she decided. There was every possibility he wasn't even married and, lost in a fantasy game of his own making, concocted the whole crazy story. She sincerely hoped she wouldn't run into him again on one of her days at the library.

With that, she let her mind relax and enjoy her few minutes free of responsibilities and problems. She turned the hot water on again and refreshed the tub, swirling her hand to make waves eddy around her. Eyes closed, the tension of the day melted away.

****

"I see you've taken on a bunny mama," Honey remarked.

Meredith regarded the rabbit hutch and smiled at the black and white lop-eared rabbit Jamie convinced her to purchase. The rabbit was cute and gentle, hopping up to the door of the hutch and nudging her hand whenever she came close. The trip out to the shed to feed the critter and clean the cage wasn't a bother, and Jamie was surprisingly responsible about giving it attention every day. The rabbit hopped after Jamie like a puppy, following her around the yard and scratching in the grass. Lately, the pet took on a roly-poly look and had its nose stuck in the food bowl most of the day.

"Jamie wanted a little girl bunny," she explained. "She named it Grendel."

Honey raised an eyebrow and looked sternly at the rabbit. "From the movie where kids kill kids?"

Meredith wrinkled her nose. "She hasn't seen the movie."

She walked over to stroke the rabbit's nose through the wire door of the cage. She was proud of the hutch, which she'd built herself, with odd pieces of lumber, chicken wire, and a little advice from Curtis. "I think a couple of her school friends have though," she added. "You'd be surprised what they talk about in kindergarten."

Honey sighed, her ample bosom rising and falling.

"I can only imagine." She frowned at the rabbit in disapproval, as though these things were its fault. "With my kids, the worry was someone would tell them the truth about Santa Claus. Today, they're talking about mass murder."

"Oh," Meredith exclaimed, snatching her fingers away from the hutch. "I hope not. Just movies."

"You've heard the saying 'monkey see, monkey do.' Kids are little sponges. They do and say whatever they're exposed to."

Meredith wondered if she should convince Jamie to change the rabbit's name to something less lethal. Her headstrong child was unlikely to be persuaded now she'd settled on a name her friends were talking about.

"Heard from our sheriff lately?"

Meredith fumbled the bag of rabbit food she'd picked up, then dropped to the ground. She felt foolish for being clumsy at the mention of Curtis. She grabbed the bag and filled the rabbit's dish. "He stops by from time to time. Why?"

"Oh, no reason," her friend said, an exaggerated innocent tone to her voice. "No reason at all."

"Honey," warned Meredith.

"Yes, dear?"

"We're just friends, okay?"

The woman rolled her eyes. "I know. I was just wondering how friendly things had gotten."

The thing was, Meredith wasn't exactly sure. She and Curtis had settled into a routine of sorts. He would visit, they'd have a cup of coffee, and then take the kids out for a walk. He taught Jamie the names of mountain peaks and warned her of the dangers from rattlesnakes and ticks. Sometimes, he performed minor chores around the house, showing Meredith how to replace the windshield wipers on the car or installing smoke alarms in the bedrooms. The last time he visited, he cleaned out a pellet stove in the corner of the living room, removed a dead bat that had dropped down the flue, and taught her how to prime and light the stove. They would chat about her class or his job or the kids. But...that was all. Every once in a while, she would catch him staring at her but he'd quickly glance away.

There was a spark between them from the first, but of course she'd been married at the time. After Brian was murdered, Curtis questioned her as his prime suspect. It was an awkward start to a relationship, to say the least. It was true she'd reflected about the appropriate time to wait after a spouse's murder...a spouse she feared. At one point, she told him she needed to learn to stand on her own two feet before starting anything new with another man. She was gun shy and worried about the effect a new relationship would have on her children. He respected those words, a fact that both frustrated her and made her care for him all the more. He was infuriatingly decent.

"Just friends," she repeated, trying to keep irritation out of her voice.

In recent weeks, with Jamie in school and Atticus settled in a new routine, she debated anew whether it was fair to force one more change upon them. She and Curtis were stuck in a holding pattern for now, and she wondered if he was just as tired as she was at waiting. Maybe, for him, the spark was fading.

Haven't I learned by now I can't have it all?

The two women turned back toward the house, walking slow and enjoying the mid-fall afternoon.

Evenings cooled as soon as the sun touched the western mountaintops, conveying a rapid chill to the nights, but the days were warm and still. Meredith wished she could hold her breath and keep the world from moving forward. Her life wasn't perfect, but she didn't need perfect. I could be happy in this place forever, she realized.

Honey stopped in the driveway next to her car and regarded the property. "You've done a lot here in a short time. The house looks better than it has in years."

Meredith basked in the compliment. She worked hard to fix up the run-down house. She'd not only painted inside, she also ripped out all the moldy carpet and scrubbed the old wood floors. New curtains, a vegetable garden and several new shingles on the rotting roof helped make the house appear lived in. There was so much more to do. Like new paint on the outside, replacing the peeling kitchen linoleum and re-caulking the windows. She tried to ignore a strange moldy smell emanating from inside the walls somewhere, but time and money limited the pace of repairs. She'd lived in worse places. At least they had a roof over their heads. Determined to give her children a stable home, she refused to behave like her mother: fleeing each place as soon as a challenge arose.

Honey opened her car door and paused. "That bunny mama. You know she's pregnant, right?"

Meredith felt a sinking sensation as Honey backed down the drive. Pregnant. She thought Grendel was just pleasingly plump, as pet rabbits should be. "Pregnant," she repeated, twisting her lips to one side. "Right."

What in the world was she going to do with a herd of rabbits?

Chapter Three

Rain pelting on the windows woke Meredith before the alarm sounded. When the sound finally registered, it gave her a twinge of anxiety about the coming winter weather. The brief warm summer lingered in her memory, with its long lazy days, nightfall not descending until nearly ten p.m.

Soon enough, snow would follow the rain, turning the hills white and blanketing her world into a polar freeze. Adjusting to the idea of layers of clothing, heavy blankets and cold noses was difficult. She didn't want to think about how she would manage driving Jamie to school and herself to work, as well as going somewhere to get her classwork done. All this in a beater of a car that she couldn't afford to replace on a minimum wage job that didn't cover the bills.

Rising from bed, she murmured her new mantra: "One day at a time. One day at a time."

The words calmed her and kept her functioning when she started to feel overwhelmed. She learned the technique from a book she found at the Twin Lakes library on coping with stress and grief. Those two words summed up her life: grief at losing a life she'd thought was real, grief at losing her marriage and husband, grief for her children growing up under the shadow Brian left, and stress over everything else.

"One day at a time," she chanted while dressing for

the day and making coffee. By the time Jamie and Atticus were up, she was ready for the day.

****

Driving up the mountain took long enough to shake loose the role of a mother with two young children and take on the persona of a college student. For a while, she was young and free, racing up the road to an exciting future. Jamie was at school and Atticus was at Honey's. One by one, troubles fell away as the narrow road climbed higher, twisting and turning toward the darkening sky.

The rain tailed off into an off-and-on drizzle, making the roads just slick enough that Meredith had to focus on driving to Twin Lakes rather than her problems or dreams. The winding road hugged the steep mountain as she drove its twining path and climbed higher, and higher still, seeing the terrain fill with emerald pines shooting straight up from the side of the mountain to the slate gray sky. Once, she braked hard and swerved when, coming around a curve, two deer appeared in the road. Her heart leaped as she missed hitting them, not quite knowing how. In the rear view mirror, she saw them trot into the underbrush, flashing their tails and white hindquarters, innocent of how close they'd all come to death.

Her mood was tense again when she arrived at the library, made worse by seeing a light frosting of snow on the ground. Of course, she thought, Twin Lake's elevation would get icy weather sooner than Hay City, which lay down in the long valley.

"Snow already?" she asked by way of conversation with the librarian when she strode in, stamping the wetness off her shoes.

"Huh." The woman shifted the graphic novel on her lap, vibrant color illustrations leaping off the page. "This is nothing. You lowlanders."

Meredith paused at the counter. She hadn't meant to really engage the librarian in conversation but being called a 'lowlander' seemed to be some kind of insult. She made herself smile at the woman in a cheerful manner and considered whether introductions were in order. "It was just an observation. This will be my first true winter out here."

"Well, buckle up, dearie," the librarian said with a mirthless chuckle. "Your little car out there isn't going to cut it on our roads much longer."

The car was visible from the narrow, front window. The vehicle was old and dented, with cracks spider-webbed across the windshield, and protested like a crotchety geezer when woken in the morning. The car wasn't likely to cut it on any roads at all soon. She couldn't risk sliding off the road. She didn't have medical or car insurance. The choice came down to insurance for the car or heat for her house; medical insurance or groceries. Which, she reminded herself, is why she was at the library: to be able to provide a layer of security for herself and her children. For now, they had a home, a car, food, and each other. It was a start.

"I'd better get to work then." She turned from the librarian, another person to list in High County's "hostile" column and headed to the computers.

One relieved glance told her no one else was at the bank of machines in the back. She settled in, determined to keep her mind on chemistry for the next hour and was able to fly through the online quiz without interruptions. She shuffled her notebook pages, proud to be a hard-working college student despite the challenges in her life. Her mother would be proud. There was only her homework left to type into the system, and she'd be done.

A figure appeared at her shoulder. "I was hoping you'd be here."

Heart sinking, Meredith swiveled on her chair. The man who'd bugged her before stood next to her. The man who talked non-stop about paranoid fears and whose wife might be trying to kill him.

She spoke quickly before he could say anything more. "I really can't talk today. I'm in a hurry."

"I don't have much time left either," he countered in a morose voice. "You're the only one I don't know in this town. Who doesn't know my wife, I mean. You're the only one I can talk to."

She shook her head at this backward reasoning. "You need to talk to the authorities…or one of your own friends." She wondered, as she spoke, whether he had any friends. His slovenly appearance would turn off even the most loyal of buddies.

"No, no, they all know her too well," he protested. "They'd never believe it of her."

In Meredith's mind, that was a character endorsement of sorts for his wife, if indeed she existed. From his description, she was religious, worked hard at a stable job, had friends who believed in her, including whatever local authorities there must be in Twin Lakes.

He scooted up a chair next to her and leaned in close. "There's just the sheriff. You know him."

She sat back. How did everyone know who she was and think they knew everything about her? Wasn't there any sense of privacy in these parts? She put her hands up, warding him off, and shook her head again. "I just come here to get my work done. Please. This is very important to me."

He prattled on as though she hadn't said anything at all. "Something changed. I don't know what, but I feel like I'm losing my wife. I've probably lost her already."

She considered getting up and leaving. There simply wasn't the time to be this guy's confessor. Her homework was due, though, and she'd already driven a long way to get to this library. One way or another, she needed to finish before she left.

She tried to sound firm but heard the hesitation in her voice. "I really have to get my work done."

He leaned in even closer and spoke in a hushed tone, breathing out the fumes of a tuna sandwich breakfast. "You were married."

The remark cut deep. People who knew she'd been married had to also know Brian was murdered. They'd been newcomers in a place where nothing much changed from year to year. Married and murdered; those were the two things people knew about Brian. The two things were intertwined with her name too, one and the same.

"I was," she admitted faintly.

He plowed ahead, barely hearing her. "You know what this is like, to love someone."

She sat unmoving. She didn't know about *this* kind of love, the kind where you were desperate about losing the other person, about wanting them to be there with you forever. Would this kind of love ever come into her life, she wondered. The thought made her sad. She was twenty-four, with two children and lived in the middle of nowhere; when would she have time or the opportunity to meet anyone again?

Curtis, a voice whispered in her mind. She tried to shut the door on this thought, but it shouldered in. He didn't signify in her life. They were just friends and, anyway, it was too soon. Way too soon. Brian had been murdered just seven months ago. Even though their marriage soured long before, her emotions were still raw. It was still possible to mourn a husband who hurt her, who was unkind and denigrating. Her heart was wounded in so many ways.

Still. She liked him. She got flutters in her stomach every time he was near, but who knew if he'd be interested when her heart was ready. He could be married with kids of his own by then.

The man took advantage of her silence and forged ahead with his story. "We've known each other since the fourth grade. Dated since junior high, engaged right out of high school. We'll be twenty years married next spring. We're going to Hawaii to celebrate. I'm planning on going deep-sea fishing for swordfish. Brooke wants to go to a luau."

Meredith nodded absently. Would he ever stop? She glanced over at the counter to the gun-packing librarian. Was it possible to ask for help? Perhaps the man could be redirected to tell the librarian his story. Or maybe the librarian already heard his concerns. She turned to her computer and started typing in her homework as quickly as she could.

Undeterred, he continued relating his childhood sweetheart story, now gone sour. "She'll never divorce me," he asserted. "We dealt with some troubles a couple of years ago. There was someone else…but…the church doesn't approve of…that kind of behavior."

She couldn't help turning to him at the remark. "I don't think churches approve of *murder* either."

He held up a shaking finger. "Here's the thing. There's confession. She can be absolved if she confesses a mortal sin. But she can't confess to divorce. The Pope is the only one who can undo a marriage. In the church, it's better to murder than to divorce."

She nearly choked. She didn't know much about religion but she was pretty confident on this point. "I doubt that very much. No priest would stand for your reasoning."

She saved her work on the computer, logged off and stood. She'd had enough of this conversation. The man was nuts. Her homework would have to be finished somewhere else. Meredith grabbed her purse and papers. "I'm not your confessor, either. Please stop telling me your personal problems. I have plenty of my own to deal with."

****

She wasn't a rude person.

The pines flashed by as she raced back down the mountain, taking the curves expertly now. If she made it to Curtis' office soon enough, she'd be able to use his computer and finish her homework before she needed to pick up Jamie and Atticus.

She hated to ask him to use his work computer, wasn't sure using government equipment was even appropriate or legal. But there were few options available, and Curtis was likely to say yes.

I'm not a rude person, she thought again. She hadn't wanted to hurt the man's feelings. His pleading affected her more than she wanted to admit. His tale of a wife who could be considering murder sounded too much like her own story. In fact, this *was* her story.

The light snow from earlier had melted off and afternoon sun beat against the windshield. Meredith felt warm and safe in the sanctuary of her car. She still couldn't get used to the idea of being safe, having a home and car, not worrying about Brian and his temper. Hay City was remote from the world at large, a haven from the troubles of big cities. She tried to push away the fear this new evolving life of hers would evaporate at any moment. The man in the library made her feel that way, with his talk of marriage and murder. The ramblings reminded her of way-too-recent tribulations. Whether or not his wife wanted to kill him was his problem. His wife probably *did* want to murder him. Didn't most wives think about it at least once? But telling him this probably wouldn't be helpful.

Ugh. Stop this! I have enough worries of my own without thinking about the problems of strangers.

Next time, she would buy earplugs. Then he couldn't interrupt her. He couldn't hijack her library time, homework time, and serenity with his insistence she counsel him. She wouldn't let another man push her around.

****

"You're leaving?"

Curtis dropped his keys, startled at her abrupt greeting. She noticed with dismay he was in the process of locking the door to Hay City's only official city building. Tall, sandy-haired and solid-looking with an easy grin that melted her heart, he was the youngest sheriff in the history of Hay City. He wore a silver star on a chamois vest like something out of an old western movie, and she knew he took great pride in his role. As sheriff, he shared the small office with the city clerk and the mayor, a rancher who held most of his office hours in Crusty Connery's bar.

He grimaced and picked up the keys. "Accident down at milepost thirty-seven. A semi jack-knifed. No one hurt, fortunately."

Meredith bit her lip, wondering if she should leave. The options for computers with Internet were limited though in Hay City. If she didn't turn her homework in on time, she'd flunk the assignment.

He peered at her. "Anything wrong? I need to get down there, but if anything's wrong…"

"No, nothing," she said, and right away chastised herself for being a coward. Of course, she needed something. She gestured with her schoolwork and took a step toward him. "Well, one thing, I guess. If it's okay, I was hoping to use your office computer, to send my homework in. I only have about an hour left to get the work done, before I need to get Jamie from school."

He hesitated, glancing at his truck and then down the road. "Don't you go to the library in Twin Lakes?"

She certainly didn't want to get into the details and waste any more time. "I did, but… It's a long story. If you're leaving, I'll just figure something else out."

He took the office key off its ring and held it out. "Let's just say I'm deputizing you for the next few hours." A corner of his mouth twitched up. "The city clerk is out again today. It'd be helpful to have someone in the office."

She paused only a second and then reached for the key, her fingers brushing his. Meredith glanced down at the key, wondering if Curtis felt the same electric jolt she did at their touch. "Oh. If you're sure. I don't want to mess this class up. This means a lot to me."

He edged sideways toward his truck, stumbling slightly. She recalled his nickname of "Barney," named after a bumbling sheriff's deputy on an old TV show. It was a bit endearing, but he hated the nickname. "Barney" smacked of disrespect for him and his position in the community as an authority figure, he explained once.

He spoke in a rush now as he got into the truck. "I know your class is important. That's why I'm doing this, even though it's probably breaking a dozen rules. The computer password's under the keyboard. If I'm not back by the time you leave, just put the key under the mat."

She watched him. She couldn't help admiring how well his blue jeans fit his chiseled physique, his wide shoulders and the light stubble he left on his face. This man couldn't be more different than the man she'd married nearly six years ago. Hay City's sheriff was easygoing, humble, and open where Brian, when not outright angry, ranged from secretive to irritable. Disappointed that Curtis was leaving to take a call, she realized she'd been hoping he would remain in the office while she completed her homework.

Afterward, she'd imagined they would chat a bit, maybe have a quick cup of coffee together before she needed to race to Blissful to pick up Jamie from school. She could even tell him about the man at the library and his crazy talk about a wife who wanted to kill him. Curtis would know how to handle the situation and might even go up the mountain and talk with the fellow.

He rolled down his window and leaned his head out. "You sure everything's okay?"

Nodding, she tried to hide her disappointment. She needed to keep her focus on what was important. Right now, her priorities were school, figuring out how to pay expenses, and giving her kids a stable home. There wasn't room in her life for anything, or anyone, else. Not the problems of a stranger from the library and not ideas about an uncertain romance with the man in front of her now.

Curtis backed the truck out, his head still partially out the window. "Up for a hike this weekend?"

Her heart flip-flopped, disappointment evaporated. A person couldn't be expected to do nothing but work, could they? She smiled her answer at him and his truck raced off, siren flashing on top of the roof, down the road to milepost thirty-seven.

Chapter Four

"I don't think so."

Jamie stood with hands on hips, feet planted firmly on the floor. It was Saturday and Meredith rose early, awakened by the rooster crowing in the shed. A long ago gift from Honey, Jamie's pet chick, 'Laf' now sprouted long tail feathers and refused to shirk his daily duty of greeting the dawn as loudly as possible. She spent the morning on a cleaning binge, scrubbing floors and counters, doing laundry, and changing linens. She pawed through Atticus and Jamie's clothes drawers and closets, putting items they'd outgrown in a heaping pile. By the time she was done, there was more in the pile than in their closets. Her children grew so fast and none of the previous year's winter clothes would fit.

"Yes," she insisted. "You two need new clothes. We need to go shopping."

Jamie shook her head, dark curls bouncing in all directions. "I don't think so," she said again, her tone firm and final. This was her daughter's latest phrase. It seemed as though everything Meredith said, Jamie responded with, "I don't think so." Her daughter spoke in such a decisive way, she had to remind herself the words emanated from the mouth of a five-year-old.

"I suppose I could just sew new clothes out of blankets off your bed." She affected an unconcerned expression. "Then, everything would match."

Jamie studied her, clearly trying to decide if her mother was serious. "You can't sew."

"I know." She heaved an exaggerated sigh. "Your clothes won't be too fashionable, but they'll be warm, I suppose. You can tell your friend Karin all about it. What do you say, Atticus?"

Her son peered up, then back down at the toys he and Jamie played with, marching them across the room and then back again in a doll and car parade. Jamie taught Atticus to line them up in different combinations: first by height, then color, then by their favorites. Meredith enjoyed listening to Jamie patiently teach her younger brother how to sort and organize their toys. While Jamie held little patience for the world, she contained an endless supply for her brother.

"No!" he answered, displaying the newest word in his growing vocabulary. "No!"

"I have an idea. You go to the store," Jamie offered. "Me and Atticus'll go to Honey's house."

She shook her head. She'd imposed too much on the woman already. "I need you two with me, to make sure the clothes fit. Anyway, don't you want to pick out your own clothes?"

"No," muttered Atticus, and she picked him up, laughing.

"Do you even know what you're saying?" she asked him.

"No," he said, giving her a grave stare. "No."

Though outnumbered, she was the adult, and this little fact made her the boss. The trick, however, was to get two unwilling children to the store and through a shopping trip without having a mental breakdown. She settled for the oldest strategy in the book. Bribery.

"Greasy grimy fast food burgers for dinner. If you're good."

Jamie's eyes brightened at the offer. "I want a chocolate shake." Her defiant pose softened, her hands dropping from her hips. "And fries."

Meredith pretended to consider this before making a show of agreeing to her daughter's terms. She held out her hand and they shook on the deal.

****

As anyone with a five-year-old would know, bargains break down quickly. By the time they returned from Mountain Home, the sun low in the sky, all three were simmering with anger and resentment. Still, Meredith was determined and a pile of sweaters and pants, socks and shoes filled the backseat of the car. She sincerely hoped she purchased enough for her kids to last through the long Idaho winter.

Even though she was conscious of every penny spent, it was a relief to know there'd been enough money in the bank to adequately clothe her children. Food, shelter, clothes. She'd known little enough of all three in her life. It was one more thing to be thankful to Hay City for—there was nowhere else they could live where money would stretch this far.

She let her kids play in the bath until the bubbles melted away and the water turned tepid. She sat on the floor next to the tub, holding her book about meditation on her lap, and breathed in the warm steam filling the room.

As she toweled off Jamie and Atticus and helped them into pajamas, she pointed out their wrinkled fingers and toes, making them laugh.

"Why don't my knees wrinkle too?" Jamie asked.

"I guess maybe they would if you stayed in the tub any longer," she said, wondering if she'd been as inquisitive a child.

Jamie threw her arms around Meredith's neck. "I love you, Mommy. Thank you for the burger and shake."

Meredith almost gasped in surprised delight. Her daughter was either storm or sunshine, each powerful enough to rock her back on her heels. "I love you too, sweetie." She hugged Jamie tight in her arms and then drew Atticus into the hug as well. "And you're welcome."

"I love you," she whispered later to each of them as she tucked them into bed, leaning over to kiss their foreheads.

There was nothing more exhausting than having children, she thought. But having them also gave her the strength to keep going when she got discouraged, to keep pursuing her dream of a college degree and to better all of their lives. As difficult as her life had been so far, she wouldn't change places with anyone.

*****

"There's this thing called mail order," Curtis said. "Ever hear of Amazon?"

Meredith shot him a dark look. She had just related her misadventures the day before in shopping with her kids. "Yeah," she quipped. "Powerful women who dominate their men."

He threw back his head and laughed. They were walking along a wide trail winding up into the foothills above the valley. He stopped by in the morning, suggesting a trail up the mountain and the three of them tied on shoes, still somewhat nursing grudges against one another from the difficult day before.

The ground was damp but far from muddy, drying quickly as the sun rose higher in the sky. From the trail, there was a view of the valley below and lush green mountains rising far on the other side. Above, snow already coated the topmost peaks. Down below, farm equipment was parked for the winter, fields were harvested and empty, and there was the small cluster of structures marking Hay City. Not long ago, she would have said the rural scene was a view of nothing; her perspective was one of a city person craving the bustle of roads, buildings, and people. Now, her mindset was changed. There was so much to take in; she could stare out at this vista forever and never truly see it all.

Curtis picked up a rock and hurled the stone far into the ravine next to the trail. "Mail order would save you a lot of grief. And time. Mail order's how a lot of people out here shop. We're just too far out to keep going into a city."

She turned away from the view and continued up the trail. "It makes sense, but I don't want to buy things using the library computer. I've heard that's not safe."

He nodded his agreement and they walked on for another minute. She didn't offer that she didn't have a credit card, and doubted she'd be approved for one. Money in her savings account dwindled more quickly than expected. A property tax bill had just arrived, swallowing a significant portion of her account and leaving her in tears. At this rate, she'd be in a serious financial crisis by spring. Money only stretched so far, no matter where you lived. She couldn't tell him any of this though. Pity wasn't an emotion she wanted to spark.

Jamie and Atticus trailed behind them, stopping and examining rocks, leaves, bugs and a hundred other things in their path. A hawk circled high above searching for its next meal.

Curtis spoke a few moments later, avoiding her gaze. "You could use my computer, at my house. To shop online. For classes too, if you want. I mean, if you trust the local sheriff."

She glanced over at him, but he was busy studying a pine tree. It was just a run-of-the-mill pine tree and she had the feeling he didn't want to look at her just then. She'd never been inside his house, although he'd been in her house several times during the investigation of Brian's murder and numerous times since then.

His house was tiny: one bedroom, a living room and kitchen all compactly fit on a sizable plot of land, an acre or more, adjacent to his parents' property. He'd told her he designed and built the structure himself, laboring alongside his father during the evenings and on weekends.

Somehow, because of this, being invited into the house seemed more intimate, an invitation to advance things further between the two of them. His parents lived within waving distance. What would they think about her showing up twice a week, disappearing behind the front door for an hour or more? What would Curtis think? Or am I making too much of this, she wondered. Maybe it was just a simple *friendly* offer.

She fought to keep her tone noncommittal. "Maybe I'll give that a try. It's nice of you."

Keeping things at "just friends" was more effort than she expected. She found herself torn between her attraction toward him and wariness about falling too quickly into another relationship. Her marriage to Brian was dreadful; she'd wished with all her heart he would disappear, right up to the moment he was murdered. Since then, she'd been assailed by a range of emotions from grief to regret to fury. More often now, she experienced an overwhelming sense of relief, a sentiment leaving her feeling guilty and ashamed.

Surely, rushing into another relationship so soon could only be disastrous for both of them. After all, what kind of man would want to get involved with a woman who wished her husband gone? What kind of woman fantasizes about murdering her husband?

Maybe this kind sheriff is just being a friend, she cautioned herself. Maybe he has his own issues to battle. Once, he'd mentioned a previous girlfriend, one who eventually married someone else. There was no question he was attracted to her, but it was also possible he wasn't over the earlier love. They'd been dancing carefully around each other for months, each worried about getting too close.

One day at a time, she breathed. Take life one day at a time.

Her book on meditation talked a lot about "living in the moment" so she forced those anxieties away. She inhaled deeply and decided autumn was her favorite time of year in Idaho. While the pines maintained a deep forest green, the underbrush sprang alive to the cooler evening temperatures. Their leaves changed to various brilliant shades of flame, orange and gold almost overnight. The occasional aspen could be seen in the hills with white branches amid their brilliant yellow coats, contrasting sharply with the lodgepole, larch and ponderosa pines. The afternoon sun lit up the aspens and gave them a golden glow as their leaves trembled and shimmered in the slightest breeze.

"I can't get over how beautiful it is out here." Meredith sighed. "I had no idea there was so much…so much…space in the world. All these trees and mountains. Idaho seems to go on forever."

Curtis chuckled. "I wasn't sure you liked it so much, way out here in the wild west." He glanced sideways at her. "This is probably much quieter than what you're used to. I wasn't sure you'd stay."

"I wasn't sure either," she admitted.

So often, after Brian first relocated them to Hay City, she felt desperate to leave. Home had been a big city in California and the city held everything familiar to her. Traffic, the sounds of people and activity everywhere, the comforting buzz and clatter of neighbors just on the other side of an apartment wall. It'd taken a while to warm up to Idaho. These days, it was the city that seemed so distant and strange.

He bent down and picked up another rock, casting it farther up the trail. It bounced and tumbled along the path. "Are you feeling more sure now?"

His question hung there for a moment, and she wondered if there was more behind his query.

"I have a house and friends here," she said warmly. "There's been a lack of both in my life and I don't want to lose them now. My kids seem happy, despite everything."

He clearly wanted her to say more. She stopped and faced him. Blood rushed to her face. "Thank you. For everything you've done for us. For me."

His gaze burned into her, his voice low. "Meredith. I don't need thanks. I'm here for you and—"

Jamie's shout startled them. "Mom! Look!"

Her daughter jumped up and down and pointed to where a herd of elk stepped into a clearing across a wide ravine. Fourteen of the stately creatures bowed their necks to the tall yellowed grass in the foothills, occasionally lifting their heads to listen and watch their surroundings for danger.

Meredith was stunned at the sight and surprised at the awe the large animals inspired. "They're beautiful."

The corners of Curtis's eyes crinkled upward. "The snow up higher gets them moving around. You'll see some in the valley now. This time of year, the animals start moving about; predators too, so keep an eye on your rabbit and chicken."

The mention of predators made her recall a recent suggestion of Honey's, that she get a firearm to protect her property. It made her realize she was in charge of the lives of two young children, a rooster and a pregnant rabbit. "What kind of predators?"

"Fox, coyote; mountain lions. There was a wolf sighting this time last year. When the game gets bigger, the predators get bigger. Black bear sometimes."

She was a city girl, unused to wild things roaming the world. It wasn't as though California didn't have bears, coyotes, and mountain lions, but those creatures stayed clear of side-walked streets and Laundromats. The word "predator" in the city usually referred to the human kind. Jamie softly counted aloud the elk on the mountainside over and over. Sometimes she counted twelve, sometimes fourteen. She edged closer. "Where do they sleep at night?"

"They live outside," Curtis explained in a gentle voice. "They know how to find their own shelter." He pointed farther up the trail. "Let's keep going and see what else is moving around today."

The day had grown crisp and clouds gathered above, blocking the afternoon sun. Jamie and Atticus were having a wonderful time, and Meredith didn't want the day to end, even as she rubbed the chill from her arms. They strolled at an easy pace up the trail, letting Jamie hunt for more elk while Atticus did his best to keep up with his energetic sister.

There was a chiming sound, and Curtis patted his pockets for his phone. He walked a few steps away and spoke in a low voice into the handset.

Jamie was peering into a bush. "Mom! I want to pick huckleberries."

Meredith nodded absently, her gaze straying to Curtis, watching as he talked into his phone with a frown on his face. At times, he seemed even younger than her and awkward. He'd earned the moniker of a bumbling "Barney" when he first started the job, but he was smarter than that. Although they were near the same age, he seemed so much older than her, competent and at ease in the adult world while she still sometimes felt like a child pretending to be a grown up. *Is there a moment when I'll finally feel like a real adult?*

Her thoughts flashed to the man in the library. A sheriff would know how to handle someone like him. It probably made sense to say something to a local law enforcement officer, especially if he was a good friend. He'd bailed her out of plenty of other messes, maybe too many. At what point would he believe she was incapable of handling her own life?

Curtis tucked his phone back into his pocket and she prepared to tell him about the stranger in the library. She'd make it a funny story so he didn't think she was a helpless female. The bottom line was she had no idea what to do.

He strode back toward them, his long legs covering the distance in just a few strides. "We have to go back," he said. "I'm sorry. Work."

She hid her disappointment, but knew he was always on call as the county's only law enforcement officer. "An accident?" she asked. There were fewer than two thousand people in the rural county and his work typically involved domestic arguments, fights at Crusty's bar or car crashes.

Vehicle smashups happened frequently on the remote roads, drivers falling asleep as boredom on the long empty stretch between rural towns overtook them. She knew Curtis suffered queasiness at seeing bodies, a normal reaction for most people, but a serious drawback for a sheriff.

He shook his head. "Not really a case for me." Wrinkles appeared between his eyebrows. "But they need me to take a look. I'm the chief deputy coroner when the coroner's on vacation."

She peered at him, curious. Having a job like his would be interesting, with something different always happening. As sheriff, you'd always be the first to hear what was happening and be among the first on the scene of the action. Chief deputy coroner though…someone would be dead, a body he'd have to view.

He was plucking berries out of Jamie's hand. "Not those. We leave those for the bears."

Alarmed, Meredith asked, "Are those poisonous? Jamie, did you eat any?"

Curtis broke in to calm her fear. "They would give you an upset stomach. Unpleasant, nothing more. But I have to get back. Right away."

They reversed direction and Curtis swung Atticus up on his shoulders so they could stride along more quickly. Jamie skipped ahead. "What happened?" Meredith asked.

"It's a strange one," he said, shaking his head. "Up in Twin Lakes, at the Catholic Church. Apparently, a guy walked in to confession this morning and just fell over dead. They're thinking a heart attack. But you never know, so they need me there to check it out and file a report. Just routine."

Her breath went shallow part way through his answer. Twin Lakes. Dead. In church. One and one and one added up to a conversation she'd had very recently. Intuition told her who'd fallen over dead in the confessional.

Chapter Five

"Can I go with you?"

The words popped out of her mouth before she realized she even wanted to go with him.

They were headed back to her house when she spoke and Curtis turned to her sharply. "To Twin Lakes?" he asked, with a quick glance to the truck's back seat where Jamie and Atticus were buckled in. He lowered his voice. "Why would you want to go up there? It's a death."

The truck bumped over the deeply rutted logging road they had taken to the mountain trail. The dirt route was graded once a year by the forest service whose rangers would drag a leveler across the ruts, but heavy logging vehicles sunk divots back into the road before summer was out. Recent rains softened the soil, settling the earth further into practiced wavy patterns.

Meredith licked her lips, debating what to say. "I know."

Her first thought upon hearing someone died in a Twin Lakes church was of the man she'd met in the library. It was ridiculous, she knew, to think it could be him. It would be a terrific coincidence the one death she'd heard of would be of this one particular, peculiar man. But Twin Lakes was barely a small village. How many people could die each year up there? There had to be some reason they'd need a coroner to take a look. If the dead person was the paranoid and unhinged man in the library, the sheriff needed to hear what he'd told her about his wife plotting his murder. If it weren't, of course, *she* would sound paranoid and unhinged. She would be the creepy one, interested in dead people.

"I could use more homework time in the library," she finished in a weak voice. "My car's having a tough time driving up and back so much."

Guilt flooded her at the outright lie. More homework time was always valuable, but her interest was in learning about the death, not chemistry. If only she'd told him about the man sooner; his death would be partially her fault for not speaking up. *I ignored his fears just like Brian dismissed me all during our marriage.* Her mind spun and for a moment, she was launched back to a year earlier when she was powerless and under Brian's thumb. She closed her eyes and trembled. Just when she was enjoying a sense of awakening and strength, the past came roaring back.

Curtis had been about to say something to her on the trail, before Jamie interrupted to point out the herd of elk. Now she was glad he was interrupted. *I'm not ready to be more than friends. I'm damaged goods.*

He was staring straight ahead at the road in front of him, apparently lost in his own worries. "It was the coroner who called; the one you met when Brian…died."

They bounced heavily once and then were on the smooth main road again, tires clicking noisily from pebbles stuck in the treads until they spun free. She recalled the short man with graying hair who showed her Brian's body so she could identify him.

"He's headed to Texas with his wife this afternoon

to visit their daughter for a month," he continued. "I'm chief deputy coroner when he's gone. Means I give the scene a once over and confirm a natural death. There's a doctor in Twin Lakes, though, so my part in this is pretty routine."

She nodded; he'd already told her this, but there was a tinge of anxiety in his tone. She wasn't the only one disconcerted by the death. "What if it's, you know, messy?" She could have bit her tongue as soon as the words were out.

Curtis took this in stride, having once before confessed his difficulty with unpleasant deaths. This was a failing he couldn't hide, having fainted in her driveway the day he told her Brian was murdered, a messy death with two shots to the head.

"It's a heart attack. The doctor up in Twin Lakes believes that's all. But I've been asked to go up. Just a report to file."

"I'd give the sheriff one of my bunnies," Jamie piped up from the back seat. "If he wanted one."

They traded glances. The tension in the truck eased somewhat. "That's very generous of you," he said. "I'm honored."

Meredith's heartbeat stabilized at the kindness in his tone. "I could go along for moral support, ride up with you. I need to go to the library anyway," she said again.

He swallowed, considering. "I suppose driving up together wouldn't hurt." He still sounded doubtful, but she knew he'd let her go. "But we don't have to talk about it, after everything you've been through…"

She didn't wait for him to say more. She twisted around to face Jamie and Atticus. "How about a visit with Honey?" she asked. "For a few hours."

****

Honey had no problem with the unannounced visitors. She produced a coloring book and crayons for Jamie and a blanket and pillow so Atticus could nap. "You two take your time, don't worry about the kids," she chirped as though they were a couple heading out to watch a movie instead of to investigate a death. "They'll be just fine here and I can give them dinner if you're late."

The woman shooed them out the door, practically shutting it on their faces.

"I think she likes my kids more than she likes me," Meredith said when they got back in the truck.

"She likes the company. It can get hard out here if you don't have family around."

Meredith hadn't considered this. If I didn't have my kids, I wouldn't stay here for a second, she thought. Hay City had grown on her but options for a social life were limited. Even if she wasn't hoping to remarry someday, there were no coffee shops, restaurants or even churches, if she was so inclined, in Hay City. No book clubs or nightclubs. No parks, shopping centers, museums or even a flea market. Just a bar and the hardware store where she worked part time. There was a small grocery store where the sullen, snarky deli boy lurked, tossing barbs at her every chance he got.

She'd met a disturbed man at the Twin Lakes library and now was on her way to see if he'd been murdered. No wonder people in far-flung areas hang out in bars, she thought. For companionship and to chase away the shadows in their own minds. If Honey wanted to babysit her children for companionship, it was a win-win situation.

****

More snow had fallen in the mountains and midway up, the road took on the appearance of a pearly strip. They chatted about neutral subjects on the way: remodeling plans for Jamie's school, a noise complaint about a neighbor snoring, Atticus cutting another tooth, a black bear sighting in the valley. Meredith tried to put the man in the library out of her mind as she soaked in the scenery through the window. The white granite rocks splintered and crumbled down the mountainside and pines were sprinkled with snow.

"May have us an early winter this year," Curtis pronounced as they rounded another corner and the road steepened in the final miles to Twin Lakes. "If it keeps up, the road'll be closed by Thanksgiving."

She considered the remoteness of her own home, in an unknown town, in a rural state, and couldn't imagine living even further removed in a place with no escape at all. "How do they get groceries? Or anything?"

He shrugged. "Most residents in these mountain areas stockpile their pantry and freezer; you learn how to cope. A lot of people have snowmobiles. Really, most people who stay up here enjoy the solitude of winter. Deep snow keeps outsiders out."

She glanced at him. This style of life didn't faze him. To her, living in Hay City was remote enough. She couldn't imagine being home bound for months in these high mountains with the unpleasant librarian as her only friend and a possible murderer living down the street. "If they don't want outsiders, why do they have the county's only public library way up here?"

"It was a pet project of a former mayor," he

explained. "Twin Lakes won the funding. The mayor's wife is the librarian. Or I should say, the former mayor's former wife. After they got divorced, he moved away."

She thought about the gun-packing librarian who read thick books behind the counter. What could her husband have been like? Was he the reason she carried a gun on her hip? Stop it, she ordered herself. You're seeing murder around every corner, in every mind.

She sought a change of subject. "How did you become chief deputy coroner along with county sheriff? That's pretty impressive, isn't it?"

He shrugged, but she noted his pleased expression. "Just the way it works; coroner's often a dual position in these areas. There aren't enough cases to warrant somebody doing it full time. Our coroner doesn't mind it being a part time gig. When he's away, he can deputize someone; typically, it's me."

"Did you go to some type of coroner school for it? To learn what to look for and what to do?"

He quickly disillusioned her, going on to explain: "That's not how the system works. It depends on where you live. In Idaho, coroner is an elected office. In theory, no experience is necessary, just public confidence. Usually, people do the right thing and a medical professional or someone skilled in investigations is elected. He or she can deputize someone they believe is capable. The process works in reverse here too; when I'm gone, I deputize the coroner as sheriff."

"Huh." She gave a small laugh. "No experience required. I could run for coroner then. And be the back-up sheriff, too."

Curtis didn't comment or laugh along with her. She shifted in her seat, aware she'd said the wrong thing. Recently elected as the youngest sheriff in the state at age twenty-seven, he was still proving himself. She could relate to needing to prove oneself; she'd been doing this her entire life.

"Your silver star," she said quickly to change the subject once more. "It's nice. Traditional."

Curtis touched one hand to his chest where the star was pinned. Whenever he was on duty, the star was there, gleaming and glinting as though he spent evenings polishing the old-fashioned badge. "This was my grandfather's," he explained. "He was sheriff out here for thirty-five years and was my best friend until he died. He taught me how to fly fish, ride a horse and build a campfire, and he made the best barbecue you've ever eaten. People out here respected and trusted him to do the right thing. I wanted to be him when I grew up. I still do, I suppose."

Meredith considered the star differently. It was a badge of honor, and a promise of sorts, to live up to his grandfather's memory. "When did he die?"

"Two years ago," he said briefly. "That's when I decided to run for election. I think most people believed they were electing him again when they voted for me."

They drove in silence for a few minutes before she returned to the reason they were heading to Twin Lakes. "This case, though...the doctor said a heart attack," she prompted. "A coroner needs to be there too? What if you disagree?"

He stared straight ahead at the road. "A coroner comes in when a death isn't clear-cut, just to look things over and make sure nothing appears suspicious, whether an autopsy is required. Apparently, there's some conflict of interest in this death. Just standard procedure."

As Meredith mulled this over, the pines thinned. The truck's tires crunched through the milky crust as they rounded the final corner. The church's white steeple rose above the frosted pines, smoke drifting from chimneys, and already a tiny snowman stood guard in front of one house. Twin Lakes made an idyllic scene, one begging to be miniaturized and put inside a snow globe. Not a scene for murder, at all.

****

He dropped her at the library, then headed to the end of the block where the Catholic Church loomed. The library was closed, not all too unexpected for a Sunday, and its interior was dark and still. Meredith stood at the glass front door staring at her reflection for a moment, knowing this is what she'd really had in mind: an excuse to shadow Curtis. Her mirror image peered back at her, a slim young woman with large eyes and worry lines on her forehead. The woman in the reflection appeared too young to have two children at home, to have gone through all the challenges she'd already faced in life. She rubbed at the lines, smoothing them flat, and then headed down the block to the church. Curtis was just stepping out of his truck in the church's parking lot.

"Hey!" she called out and then jogged toward him. "Library's closed today," she panted when she was a couple of yards away. She stopped before him, her lungs laboring to draw in the thin mountain air.

He regarded her, biting his lip. "I guess you could wait in the truck."

"I don't mind..." she started. "I don't mind what's inside. I can take notes for you if you'd like, while you check it out."

He shook his head firmly. "The scene's bound to be unpleasant. Anyway, you're not official. Your being there wouldn't look good."

"I've seen bodies before," she said. "I can handle the situation. I promise."

She'd seen her mother, and her husband, dead. Her mother died slowly at first, one drink at a time, with her body wasting away to nearly nothing. The end was terrible and fast; her mother suffered hallucinations about a man chasing her and refused to come out from under the bed. By the time paramedics arrived, she was convulsing. She died three days later in the hospital.

Then there was Brian, murdered in the spring, with two bullets in his brain, laying cold in the coroner's office. So, no, there would be nothing to fear in seeing a stranger's body, an empty shell devoid of life. She'd never been superstitious about death. In any case, she was determined to know who died in the church. The man in the library never introduced himself so she didn't know his name; the only way she'd know if the dead man was the same person was to go in the church and see for herself.

Curtis handed her his notebook with a shake of his head. "Stay back a bit. If you need to leave, don't worry about it."

Clutching the notebook, she followed him up the steps and into the church.

Father Michael, the church's only other priest, met them as they entered. "It's the first time in eighty-four years our church hasn't held Mass on Sunday," he explained dolefully. "Father Karl, the elder priest, is holding Mass over at the grange hall down the block."

"We're not here for Mass," Meredith piped up, drawing a sharp nudge from Curtis.

"This way," the priest said, and led them farther into the church.

The church was hushed, echo-y quiet as only a church can be, and filled with the scent of burning candles and incense. As they approached the booth, she spotted a man's leg sticking out from the bottom of the enclosure, the rest of the body still hidden inside.

Father Michael gave his report of the morning's events. "I don't know what happened," his tone monotone and indicating he was repeating his story yet again. "I was inside early, waiting. Today was a slow morning. Some Sundays are just slower than others. Either everyone in town wants to confess or no one does. This was one of those slow mornings."

Itching to ask questions, and peek inside the confessional to get her own look, Meredith scribbled notes from her place a few steps to one side.

"I took advantage of the quiet to pray," the priest continued. "I heard a bump as the door opened on the other side of the booth. There's a screen that opens between the two sides, but he never opened the screen. I just heard him coughing and then choking, and then…"

The priest paused, then gestured toward the floor. The three of them stood there, silently staring at the man's leg, as though paying respect for his untimely passing. She felt terrible for the dead man, whoever he was, left for hours waiting for the county sheriff-deputy coroner to make his routine report. A pungent odor emanated from the confessional booth, a smell unlike incense and candles.

"Did he say anything?" Curtis asked the priest. "Last words?"

"Nothing." Father Michael pressed his lips together and shifted on his feet. "Of course, even if he'd said something, it would have been in the confines of confession, privileged, inviolable. I told all this to the doctor. We've waited a long time for you to get here."

The priest glanced at her and then gave the slow-arriving sheriff a disapproving stare. She sensed they'd been judged and found wanting. Today was Sunday and neither of them were wearing church clothes. She studied the priest, thinking she saw something change in his demeanor. Defiant, she thought. And anxious.

She glanced up at Curtis, wondering if he was nervous about approaching the dead man. "We had to drive up from Hay City," she broke in, trying to sound official. "The sheriff got here as soon as he could. He's chief deputy coroner, you know; he has to sign off on the death certificate."

The priest frowned at her, as though he knew more about her than she knew herself. She glanced away from him and to statues of saints, the large crucifix behind the altar and rows of pews. Guilt washed over her even though church was never a part of her upbringing. She was suddenly glad she didn't belong to a religion requiring confession. Where would she begin? Where would she stop? *I could go on for days.*

"Who are you?" Father Michael's tone sounded as if he wasn't prepared to believe anything she would have to say.

"Just a helper," she answered, guilt intensifying. This wasn't technically a lie. She was helping, after all, even if she had somewhat ulterior motives for doing so.

"She's my assistant," Curtis said at the same time, then gestured toward the confessional. "I guess I should take a look now."

He paused, took a deep breath, and squared his shoulders as though preparing for battle. "I'll talk and you take notes," he murmured, a slight tremor in his voice. "Let me know if you need to leave, if it's too much for you."

She followed close behind as he stepped closer to the booth. Without touching the body, he peeked inside the half-opened door and started his observations. "The body is inside the confessional except for one leg," he intoned, his voice cracking. "It appears he was already inside when he collapsed. There are no marks on the body. The man is mid- to late-thirty's, maybe older, Caucasian…"

"Excuse me," the priest interrupted, exasperation in his tone. "I know this man. Jacob Burns. He lives around the corner. And the doctor already knows this. Why don't you just talk to her?"

Meredith had been waiting all this time, wanting to see the man's face, to see if she recognized him. The name meant nothing to her since the man in the library never introduced himself. She needed to see him to know for sure. If it was the same person, Curtis would be impressed by her insider knowledge.

"This is just procedure in deaths like this." Curtis glanced over at the priest and then returned his gaze to the crumpled body. "I need to make my own observations and make my own report."

Father Michael made an impatient sound. Meredith watched him from the corner of her eye. She didn't have much experience with churches and especially not the Catholic Church. Priests, with their black garb and white cutout collars, made her think of chanting and vows of silence, although it didn't make sense someone taking a vow of silence would chant so she wasn't quite sure about that. She did know priests took a vow of chastity and for some reason that made her uncomfortable in his presence. She wondered why such a normal looking man would enter the priesthood, and then immediately chided herself for stereotyping. People of all sorts would get callings for religious service: tall, short, handsome, homely.

"...puddle of vomit on the floor," Curtis was saying, his head back inside the booth. She hurried to write his comments down, worrying she missed something important while she'd focused on the priest. "No wounds on the body."

He backed out of the confessional and wiped a hand across his mouth. His face was pale; she hoped he wouldn't faint. He took a deep breath. "I guess I'll go talk to the doctor now. Compare notes. We'll get someone to remove the body."

Father Michael nodded and gestured toward the church doors, as if inviting them to leave.

Meredith peered over at the confessional, trying to see inside at the man's face. She crept closer, feeling ghoulish but needing to know. The man she'd met in the library was so certain he was going to be killed by his church-going wife. Then, here was a man, about the same age, coincidentally dead in a church.

"Probably a heart attack," the priest was saying. "The doctor said so several hours ago."

She turned toward the priest. "Wouldn't you need

an autopsy?" she asked. "To confirm a heart attack?"

His Adam's apple twitched beneath his collar. She sympathized; he'd have had a terrible shock, with a man dying right in front of him. "That's up to the doctor," Father Michael said. "She would know, as a medical professional. I'll pray for the family."

Curtis cleared his throat. "I'm done here. We'll get him out of your, uh, box soon enough. I'll talk to the doctor about this...this unfortunate event."

As Father Michael took a step toward the entrance, she saw her opportunity slipping away. "Curtis," she whispered. "Flip him over."

He looked horrified at the suggestion. "What?"

"Flip him over," she hissed. "So you can see the rest of him. For your report."

Father Michael took another step toward the entrance. "I don't know if that's necessary," he said. "The doctor will examine the body in more detail later."

Curtis focused back on the booth and his shoulders slumped. She sensed he didn't want to touch a dead body and felt sorry for him. On impulse, she stepped in front of him, grabbed the man's leg and tugged, hauling him out of the confessional. The two men stood frozen, as though in shock.

"Meredith, stop!" Curtis protested. "What are you doing?"

"Assisting your investigation," she grunted as she dragged the body out of the confessional. After heaving the body over, it flopped face up on the wood floor. A sour stench of vomit rose up. While sheriff and priest winced at the smell, Meredith's focus remained on the man's features cruelly twisted to one side.

"It's you," she said. "I knew it would be you."

Chapter Six

"Tell me again," Curtis queried, his tone puzzled. How did you know this man?"

They stood outside the office of Doctor Rose, the county's only physician, who had gone to the late afternoon Mass at the grange hall. From the front stoop, they watched the quiet village come alive as churchgoers filled the streets on their walk home.

The peaceful tableau was very nearly a timeless scene, with villagers living close enough to forgo using a vehicle. Even the older residents walked, assisted by family members or fellow parishioners.

While they waited, she related how she met Jacob Burns, about how he rambled on about his marriage and his certainty his wife was going to kill him. "I didn't believe him," she said. "I just thought he was this weird Idaho guy, so I never said anything about it. But see what happened. I should have told you."

"'Weird Idaho guy'," he muttered. "Okay, you didn't say anything to me. How could you have known this would happen? He must have been very sick."

"No," she protested. "That's not what I'm trying to tell you. He predicted his own death, his own *murder*."

"You." The accusation came from the street. The librarian glared at her.

Meredith stood still, stunned at the venom in the woman's voice. Had she kept a book past its due date?

Other church-goers glanced at them curiously and hurried past.

"Hiding in corners with him," the librarian spat. "A married man. See what comes from deception?"

Another woman hurried up and touched the librarian on her arm. "Leona, go on home. Today's been an upsetting day for all of us."

Leona the librarian shot Meredith a distasteful scowl before stomping off through the thin snow. The other woman strode up, shook their hands in a firm grip. "I'm Doctor Rose. Glad you made it. The whole town is topsy-turvy this morning over Jacob Burns' death. Father Karl forgot the words to his sermon twice and, well, you saw how upset Leona is. Come inside."

They followed the woman into her office where she waved them into seats before a broad desk. Doctor Rose settled behind the desk and folded her hands together. The room was stark, the desk free of clutter. A diagram of a human body hung on one wall, skin stripped off so bones, organs and veins could be visualized. Behind the desk hung three framed diplomas, with type too small and ornate for Meredith to decipher. Her gaze settled on the woman before her: mid-forties perhaps, wavy black hair shaped in a severe bob that accentuated an unfortunately long nose. There was a clunk under the desk, indicating the doctor had kicked off her shoes. "I guess you've seen the body?"

Curtis nodded with a grimace. "Father Michael showed us everything."

Dr. Rose eyed Meredith but spoke to Curtis. "You have a deputy, too?"

"Meredith is assisting today, taking notes," he explained, his cheeks coloring.

"Ah, the deputized coroner has a deputy," the doctor said with a laugh, and quickly continued in a serious tone. "Jacob Burns wasn't well. In fact, I'd seen him a few times recently. High blood pressure. High cholesterol. I told him just last week he needed to change his lifestyle right away. I'm not a magician, just a doctor. He didn't want to take responsibility for his own health. I see this all the time. 'Give me a pill,' they say. Then they can hold onto their bad habits."

Taken aback at the doctor's lack of empathy, Meredith protested. "His death wasn't his fault."

Again, Dr. Rose frowned at Meredith; again she spoke to Curtis. "Is she a doctor as well as the deputy coroner's assistant?"

"I'm not a doctor, but I met Jacob a couple of times," Meredith said. "He told me…"

The doctor interrupted her. "You met him a couple of times? I've been his family doctor for nearly ten years." Dr. Rose continued to direct her attention to Curtis. "Is there a problem here?"

He held both hands up in a gesture of peace-making. "There's no problem. Meredith just informed me of some disturbing information about the victim and some claims he made recently. In view of what's occurred, we need to talk about it."

Dr. Rose sat back in her chair and tapped her fingers on the desk in front of her. It was clear her pride was injured. "In the past, I've been deputy coroner for the deaths up here, since I'm a *medical* professional. The only reason you were called in this time is because of the location, in the church. And, I suppose, my brother."

Meredith was puzzled at the comment. What would

the doctor's brother have to do with anything?

"Your brother?" Curtis asked.

The doctor gave a small, mirthless laugh. "My brother, the father. Father Michael is my brother. He returned here after he was ordained. I guess my brother is now my father. Anyway, it's best you confirm the death certificate, considering the relationship. We don't want the perception of anything done wrong, do we?"

"He didn't die of a heart attack," Meredith broke in, annoyed at the doctor's pushy attitude. "Jacob told me his wife wanted to kill him."

Doctor Rose blew out an exasperated breath. For the first time, she spoke directly to Meredith, glaring at her as she did. "Do you know how upsetting an autopsy is to a family? I take my job and my role in this community very seriously. Jacob was under my medical supervision and he was unwell. In my medical opinion, this is a clear case of myocardial infarction, provoked by a documented lipid disorder, chronic hypertension and ongoing stress." Meredith's head swam at the doctor's continued recitation of medical terms. "The signs of an MI include vomiting and wheezing, both of which were evident at his death. Other symptoms are self-reported, which obviously can't occur if the victim dies suddenly."

The doctor turned to Curtis. "My understanding of state law is no autopsy is required in this instance. I won't even comment on the tasteless accusations against his wife. Jacob was known for saying a lot of strange things."

"We've all had a tough day here," he started, speaking slowly. "There are some personal connections here, too, which means we need to proceed carefully. It seems I was called in so there's no perception these personal connections taint the record. We all have the same goal: do the right thing. So, let's start there."

Meredith was impressed how he took control of the conversation. She wished people who called him "Barney" could hear him stand up to this bossy doctor. Something akin to pride surged through her. "I think we need to consider a limited autopsy to examine his heart," he continued. "A limited autopsy would focus on the heart alone and not be as invasive. I'm sure the family would want this confirmed for their own peace of mind. Could we agree on this, Doctor?"

Doctor Rose's face turned stony, but she gave a brief nod before standing. "I'll arrange for a *limited* autopsy and have the report sent over to you."

Once the decision was made, their departure from the doctor's office was swift. Within minutes they were back in the truck. "He was so certain the wife wanted him dead," she said. "I didn't believe him, no matter how many times he said it. I didn't listen to him. I didn't say anything other than tell him to leave me alone because I had enough problems of my own."

The truck rumbled past the library, past the "Welcome to Twin Lakes" sign, and out of town. "What could you have done?" he asked.

She glanced up and, with a jolt, noticed they weren't in Twin Lakes anymore. "Wait. What about the wife? You need to ask her some questions. Hear her story, her alibi."

He raised one eyebrow. "His wife's just had a terrible shock and now Doctor Rose is going to tell her there's going to be an autopsy. We need to wait for the doctor's report. Give Jacob's wife a bit of time with family for now."

"But if she killed him, she's not in shock at all. You need to talk to her, right away, before she covers everything up."

Curtis pulled to the side of the road and turned off the engine. He rubbed one hand at the back of his neck and twisted in his seat to face her. "I hear what you're saying, I promise. There's just a process I have to follow. I can't just barge in with allegations of murder without any proof. We don't even know a crime's been committed. Just think if it's not true."

She knew exactly how that felt—being accused of a murder you didn't commit—but bit her lip from saying so.

"This wasn't a gunshot, something clear cut," he added, as though he knew what she was thinking. "This man had some kind of medical episode; the doctor's certain it's a heart attack. We'll see if the autopsy confirms this diagnosis. If not, we continue to the next step. But I didn't see anything on the body or in the church pointing to anything suspicious."

She couldn't argue with this, but he could at least talk to the wife. He could size her up, judge for himself whether the woman wanted to kill her husband. A small voice inside warned her she was being unreasonable, but she couldn't stop tears from springing to her eyes. The man's accusations echoed now he was dead. The situation was Brian's murder all over again, with another unhappy wife and a murdered husband.

Brian. She'd done her best to put him in the past, but he wouldn't stay there. She would carry a share of guilt for his murder the rest of her life, even if she hadn't squeezed the trigger. She'd considered killing him herself, after all, to escape her marriage. It was as though she'd wished his slaying into reality. Now another man was dead.

Curtis laid a hand on her shoulder. "I shouldn't have let you come with me today. What was I thinking?"

Meredith gazed out the passenger window and breathed deeply, willing her tears away. She'd made it this far without breaking down. The forest was all around them, the trees packed tight together, branches intertwined with branches, creating an impassible thicket. A squirrel perched on a nearby limb stared down at her. The critter twitched its tail and chattered at the truck. "I'm okay," she said, even as a tear slipped down one cheek.

His hand shifted from her shoulder and a moment later he pressed a tissue in her hand. She wiped her eyes and blew her nose. "You were good back there," she said softly. "In the doctor's office. I was proud of you."

The truck rumbled to life. He cleared his throat. "Let's get you home."

****

Jacob's not Brian, she told herself later. Two dead husbands, two unhappy wives. Those are the only similarities. Just because one was murdered didn't mean the other one was as well. What was it called, when terrible events from the past came alive in the present? Post-traumatic stress.

One day at a time, she breathed, eyes closed.

She needed to get Jacob and Brian out of her mind, so that evening she turned to the topic of rabbits.

Jamie hooted at the news. "Babies? Grendel's going to have baby rabbits?"

Meredith nodded, her mouth twisting to one side. What was great news to Jamie was worrying news to her. The hutch was big enough for one tubby rabbit, but wouldn't hold six to ten rabbits.

She tried to explain to Jamie plans for getting rid of the coming bunnies. "Crusty's going to let you sell the babies at the hardware store and you can keep the money." This was the best way out of an emergency situation.

Jamie's tone was indignant and she anchored her hands on her tiny hips. "I don't think so. I'm not selling Grendel's babies. I'm keeping them."

She shook her head. "No way, kiddo. This isn't a rabbit farm. Anyway, we can't keep them warm during winter. They would die in the shed."

Jamie's mouth rounded in horror. Tears glistened in her eyes and Meredith knew she wasn't handling the situation well as a mother. "What about Grendel? Is she going to die out there?"

The fact was, she had no idea how an adult rabbit would survive an Idaho winter in their shed. This was a question for Honey, who raised chickens in her large barn. "Big rabbits have lots of fur…" she started in a soothing voice.

A wail from Atticus interrupted her and she turned from Jamie to her son to see his hand stuck in a narrow jar. She spent the next ten minutes trying to get his chubby hand out of the too-small opening, wondering how it had gotten there in the first place, and finally rubbing hand cream along his arm and slipping it out. He sobbed and whimpered through it all and then five minutes afterward was chortling happily and working puzzles with Jamie.

Every once in a while, Jamie would flash a glare Meredith's way, letting her know giving away the baby bunnies was not an option. She slumped back on the couch, emotionally exhausted, as her kids played. Baby rabbits were the least of her worries.

****

Her car chugged to life the next morning, coughing once or twice as though in protest, and then growled to a start with its usual puff of angry exhaust. Jamie coughed along with the car each day, mimicking the vehicle's rough start-up and then cheering when the engine turned over. Meredith laughed at this routine, but it was a weak laugh, knowing one day the car would continue to cough and chug sickly without starting.

Their first stop was to meet the school bus just outside the grocery store, where Jamie hopped aboard three times a week, riding with two other kindergartners, three second-graders and a fourth-grader from Hay City. From there, she headed to the hardware store with Atticus to work her four-hour shift. The store owner, Crusty Connery, with a mountain man beard and surfer-dude ponytail, was easy-going about Atticus being with her at work. Now at eighteen months, her toddler was walking everywhere and there was nowhere less childproof than a hardware store. Somehow, from some remote and magical corner of the store, Crusty had produced a playpen for Atticus. When she was distracted with the rare customer, she was able to put Atticus there without worries he would be eating nails or opening lethal packages of ice melt.

There was relatively little for her to do since customers were few and far between. Because the hardware store doubled as the post office, with Crusty serving as the county postmaster, Meredith sometimes oversaw the mail delivery, distributing letters and bills in mailboxes customers kept at the store. Even when she took the time to peruse the return addresses and speculate what was inside each envelope, the chore took less than fifteen minutes.

Her first day at work, she'd tried to rearrange items into a more logical assortment, putting men's socks near hats and wind chimes near gardening items, but her boss had been horrified.

"Those ceramic snails have been there for years, and I know exactly where they are," he protested, his bushy eyebrows twitching from side to side.

She pointed at the stack of tires, none matching each other, rising to the ceiling. "They've been here for years because no one can see them behind those car tires. Now there's a chance someone will buy them."

Crusty stamped a foot, one of his giant size fourteen feet, causing years' old dust to rise from under the wooden floorboards. "If someone wants to buy one of my snails, they have to really want one," he explained, his voice rising. "They have to ask for one. They can't just walk in, see one and decide on that particular moment they want it."

She stared at him. The man's reasoning made no sense. "That's how people buy things all the time." Even as she said these words, she was left feeling she was in the wrong, but not knowing why. "Customers see something and then decide they want it. That's exactly how things are done, how stores make money."

"I've been doing just fine here the way things are."

He gave her a dissatisfied stare making Meredith think he was reconsidering hiring her. She needed this minimum-wage part-time job and so she promised to stack the ceramic snails back where she'd found them, tucked away behind the stack of tires, and also not to do any more rearranging of the store.

As far as she was concerned, hiding goods from customers was a terrible idea. Crusty couldn't net much from his hardware store, judging by the number of people coming in. During her first week of work, she counted five customers, with total sales of a little over two hundred dollars. After he paid her wages, plus all the other costs of her employment, he had to be losing money. She hoped he did better with his bar, which shared a wall with the hardware store.

The bar seemed busy enough, with customers filing in as soon as the doors opened each morning. Rumbles of laughter and the sound of clinking glasses seeped through the wall through the morning and afternoon, regardless of what time she was in the store. She figured perhaps since Crusty no longer had to deal with hardware store customers, he was able to sell more in the bar. Certainly, he was now free in the mornings to carry on his lusty affair with Honey, the details of which she tried not to listen to.

Since she was forbidden from rearranging the mish-mash of goods, and her boss frowned on much cleaning being done—explaining fingerprints in the dust let him know what customers had touched—there was plenty of time to study and take care of Atticus. Sometimes they even went for short walks behind the building, keeping an eye on the hardware store door for any arriving customers.

On the day after Jacob's death, Atticus was down for a nap in the portable pen while Meredith had her head buried in her book, trying to understand the concept of absolute zero. She'd slept uneasily, waking from dreams about Brian. In one, he was chasing her down a foggy street. She ran and ran, waking just as his raspy breath sounded at her shoulder. In another, he sat next to her, complaining matter-of-factly how his wife wanted to kill him.

She struggled to concentrate on the chemistry book in front of her. Absolute zero made no sense at all. To her, zero had always been absolute enough. Shouldn't zero always mean zero? What was the point of having a temperature scale where zero was just another number?

A quiet footfall broke her concentration. She glanced up and gasped.

A man, unshaven with a scruffy auburn beard, was at the counter eying her in an unpleasant manner. He wore blue jeans and an untucked blue plaid shirt. She recognized him instantly even though she hadn't seen him in months, and then only once. That time, he'd been on a snowmobile in front of her house with another man, both dressed in camouflage, shotguns strapped to their vehicles. He hadn't talked then, just glowered at her in an uncomfortable, searing manner. Brian was there then, and he'd sent her and Jamie into the house. With her out of hearing, she watched through a window as he spoke with this man and his friend in a way indicating they knew each other, although he denied it later.

"I didn't hear you come in." she stuttered, stumbling off her stool. "You surprised me."

Shoulders hunched, he said nothing, hands buried in the pockets of his jacket. The surly attitude was the same as before, except this time she was alone in facing him. She wondered if Crusty was busy on the other side of the wall and whether he could hear what was going on in the hardware store. "Can I help you?"

She took a slight step back toward the wall, thinking she could knock against it if needed. Hopefully, that would make Crusty come over to see what was going on.

The man took a deep breath, not taking his gaze off her. Meredith glanced over at Atticus, sleeping the deep sleep of babies and she knew the walls would have to come tumbling down before he would wake up.

Why didn't this guy say anything?

"Do you want something from me?" she challenged, standing tall as she could in her worn tennis shoes and tried to keep her breath even. Isn't that what you should do when confronted by a bear? Stand tall and make yourself appear big and challenging?

He shifted on his feet as though deciding something. She figured he was there to rob the store, an easy mark except it must be clear she recognized him. With the wall behind her, there was nowhere for her to go. He had her trapped. For the first time in her life, she wished she had a gun. Why, oh why didn't she have a gun? If she survived this situation, she was going to buy a gun or learn a martial art.

When he finally spoke, his voice was barely above a whisper. "You know about Gemma?"

Gemma.

The name hit her like a slap, making her knees buckle. This was the last thing she expected him to say. She thought he was going to rob her or...something.

She shook her head quickly, as a much a rejection of the name as it was an answer to his question.

He spoke a little louder. "You do. I know you do."

She shook her head again. "I don't know her."

"She knew your dead husband." His voice was bitter, sad, and angry, all at the same time. The tone indicated there was a history between this man and Gemma, perhaps with Brian. Her intuition that Brian had known the two men on snowmobiles was correct after all.

"I don't know anything about all that. Just…just…" She stopped. Why would she tell him anything? She didn't know him at all, not even his name. "I don't know you either," she finished firmly.

"Barker," he said. "Egan Barker. Gemma was my girl before she met your husband. Before he took her away. With his city talk and promises."

A headache settled right between her eyes. Now that she knew why he was there, her breath came easier. But she was the last person on earth who would keep track of Gemma. No wonder he gave Brian and her the stink-eye when they first met. He'd been jealous and angry. He must have been outraged they'd moved to Hay City, into Gemma's old family house. *What did Egan think of me that day, Brian's fool of a wife?*

"I'm sorry." She stopped, biting her lip, and wished she hadn't apologized. Nothing that happened was her fault, and certainly not because Brian had seduced this man's girlfriend. "I don't know where Gemma is, where she lives, anything about her. Maybe you should talk to her grandmother. Honey."

His shoulders slumped; his Adam's apple worked below his beard. He appeared far too young to be of interest to a girl with lofty aspirations like Gemma. At first, the beard made him appear much older and more gruff, but overgrown whiskers couldn't hide the boyish pain in his expression. The pain of losing his first love to an older, more sophisticated man. "I've tried. She doesn't like me much."

Meredith couldn't help but wonder about Gemma and Egan, what their past was and why Honey didn't like him. Had they been dating when Brian arrived in her life? Could Egan possibly be worse than Brian, an abusive, married man?

"I'm the last person Gemma would talk to," she said in a gentler tone, finding herself feeling a little sorry for him. Like her, he'd gotten shunted aside by someone else. "I can't help you."

He swiveled and strode toward the door, work boots thumping heavily. His wet shoe prints tracked across the floor and she wondered if Crusty would be upset if she at least mopped them up. Egan turned toward her just before he left. His mouth twitched downward and his eyes were narrowed. "I bet you know more than you let on," he snarled. "I've heard about you."

The door banged shut behind him and she glanced over at Atticus, who slept on and on. The tension from the encounter with Gemma's old boyfriend ebbed away. She took a deep breath, released it slowly and then repeated, intoning her mantra, "One day at a time" over and over.

A burst of laughter permeated through the wall and the world seemed steady again. Needing to move, she mopped up the muddy footprints, then paced through the aisles, giving herself the chore of learning the many and varied items carried in the hardware store. Cans of extra hot chili, bear spray, cast-iron pots, twin bed sheets, rain ponchos, pick axes, hand warmers, bird seed. All these items and more were stacked to the ceiling and three deep on the shelves. Every time she walked through, the store's aisles appeared to have changed and more items materialized. Sometimes she suspected her boss of slipping new items onto the shelves at night, packing more and more into the already overstuffed room. The activity and stroll around the aisles calmed her.

Atticus stood in the playpen, watching her when she returned to the front of the store. She held up a potty training seat she'd discovered on aisle three. "Hey kiddo. Guess what?"

She gave the encounter one more thought before she gave her son her full attention. Egan's relationship with Gemma would have been more than a year ago and he was still pursuing the girl. If he hadn't given up on Gemma yet, it was unlikely he would now. What did he mean when he said he'd heard about her? In Hay City, everyone was in everyone else's business.

Meredith had a feeling the surly young man was going to create a few more complications in her life.

Chapter Seven

No word about a murder filtered down from the mountain that day. Meredith was unsure how long an autopsy took and she hadn't thought to ask. Would it be a day or a week before results were known? She was certain Curtis would let her know one way or the other; he knew she was involved and waited to hear.

"I need a Halloween costume," Jamie announced when Meredith picked her up from school. "I'm going to be a lion."

Meredith's heart sank. Halloween. She'd totally forgotten about the holiday, but there it was, just two days away. When they were in California the previous year, they put an old shirt of Brian's on her, with one of his baseball caps, and pretended she was a man. They went door-to-door in their apartment building, where most people didn't answer their knock. Afterward she let Jamie keep just a couple of wrapped candies from their next-door neighbor. You never knew what strangers might drop in a child's bag.

She hoped they might skip things this year. "There's nowhere to trick or treat here. I'm not sure they celebrate that holiday in Idaho."

"They do," Jamie informed her in a serious tone. "I have to have my costume tomorrow for school. Mrs. Beebee...the princi-pess...says we're having a parade and a party. Karin's going to be an elephant."

This left only hours to figure out a costume. Something simple, she thought. Something she could whip up with existing materials at home. "How about being a ghost?"

She remembered the once or twice she had trick-or-treated wearing an old flowered sheet draped over her head. The basic costume was quick, cheap, and then could be recycled into dust rags afterward.

Jamie remained firm. "I'm going to be a lion. All the other moms are making costumes. You need to make mine."

Meredith's heart sank even lower. Making a lion costume was far beyond her skills. There was only one solution. As ever, its name was Honey.

****

Honey licked a thread before she squinted and poked the strand through the needle's eye. "It's so easy. Sew easy. Get it?" She tittered at her own joke.

"I'm grateful," Meredith said. "I'm the worst mom in the history of the known universe."

Her friend rolled her eyes. "We all think that at the time. You're doing the best you can. And your kids are doing great, too."

Honey threw the door open when they arrived, a wide smile on her face. Upon hearing their quandary, she immediately beckoned them down a hallway to her tidy guest room where a sewing machine sat, ready to go, on a desk. She rummaged in the closet, pulling out stacks of fabric scraps of all colors and sizes. They settled on a combination of light and dark yellows for the body, with dark yellow yarn for the tail and mane. Within minutes, the older woman put Jamie to work, giving her instructions on looping and cutting the yarn.

As Meredith watched the woman's efficient movements, she was again thankful for her friendship. Honey seemed to be a stand-alone fixture in the world. Over the past months, Meredith had learned about her abominable first marriage to Shorty Harris, the man who murdered Brian. Her granddaughter, Gemma, had an affair with Brian and now had a baby from the relationship. This was enough of a link for Meredith and her children to be quasi-adopted as part of her own family. There was nothing the woman wouldn't do for family and she'd latched on tight to Meredith and her children.

She knew little about Honey's children, except one was from her brief first marriage to Shorty. "Where are your kids?" she asked, realizing she didn't even know where her friend's five adult children lived.

"All over the place. One ran off to Australia. Two are on the East Coast somewhere, another in Florida. The closest one's in Utah but she doesn't come to visit much."

The tone was light, but her voice wavered slightly as she spoke. Her children had ended up settling far from Idaho. It was impossible to ask about grandchildren. One of them was Gemma, the young woman who returned to Hay City and met Brian, prompting a string of calamitous events and changing their lives forever.

"And you?" Honey asked. "How's the class and the *homework* going?"

Meredith glanced at Jamie, knowing 'homework' referred to Curtis. It was challenging to talk about him in front of Jamie and Atticus. The subject would lead to her worries about supplanting Brian as her children's father, her nervousness about not being ready for a new relationship, her guilt over Brian. These were topics she couldn't discuss in front of her kids.

She drew out the next word slowly. "Okay. Difficult subject matter."

"Hmmm. Sounds like you need to invest a little more time in the project. You don't want to see this opportunity slip by." The sewing machine hummed and stitched. At times, Honey wrapped fabric around Jamie, barking directions like a general on where to set pins.

The older woman chatted nonstop, clearly enjoying the project and the company. "How was Twin Lakes? You were a doll to ride up with our sheriff. Jamie, dear, give me your arm; no, the other one...Curtis must have enjoyed having you alone to himself for a while. Jamie, let's have the other arm now. Meredith, hold those seams together for me a moment...I bet you enjoyed the drive, too. The two of you make a good team."

"Please...the costume," she interrupted, desperate to make her stop. Jamie was exceptionally bright for a five-year-old and she didn't want her daughter asking questions.

Honey spun Jamie around. "Now, look at this. A ferocious lion ready to roar."

Covered head to toe in an orange costume, and with a long tail trailing behind, Jamie raced around the room. The five-year-old threw her head back and let out a roar in front of Atticus, who chuckled deep in his throat at his sister's antics. The two children ran down the hallway and then back again.

"The costume is a success," Meredith said, glad the subject was changed. "I can't thank you enough for doing this."

A satisfied smile filled her friend's face. "Let's get you some eggs to take home."

****

Honey first spent a few minutes convincing Jamie to take off her lion costume, telling her the chickens wouldn't appreciate a lion in the hen house. Then they all headed out to collect eggs. Meredith protested they couldn't eat more than a dozen and finally limited the pile of eggs in her basket once she counted out eighteen.

Back out in the yard, Jamie practiced her lion's roar and tormented a handful of chickens running loose. She tried to get Atticus to share in the fun, but he was content splashing in a puddle left from the recent rain. The afternoon chill settled in, the sun lowering earlier in the day now autumn was in full swing, and it soon would be time to return home. They'd encroached too long on Honey's hospitality for one day. For the moment, it was comforting sharing the moment with a friend and watching her children play.

"Now, tell me all your news," the other woman demanded. "How's school going for you?"

"Fine. Good."

Atticus walked through the puddle, squealing, and Meredith considered calling out to him to stop. His shoes would be wet, but there were other shoes in his closet for tomorrow.

"There was snow up there the other day," she added.

Her friend gave a satisfied sigh. "Oh, there'll be a heap of the stuff. It sneaks up on you, keep an eye out on those roads."

Jamie left the chickens and joined Atticus. They

raced through the puddle, kicking mud up the knees of their pant legs.

"About the man in Twin Lakes. I'd met him before he died." She stopped. She hadn't meant to say anything but the words popped out. That was the problem with holding onto things; they bubbled up and out at unexpected moments.

Honey's eyes glittered at the information. "Well, this is news. You didn't say anything earlier."

She swallowed tightly. She wasn't sure how much she should divulge; the woman was a tremendous gossip, avidly trading information around the valley. But it was good to talk about Jacob to someone. "I met him in the library. He was creepy. Pushy. He knew about me…and what happened to Brian."

The other woman gave a knowing nod. "There are men who'll prey on you, take advantage of a grieving widow. Doesn't hurt you're a looker, too."

Perhaps that was all it was, a way to get her attention with a common story of murder. Not the best come-on line, but a compelling one. Still, he'd talked of death and then died shortly afterward. The occurrence was all too strange to be a coincidence, surely.

"Probably was married as well," Honey continued, pursing her lips as she further developed the story in her mind. "Creepy married men are the worst type. Just as well he's dead, I suppose."

Meredith glanced at her, startled at how casually she tossed out the heartless comment. Her friend had a sharp edge to her personality that rose to the surface from time to time. She had little patience for creepy men who took advantage of women. She decided not to say anything about Jacob's plea for help. The woman was the biggest gossip in the county. Curtis would be furious if this kind of talk muddied his investigation.

Atticus sat in the puddle and Jamie danced around him, splashing water high in the air. The older woman gave a happy sigh, a wistful expression softening her features, as though she were remembering her own children getting muddy in the yard. "You might reconsider learning to handle a gun."

This was the last thing she planned to do. She was surprised anyone would suggest a gun to her, after what had happened to Brian. "No," she said firmly.

Honey ignored the flat rejection. "I have extras. You could do some target shooting over here."

There was no way, absolutely no way, she would allow another gun into her house. The last and only gun they owned had been used to murder her husband. On one terrible night, she'd been tempted to use it on him. Best to not have one at all. "I'm not getting a gun," she stressed.

"Next time then, when you all come over," Honey persisted. "A single mother way out here in the country; predators lurking. I have this little Ruger that doesn't have too much of a kick. You'll enjoy a bit of target practice."

The conversation was going sideways. "I'm more into meditation these days," she said, trying to change the subject. "It makes a lot of problems disappear."

"No, no, no," the other woman said, with a solid shake of her head. "That's not how meditation works."

Meredith wished she hadn't said anything about her meditation now. Only, she'd felt so very proud of herself for taking a step toward becoming more confident and taking care of her own problems. Isn't self-sufficiency the number one priority of becoming a real adult?

Honey heaved herself to her feet with a grunt and a huff. "Meditation isn't meant to push away your problems," she added. "It's there to help you deal with them, to put you in a state of mind where you *can* deal with them. Trust me, a gun is much more efficient."

Leave it to Honey to have a better way of doing everything, she thought. Her friend meant well, really was a godsend to her for taking on Atticus while she drove to Twin Lakes. But did the older woman always have to be right?

Jamie sat in the puddle next to her brother and jammed both hands into the mud. Both her children were as wet and filthy as they could be. They also were happy and healthy.

She was on the verge of mentioning her encounter at the hardware store with Egan and then reconsidered. The subject of the young man would prompt the subject of Gemma and that was an explosive subject. The last she heard, Gemma had given birth to a baby boy. Brian's child and this woman's first great-grandchild. Her friend was clearly thrilled at witnessing a new generation being born, regardless of the calamitous circumstances. Gemma and her baby was a delicate subject between them.

Meredith decided to wait until there was more time to talk about Egan and what happened with his relationship with Gemma. She'd meditate first to get her state of mind in a place where she could deal with the awkward topic. "I'd better go."

Her friend appeared unfazed by the refusal to get a gun. "My goats are arriving in a few weeks. They should keep the kids entertained and out of puddles. Let's get your things."

Meredith forced a grin although she was less than happy at the idea. Goats. Jamie would start a campaign for a baby goat. This news was potentially more dangerous than a creepy married man and target shooting with this older woman.

In the house, they toweled off the wet children and Jamie immediately put on her costume. She resumed roaring and pouncing on a squealing Atticus all the way out the front door to the car. Honey followed them out and they stepped over the mud puddles in the walkway.

Her friend sidled up close. "Don't dally too long. Opportunity's knocking, my dear," she advised. "Do your homework and open the door."

****

The sunset flamed red before it was extinguished behind the mountains. Meredith checked her phone for messages, frustrated at not hearing from Curtis. She debated calling him but held back. He believed she was interested in the case because of Brian's murder. She'd play it cool.

The house was quiet, with both kids tucked in bed, and she curled up on the couch rereading a section of her chemistry book. It was difficult to stay focused when there were so many distractions in her life: her children, Jacob Burns, Egan Barker, work, Curtis. In her shed was a noisy rooster and a pregnant rabbit; her house needed repairs and her car...well, her car was flat-out hopeless. What was she doing staying in this middle-of-nowhere town? A reasonable woman would head to a city where she could find decent employment and give up on silly dreams of a country house and a county sheriff. There was a reason rural places stayed rural; there was nothing out here for sensible people.

The phone rang and she dropped her book. She ran to the kitchen to answer it. Curtis's voice rumbled through the line and sent a charge down to her stomach. She clutched the handset a little tighter. The hell with being reasonable. There was no way she could leave and not find out if there was something between them.

"Meredith," he said, then paused.

"Yes, yes it's me. Who else would be here?" She laughed lightly to soften her tone. "Did you hear anything? About the autopsy?"

He spoke slow and even. "I knew you'd want to hear as soon as I heard, to settle your mind about Jacob, to give you closure. Doctor Rose did a limited autopsy to examine his heart and said there was significant damage. He had a fatal heart attack. That's all."

She stared blankly at her refrigerator in disbelief. A piece of paper stuck on the door listed her bills, one by one. Tiny check marks were by some, indicating they'd been paid in full, but the list had grown lately. There was little closure in her life. Problems didn't get solved so much as they morphed into yet another.

"Heart attack," she repeated, feeling a strange sense of disappointment. Jacob hadn't been murdered.

He cleared his throat after a moment passed. "You confirmed he was acting very stressed, when you talked to Jacob in the library," he said in a gentle voice. "Stress puts a heavy burden on a person's heart. A heart attack makes sense if you think about it."

Rain pattered against the window and roof. The sound grew louder, like water bullets hitting her house, trying to get inside.

"Hey, are you okay? Want me to come over?"

"I'm fine," she mumbled, not feeling fine at all. The news cut deep. Jacob's death wasn't like Brian's at all. In some strange way, she'd merged the two cases in her mind. She rubbed her temple. *I've gone crazy. No one cares about a stranger this much. No one wants to hear someone was murdered.*

They both breathed into the phone line for a moment.

"It'll take time," Curtis finally said, breaking the silence. His tone was pained. "You have two children and…you're not over what happened. You don't get over something like that in six months or even a year. Maybe not ever."

She heard a surrender in the phrasing. He was telling her he would wait no longer. She couldn't blame him. Her behavior over Jacob's death made no sense to her either. She cared more about dead Jacob than a live Jacob.

"I'm going back up tomorrow afternoon, to let his wife know the official manner of death," he said. "Doctor Rose would have told her already, but the outcome's not official until I sign the papers."

She gave a soft humorless laugh. "I'll be up there too, in the library. The librarian…what's her name, Leona…she'll be happy to see me again."

"None of this is your fault. He was going to have a heart attack, regardless. Don't listen to her. You know by now how these small-town people can be."

"I know. Small-townish."

He chuckled, though it sounded forced. "Exactly."

She considered asking for a ride up the mountain, but recalled how the last trip ended. "I guess maybe I'll see you on the road." *It's up to him to offer me a ride. If he wants to be with me.*

"Right. Have a good night, Meredith."

She said goodbye and hung up, her heart leaden in her chest. That was that.

****

Deli boy raised his eyebrows, waiting. She glared at him, waiting, too. The phone call the night before plunged her into a dark and edgy mood. "Turkey and ham," she ordered, giving in to his game. It was her standard order, week in and week out for months, never changing, but the pimple-face teenager always pretended he was seeing her for the first time.

He examined a fingernail and then veered it up to his mouth to nibble at a jagged edge. "How much of each?"

"Half pound."

He pulled on plastic gloves with a flourish, stretching them on each finger as though he was getting ready for a surgery. No matter how hard she tried, she couldn't help rising to the bait. Aside from his attitude toward her, there was something about him that provoked her. She forced a hopeful tone to her voice. "I saw the 'help wanted' sign in the window. Are you moving on?"

He ran the slicer and then, not missing an opportunity, added, "Just temporary help, but I don't think you're quite right for us."

Her nostrils flared, her hatred renewed. From the start, they were enemies. "I wasn't applying."

He wrapped her turkey and ham slices in white paper and slapped the packages on the counter. "It's hunting season." Deli boy puffed his chest out, tucked his chin in a strange pose he must have thought adult-like, and deepened his reedy voice. "I get busy this time of year. Someone else needs to man my counter for a few days a week."

Meredith couldn't imagine this boy with a gun in his hands, aiming at deer or elk or passing cars. She was horrified at the idea of him prowling the mountains where she and her kids hiked. "What are you shooting at?" She waited for him to say something terrible.

He shook his head, giving her a derisive look. "I hunt mushrooms." His face lit up in a glow as he said the next two words. "Black chanterelles. Something only true locals would know about. Finding them is like finding gold. I earn more in a week out there hunting mushrooms, than I do working here in a month."

She wrinkled her nose. Leave it to deli boy to spend his free time prowling the countryside for something as disgusting as fungi. She detested mushrooms and the way they tasted of dirt and slid around like snails in her mouth. Fool's gold for a fool, she thought. *At least I won't have to see this kid every time I come in to the store.*

Thankful also at the news deli boy wouldn't be wielding a deadly weapon, she grabbed her packages and turned away without another word. She had more important things on her mind than deli-boy crawling around plucking slimy growths from the muddy earth. An idea came to her in the night after hours of tossing and turning. Today, she would visit Jacob Burn's wife and see for herself what the woman was like.

Closure, she decided.

Julie Howard

Part Two

"The great question that has never been answered, and which I have not yet been able to answer, despite my thirty years of research into the feminine soul, is 'What does a woman want?'"
  - Sigmund Freud

Julie Howard

Chapter Eight

The day ripened crisp and clear over the valley. Gray clouds swathed the mountains, cutting off the tops from view. In California, there'd been plenty of foggy mornings shrouding the rolling hills of Oakland, enveloping the city in gloom only to melt away as the sun rose in the sky. A little bit of early gray was nothing to fear.

She headed up the mountain after she stocked her groceries away in the refrigerator. The clouds only thickened as morning edged toward noon, but the weather didn't appear anything to fear. The season was still autumn, after all. When snow fell in earnest, as it certainly would soon enough, she would figure out another option for getting her homework done. It would be awkward asking Curtis for help, considering the conversation the evening before. Worse than losing an option for doing her homework, he surely implied he was giving up on her. Brian's murder cast a shadow over her life and his abuse had bruised her psyche. She'd felt so good through the summer—healthy, strong and in control for the first time and perhaps ready for a new relationship. The chance meeting with Jacob and his talk about murder showed her how fragile her recovery was.

Jamie and Atticus didn't deserve to suffer from imperfect parents. She needed to dig in deeper and fight to give them a stable home. A house and a decent job—those are my priorities right now, she vowed.

Just a few weeks remained in her class before she took her first college final. She'd achieved a solid B-minus so far, and was pleased with herself for this result. A B-minus was still a B, after all. Considering she'd since discovered in herself a true lack of interest in chemistry, a B wasn't bad at all.

White flakes drifted down in slow motion halfway up the mountain, creating a snow globe effect both mesmerizing and dizzying. By the time she reached the Twin Lakes library, the size of the flakes had grown and white flecks polka-dotted everything. Parked cars, trees, telephone poles. The new snow merged into the existing slush, one flake followed by another and then another. Meredith glanced up at the sky, willing the sun to burn through as it was supposed to have done. Fall had scarcely arrived and already winter was in sight.

The library parking lot was deserted when she arrived. Jacob, with his wild stories, wouldn't be playing computer games in the library today, or ever again, interrupting her. She wondered whether Leona would speak to her and repeat her veiled accusation about an affair occurring in the library's dark corners with Jacob. She glanced down the block, wondering if Curtis was already in Twin Lakes talking to Doctor Rose and Jacob's wife. The only person visible was a man walking his dog. Such a peaceful, lonely place, she thought.

She strode into the library, her gaze darting to the counter, but Leona wasn't there. A rustle alerted her to a far corner where the unfriendly librarian was shelving magazines. Her back was to the door so Meredith tucked her head down and hustled to the computers.

The library remained quiet and Leona, who must have known she was there, ignored her. Class work kept her occupied for the next ninety minutes and no other patrons came through the doors. Once again, she wondered why a county government would place its only library in a remote mountain location snowed in a third of the year. No matter. A few more weeks and she'd have one class done. After finishing her work, she logged off and shrugged her sweater back on.

There was no avoiding Leona on the way out. The woman sat behind the counter with a thick book on her lap, the kind of book you pick up when you have all the time in the world to do nothing but read. Meredith's gaze flickered to the woman's hip to see if the holster and gun were visible and noted they indeed were present and accounted for.

"We don't get too many strangers up here."

She stopped, unsure if she really wanted to engage the librarian in conversation. But if there was one conclusion she'd arrived at in the past year, it was she would no longer be bullied. She would stand up for herself. In this instance, the librarian developed the wrong idea about her and Jacob. Gossip had a habit of traveling far and wide in a sparsely populated place like High County. Rumors needed to be cut off at the source.

"I didn't know him," she started. "Jacob, I mean. I'm sorry he died. You must have known him well."

Leona closed the book on her lap with a thump. "Most of my life." She stood and touched the holster at her hip. "You know he never was able to make his confession, before his heart attack. There must have been something terrible weighing on his mind."

Meredith frowned, not sure where the conversation was heading. "I didn't know him," she repeated. "I just come in here to do my schoolwork."

"What was he talking about with you, all that time back there in the corner?"

The conversation with Jacob flashed through her mind: his fear of his wife and his certainty she wanted to kill him. "He said their anniversary was coming up."

Leona appeared grudgingly satisfied at the answer. "That's right. He was a happily married man." The librarian set her lips firmly together, as though she were defying any contradiction. Then she added, "Your husband died too, didn't he?"

Meredith hid her discomfort. Brian and Jacob, two dead husbands. "Yes. Recently."

"We don't get that sort of thing up here."

Unwittingly, a laugh bubbled to Meredith's lips. "People dying?"

"Murder," the librarian said, her face screwing up as though the word tasted bad coming out. The word was just short of a reproach.

The breath stopped in her throat. She swiveled and walked out without glancing back. No wonder she was besieged with guilt over Brian's death; others treated her as though she were guilty, too. It was impossible to go anywhere or do anything in these tiny towns without someone watching, judging, and gossiping. She'd suspected the man was going to cause headaches for her and, sure enough, here was this bored librarian creating drama out of thin air.

Even in death, Jacob was a problem, conjuring Brian back into her life. Honey was right; Jacob had been a creepy married man and that was that. She wished for the thousandth time she wasn't reliant on others for help and she didn't need to use the Twin Lakes library. Her own life was complicated enough without getting involved in the lives of others.

Someday, I'll get out of the dark ages and have a cell phone, cable TV, a computer and Internet like the rest of the world. All those things cost so much money. How do people afford them all?

A thin film of white had accumulated on the walkway and she walked slowly with her feet wide apart, trying not to fall. She wasn't entirely clear what her intentions were in talking to Jacob's widow. It didn't make sense she'd be able to spot a murderer just by studying her. This was ridiculous. She figured the older priest, Father Karl, might tell her something about Jacob's widow. At the very least, he could point her toward Jacob's house. She headed toward the church at the far end of the street.

The church's heavy wooden door was twice her height but swung open easily. Again, the interior of the church was hushed and votive candles flickered at one side. Neither priest was in sight and no one sat in the pews. The confessional where Jacob died was empty and silent. Meredith gazed down the center aisle and considered what life would be like to belong to a community such as this. There'd be comfort in the rituals and formalities, and especially being accepted as part of a congregation. Church picnics, family gatherings, shared experiences.

Belonging. I want to belong somewhere, but how?

People in small towns closed ranks, were generally distrustful of strangers, and made it difficult for someone new to join in. She didn't always want to be an outsider peering in.

She shifted on her feet, unsure if she should call out. Unnerved by the quiet, she backtracked to the entrance, her footfalls echoing. If anyone was inside, they were staying hidden. She shoved against the door and emerged again into the cold, standing at the top of the steps. More snow was falling now and her thoughts flew to the road down the mountain. She was unused to driving in slick conditions. Rain and fog, no problem; the general rule was just slow down. Snow was different. Handling a car in these conditions was like the difference between roller skating and ice skating. Anyone would tell you ice skating was much more difficult.

She gazed down the street, wondering if she should give up on Jacob's wife and simply go back home. Meredith blinked snowflakes away as a figure appeared at the end of the street, in front of the library. Leona stood watching, arms crossed in front of her.

This decided her. She wouldn't let small town people chase her away. Let the librarian watch her and gossip all she wanted. She would find Jacob's wife and look her in the eye. The visit would be masked as a simple condolence call, from someone who'd met her husband. This decision made, a truck came into view, driving slowly past Leona and turning to go behind the library. Curtis, she thought; just in time to lead the way. She drew her sweater more tightly around her and flipped up the collar to shelter her neck from the wet flakes. Leona disappeared back into the library as Meredith hurried by, hoping to catch sight of the truck again before she froze to death.

She didn't expect Idaho to get so cold this soon; it was still autumn, after all. Autumn was supposed to be a time of warm breezes and trees taking on subtle colors of rust. The season was supposed to gradually edge toward winter; instead it burst in within a week. Meredith expected to have at least until after Thanksgiving before she needed to worry about snow. Winter apparently arrived earlier in this part of the country, especially in the higher elevations.

Bingo, she thought, as she rounded the corner to the street behind the library. The truck was parked in front of a tidy house halfway down the block. Jacob lived right there, with the library practically in his front yard. She hesitated only a moment, and then shunted the last misgiving away. She had every right to make a quick stop, one widow consoling another. It wasn't strange at all.

****

Jacob's wife wore black from head to toe, from the lacy veil perched on the crown of her head to the three-inch heels below a narrow pencil skirt. She made a comely widow, demure and alluring at the same time. Such effect didn't come without some effort and care, and she wondered at how the woman considered these things so soon after her husband died.

"I'm Brooke." The woman's voice was hushed and gaze downcast as she introduced herself. "Thank you for coming."

Jacob's wife was much prettier than expected and Meredith was instantly aware of her own appearance. Her chunky pea green sweater, found at a secondhand store, sported a small moth hole at one elbow. She'd worn the same jeans twice already that week and a strand of hair had fallen from her usual ponytail. "I...I just wanted to say how sorry I am," she stuttered, overly conscious of her lie.

Brooke gestured to one side of the entry to the living room. "Please come in."

Father Michael and Curtis stared as she entered, both wore similar expressions of surprise and dismay. The window shades were drawn, shutting out the purity of the early winter light, and a single lamp lit the room. The space was uncluttered and neat, with no sign children lived in the house. Certainly, Jacob hadn't mentioned any. A few books sat stacked neatly on one table, but otherwise, there was little to indicate real people occupied the home. The room was neat to the point of being sterile. Cups rattled through a doorway apparently leading to the kitchen.

"You know Father Michael?" Brooke asked. "And the sheriff, of course."

Meredith smiled weakly at both men, her gaze lingering an extra second on Curtis before flickering away. "We've met."

Brooke gave a charming shrug and sat in a chair next to the priest, gesturing that she should sit on the sofa next to Curtis. The four of them faced each other.

"Tell me," Brooke said. "How did you know my husband?"

"I didn't really know him; I met him at the library. We talked a couple of times, that's all. He seemed upset about a few things." She studied Brooke carefully as she made this last statement, to see if her words rattled the woman.

Brooke nodded, her chin jutted forward. "Jacob was under quite a bit of stress," she acknowledged. "He lost his job last year and wasn't able to find anything else. Jobs are scarce around here. I told him we could move but he didn't want to leave. We both grew up here, you know."

"He's at peace," Father Michael murmured, then to Meredith said, "As is your own husband."

Meredith wiped her palms lightly against her pants at the mention of Brian. Sitting in this newly widowed woman's house took her back to the days when her own widowhood was fresh. Death, murder, and suspicion haunted her for months before she regained a semblance of normality.

I'm here for closure, she reminded herself.

Curtis cleared his throat. "The doctor confirmed a heart attack, in the autopsy report. We were discussing this when you knocked."

The priest leaned forward. "In my experience," he offered, "heart attacks can come on suddenly."

"He was awfully young to have a heart attack," Meredith interrupted, her heart in her throat. "That's unusual."

They all stared at her.

"Excuse me." Brooke's voice sounded small and whispery. "Are you implying you don't believe Jacob died of a heart attack? Doctor Rose confirmed it."

There was another clatter in the kitchen and then a woman emerged carrying a tray filled with coffee cups. The sour-faced, romance-reading woman she'd seen talking about handguns with the librarian hesitated for a moment at Brooke's side.

"This is my good friend, Carolyn Reynolds," Brooke said, gazing up at the woman. "She's been such a life-saver, helping out, cooking and cleaning."

"I go by Caro," the woman corrected, setting the tray down on the coffee table. She looked around the room for an extra chair and, not seeing one, perched on the edge of the sofa hovering over Meredith. "Have some coffee."

It came out like an order so everyone leaned forward to get a cup except for Meredith. Already on edge, she bristled at Caro's tone and didn't like how the woman loomed at her shoulder. For a moment, there was just the sound of gentle slurping. Meredith eyed Brooke and recalled Jacob talking about his wife working long hours. What kind of work did this pretty woman, one who wore heels on a snowy day, do in a rural area?

Father Michael broke the silence, balancing his cup and saucer expertly on one knee. "It was nice of you to stop by. Brooke is fortunate to have so many friends, like CeeCee here."

"*Caro*. I don't go by CeeCee anymore," she corrected. "Doesn't suit me. Not like Bee." She nodded at Brooke and the hint of a smile touched the corners of her mouth.

Brooke smoothed her skirt of unseen wrinkles, running one hand slowly from hip to knee, like a cat preening at the praise. Everyone in the room—Curtis, the priest and Caro—watched as she repeated the motion down her other side. Irritated, Meredith was certain she knew the effect she made. What would life be like to be so beautiful, she wondered. Life must be easier; doors were opened for you, people were kinder. Then she blinked, realizing she was staring too.

"Bee for Brooke, Cee for Caro," Father Michael explained. "I always used to say they needed a friend whose name started with A so they could be the ABCs."

Meredith didn't want to be on friendly terms with these people. There was a grim purpose to her visit, so she changed the subject. "Have you made funeral plans?" she asked, and mentally kicked herself. This wasn't the hard-hitting question she was here to ask *Why was your husband so afraid of you?*

"The service will be at the church," the priest said, his attention focused on Brooke's face as he spoke. His gaze was soft, filled with compassion. Brooke rewarded his sympathy by reaching over and touching one of his hands. Her eyes glistened with unshed tears.

Meredith raised her eyebrows. "The funeral will be in the same place where he died? Won't it be uncomfortable for everyone?"

Brooke's tears instantly vaporized. "What else did you and Jacob talk about?"

Caro stood up and her coffee cup upended onto the floor. "Oh," she cried. "Look what I've done. I need a dish rag."

Caro dashed to the kitchen and Curtis stood, setting his cup on the table. "We should go." He gestured to Meredith. "I'll walk you out."

She ignored his prompting and kept her attention on Brooke. Now or never, she thought. "You asked me what your husband and I talked about," Meredith said in a rush. "He told me you were going to kill him."

Chapter Nine

The priest gave a choking cough. Curtis blew a regretful sigh and didn't speak. Brooke simply nodded, appearing unperturbed at the accusation. The widow set her cup on the table at her elbow and lifted deep blue eyes to Meredith. For the first time, she noted puffiness below the woman's eyes, covered expertly with makeup. She felt a twinge of guilt at her harsh words. For the first time, she wondered whether she was mistaken.

"Thank you." Brooke spoke quietly. "I appreciate your bringing this to me."

The woman's poise was impressive. Defensiveness or anger, maybe even a run for the door, would be expected, but not this calm gratitude. "Why would he accuse you? He was very upset, and very sure."

Brooke didn't blink, her expression gentle as if talking to a recalcitrant child. "As I said, Jacob lost his job a while ago. When he couldn't find another job, he became very depressed and started acting strangely. Anxious. Angry. The last few months, he wasn't the same man anymore. It was as though I'd lost my husband already."

Silence descended on the room. The priest paled and his fingers fidgeted at a rosary he'd drawn from his pocket. Meredith glanced sideways at Curtis, but he stood stock-still next to her. His mouth was set in a line, lips unmoving, offering her no assistance. Perspiration formed at her upper lip, but she couldn't stop herself. *Brian and Jacob. Jacob and Brian.* Her heart jumped in her chest. "You told Jacob you fixed the brakes on his car, but the mechanic said they weren't touched."

"Stop it." The statement came from the kitchen doorway, the words dripping with venom. "Everyone knows who you are," Caro said. "You don't belong here." She took a step forward and then strode across the room to stand next to Brooke.

Curtis put a steadying hand on Meredith's shoulder. "This is an emotional time, for everyone. Let's remember that. There's no point in making this worse."

Caro hadn't finished. "Your husband's murder was big news," she said. "Everyone knows about you, your family. Don't drag those city lifestyles up here."

It wasn't fair. She'd been vindicated. Besides, murder wasn't a city lifestyle. These words were on the tip of her tongue, but Curtis gripped his hand under her elbow and tugged her up and off the sofa. "We need to go now." His tone indicated there would be no debate.

Father Michael stood as well, his face stern and reproaching. The chilly atmosphere took her back to the previous spring when she was the accused, a murderess. Brooke watched coolly as they went to the door. "Forgive me if we don't walk you out," Brooke said, rooted to her seat. One of her hands clutched the priest's, the other held Caro's. The three remained riveted in place.

Curtis and Meredith were at the doorway, then out the door. He led her to his truck. "Get in," he ordered.

****

He drove around the corner, out of sight of Brooke's house. She waited for him to blast her and so prepared her arguments for why she confronted Brooke. They drove up a hill, the snow crunching under the tires and his hands squeezed the steering wheel. His knuckles squeezed and released, and she wished he'd yell at her and get it over with.

"I have to pick up Jamie soon."

"Hmmm."

"Curtis. Say something."

"Look up there. By God, that's a beautiful sight."

She gazed up to where he pointed at a bald eagle high in a pine, its white head shimmering as though snow-capped. As they watched, the huge bird lifted its wings and with a weighty flap soared off over the trees.

"Where are we going?"

"Don't you trust me?" His tone was jesting although his expression remained serious.

Meredith twisted in her seat to face him. Her gaze traced his lips, chapped in the cold, and over his solid jawline, covered with his ever-present two-day stubble. His profile was so familiar and dear to her now.

She recalled their hike—was the outing just a few days back? —when he started to say something to her: "You know I'm here for you and…" Jamie had interrupted to point out a herd of elk, then Curtis's phone rang to alert him to Jacob's death. It was the moment everything went wrong. She wondered what he was going to say next and what would have happened if he had a chance to say it. His expression was warm as he gazed down at her and her heart had quickened. Only two others before affected her the same way: Brian and a boy in high school years ago.

The boy in high school was skinny and his ears stuck out, but he'd been sweet and shared her circumstance of being in the group teachers categorized as "disadvantaged." His name was Sam.

A smile crept to her lips in recollection. They'd been best friends for a year before he gathered the nerve to kiss her. Then her mother got sick and there was no time for school, or Sam, or anything. When she returned to classes after her mother died, Sam was gone. A note in her locker explained his family planned a move to Tennessee. There was no forwarding address. Neither of them was the type of people who stayed anywhere long enough to have permanent addresses. This was understood.

Then there was Brian, and their marriage didn't end well. Maybe she was fated to be unlucky in love, attracting men who would leave her. Maybe she was doomed to repeat her mother's life of drifting and poverty, and never having a place to call home. Her life wasn't like Jacob's, who loved his wife since grade school. Not like this sheriff sitting next to her, who lived in the same town nearly his entire life.

Curtis cleared his throat, halting her musings. "I thought we both needed a bit of a drive. To reset our thoughts."

"I needed to see her," she explained. "After what Jacob told me."

"Meredith, my hands are tied. There's no evidence of murder. The doctor confirmed a heart attack, did an autopsy. I don't have a murder investigation without a murder. Trust me, I believe what you've told me, about what Jacob said. I believe he said those things to you, but a man's fear isn't evidence."

He turned the steering wheel hard onto another road which angled them back toward Twin Lakes. "I'm more worried about you right now," he added, glancing at her. "Just so you know, I didn't sign the death certificate before visiting Brooke, but now I have no choice. This is how my job works."

His words made sense. Of course, there was no murder. There'd just been a sick man obsessed with murder fantasies, leaving a grieving widow. Jacob's anxiety was the last straw for an already stressed heart.

Meredith gave a short laugh. "I'm a little crazy, right? Showing up out of the blue?"

He kept his gaze on the road in front of them and she took his silence as agreement. Crazy. Yep. "I'm not sure there's a normal for all you've been through," he finally said. "My impression is you're handling it all pretty well. Definitely not crazy."

They rounded a corner and parked in front of the library, next to her car. The windshield was covered in a sheet of white, and its tires were frozen against the pavement. She didn't want to get out of the truck, a foot away from a man she was more than half in love with.

"Be careful driving down the mountain. Remember to turn the wheel into a slide if you start slipping. It's the cardinal rule of driving out here."

She couldn't help but smile at him. "You've told me already, a few times."

Curtis returned her smile, and then his gaze dropped. "Like I said, I worry about you."

It took everything she possessed inside not to throw herself into his arms. Instead, she opened the door and stepped into the cold.

****

Honey's head poked deep into Meredith's refrigerator as she examined the expiration dates of mayonnaise jars and milk cartons. "How long are you going to keep your husband in a box?"

Meredith nearly spat out her coffee.

"It's high time you buried him," her friend continued, as she stacked containers with remnants of moldy cottage cheese and old leftovers on the counter. "It's not healthy to keep those ashes sitting around."

Brian's ashes were in a plain cardboard box, the cheapest container offered, which was the only affordable option at the time. She had no money for a cemetery plot, a stone, or a niche in a wall to place his ashes. Now she had a small sum in the bank, enough to do something modest and more respectful with his remains. The other woman was right. Certainly, it would be better than having them in the back of her closet, where Jamie and Atticus could come across them. The idea made her wince.

Meredith blew out a breath and set down her coffee cup. "I've been thinking about burying him back by the tree in our yard. Where the kids can visit him."

Honey made an exasperated sound and closed the refrigerator door with a thud. "You absolutely, positively are not." Her tone was firm. "You want to frighten your kids? Having their daddy buried in the back yard?"

She still wondered if her friend was behind Brian's murder, even in some subtle way. Even though Honey's long-ago ex-husband readily confessed to the murder, Meredith continued to get the vibe someone prodded him into killing Brian. Shorty, who scarcely knew the family he treated poorly so many years ago, didn't have enough reason to murder someone hurting a granddaughter he barely knew. Her friend, though. The unshakeable woman was someone who would do anything to protect her family...even, she suspected, encouraging her off-kilter ex-husband to murder someone.

Honey plucked up their coffee cups from the table and set them in the sink. Her plump grandmotherly face was in sharp contrast to her stubborn nature. "Get up," she ordered. "We're going to the city cemetery. That's where I buried my Milt. You're going to get something appropriate, where Brian's kids can visit when they're older. Whatever that man did, he's still their daddy."

She rose obediently. In the few days since confronting Brooke, she'd learned one lesson. Her obsession with Jacob's death most certainly was connected to her inability to let go of her past. It was time to bury her past, literally and figuratively. It was time.

****

She chose a simple niche halfway down a wall and paid for a small plaque etched with Brian's name, along with his birth and death dates. It struck her for the first time how young he'd been when he died, even though he always seemed so much older than her in life. Thirty-three was much too young to die. How long would it take her to forgive him for all he did in the few years they'd been together. Was forgiveness even important or necessary? Her book on meditation instructed to let the past go and to focus on the present. Her past haunted her and invaded her present; it would be a relief to be able to let it all go. Meredith recalled the scene at Brooke's house. She closed her eyes.

"...joint niche?" the man was asking.

Her eyes flew open. "What? I'm sorry."

The man at the cemetery was all sympathy and understanding, tilting his head to one side with a practiced frown. "This is a difficult hour," he intoned. "Take your time. I was just asking if you wanted to pre-pay for a joint niche, so you can join your husband when the time comes."

She shook her head. "I won't be joining him." She fumbled in her purse for her wallet. "How much?"

****

Finished with the details, she strode outside where Honey strolled with Atticus and Jamie by the memorial wall. The cemetery grounds were sparse, with fewer than a hundred flat stones and a few older upright markers set into an acre of close-cut yellowed lawn. The wall, rising up six feet, was down a brief sidewalk from the office building.

"I explained to Jamie her daddy's ashes will be right here, so she can come talk to him whenever she wants," Honey said.

Jamie studied the blank niche with a frown. "I don't think so. My daddy's dead now."

The five-year-old clutched the tail of her lion costume to her chest as she stared at the wall, full of dead people. She'd refused to take off her Halloween costume for anything except a bath for days. After wearing it to school, serving as pajamas at night, and absorbing various spills at meals, Jamie would eventually have to relinquish the costume to the washing machine. *Heaven help us all if the mane unravels or the tail comes off*, Meredith thought.

Honey heaved a sigh, her shoulders rising and

falling heavily. "Come with me."

Not looking back, she marched across the grass to a small flat stone at one edge of the cemetery, weaving among the markers. They followed her, Jamie first, then Meredith hand-in-hand with a toddling Atticus, his chubby legs pumping up and down. There was no path so they walked across the dying lawn and likely, Meredith imagined, on top of people's caskets and bones. Cremation made so much more sense to her than burying one's dead. She'd read of one cemetery, so crowded the caskets were buried on top of one another. Someday, those coffins would rot away, raining bones down on others below, all sinking deeper into the earth together. There was no guarantee at some far-off future date, a stranger wouldn't be buried above her. She'd rather blow away in the wind.

Her friend stopped before a stone and tapped the marker with one foot, like she was knocking on a door. "Hi-ya Milt," she called out. "You have visitors."

They stared down at the stone, etched with "Milton Jackson Stohler, Sprouted 1947, Replanted 2015." Honey's second marriage was idyllic, and the woman truly mourned Milt's loss to cancer. People called them "Milk and Honey," the story went, because they fit so well together as a couple. Even the road they lived on was named "Ham and Eggs Road" because the couple raised pigs and chickens on their small farm.

"Death is a mystery, for sure," the woman explained to Jamie. "We don't know if your daddy can hear you or not. But I talk to my Milt all the time and I think he hears me. If there's even a chance he can hear me, I don't want him wondering why I'm ignoring him. It's good enough reason for me."

Jamie bit her lip. "I can tell my daddy about school," she started in a hesitant voice. "He'd want to know about Karin and the princi-pess. And my rabbit being pregnant. And Laf being a boy chicken, not a girl chicken."

"Exactly," Honey encouraged. "There's a lot to tell him."

Jamie nodded. "Okay," she agreed, the subject settled. "I'll come and talk to him."

Meredith appreciated how the older woman could talk so easily to her kids. Both of them adored her and the woman soaked in the adoration like a thirsty sponge gone too long without water.

"You can give a hello to Milt too whenever you stop by," said Honey. "He was always a talker and he's a great listener now." Meredith wondered if she was making a morbid joke, but her friend was blinking back tears. The older woman spoke as though to herself. "Milt has a very forgiving nature. I'm not sure I ever deserved him." Honey shook her head as though conveying herself back to the present and smiled at Jamie. She nodded toward the car. "I always eat some cookies after my visit. Oatmeal or ginger snaps?"

****

Jamie ran into the master bedroom that night and jumped into her bed. Her daughter tugged at the blankets, burrito-ing herself inside them until Meredith possessed nothing but a sheet on her side. Within minutes, Jamie began to snore in a soft rhythm.

Rain pounded the roof, causing a steady drumming above their heads. Meredith rose. She checked on Atticus, who had one thumb firmly stuck in his mouth, and then she wandered through the living room and into the kitchen. The house was taking a beating but the roof Curtis patched for her appeared to be holding and all was dry and snug. It was small and shabby...maybe a shade below shabby...but the house was all hers. Outside, there was a garden, a tree swing and a walking path cutting through the fields to the tall eastern mountains.

My house. My home. Two healthy children. I have a job and I'm taking a college class.

They were getting by, but just barely. Was it wrong to be happy with so little? There had to be more to life than money in the bank. Curtis told her there was no normal for what she'd been through—the years of living with Brian's cruelty and betrayal, then his murder. She felt safe here in Hay City, with a growing sense of belonging, and this seemed like everything. With Jacob's death settled once and for all as a natural occurrence, she could return her focus to her own life.

She checked on Jamie again who by now had rolled her mound of blankets to the middle of the bed, taking the rest of the sheet with her. She sighed and then went to Jamie's room, stepping gingerly over dolls and shoes, before climbing in her daughter's narrow bed. A lump at her feet made her grope under the blankets and she plucked out a stuffed rabbit Brian gave to Jamie one Christmas. One ear was missing as well as most of the fur on the front legs, but since Brian's death, Jamie wouldn't go to bed without it. She dropped the toy to the floor and then, reconsidering, stretched over and retrieved it. She hugged the rabbit to her chest and listened as the pitter-patter of rain on the roof softened and then disappeared.

She closed her eyes and slept, without dreams.

Chapter Ten

"Mom! I'm gonna be late for my bus." Jamie stood over her, a bedraggled lion wearing a backpack.

Meredith's eyes flew open to bright sunlight. The stuffed rabbit dropped to the floor. "What time is it?"

"I made my own breakfast." Jamie's tone accused her of being a bad mother, once again. "Atticus's, too."

She scrambled out of her daughter's bed, stumbled on a doll, and raced to her room, Jamie following. "You don't have time to get dressed," she said. "I want to ride the bus."

"Okay, okay." The clock by the side of the bed confirmed there was little time to spare. The bus would leave in ten minutes; it took nearly five minutes to drive Jamie to the bus stop in front of the grocery store. It'd be close. "Get Atticus into the car seat. Pack his day bag. I'll be out in thirty seconds."

She slid a sweatshirt over her pajama top, tugged on old jeans, and took a quick glance at her hair in the mirror. The stubborn cowlick at the back of her head shot a poof of ash-brown hair up like a geyser. She pawed through the closet and found a baseball cap, which she set firmly in place to cover the damage. Another glance in the mirror assured her she still looked like she'd just climbed out of bed. No matter, she was late. This was her morning to open the hardware store and she'd promised to stay all day.

Since she wasn't at her most glamorous, it was a good thing few people patronized the store.

Something nagged at the edge of her memory, a phrase uttered or…something…at Brooke's house. What was it and why did it flash through her mind just then? She paused, frowning.

"Mom!" Jamie shouted one last time before dashing out the front door with Atticus.

No time for coffee or breakfast. It was a rough way to start the morning, this day of all days.

Outside, a dusting of snow covered the valley, the road, and her car. *Not so soon. It's too early for winter.* Her feet skidded on the slick gravel as she made her way to the driver's side of the car, scrambling to keep from falling.

"Mom." Jamie bounced impatiently in her seat. "Hurry, hurry."

The car chugged, the battery protesting the sudden drop in temperature overnight, but then started, belching out its usual gray smoke. Meredith raced down the road, trying to make up a few seconds and terrified they'd miss the bus and she'd have to drive Jamie all the way to school in Blissful. The short yellow bus was at the store when they drove up, blaring the car's horn so the driver wouldn't leave.

"This is so 'barrassing," Jamie complained as she jumped out of the car and ran to the waiting bus where her friend, Karin, waved an arm out a window.

Meredith took a few deep breaths to recover her equilibrium as she waited for the bus to pull away in the direction of the Blissful school. She glanced in the back seat. Jamie had dressed Atticus in layers of heavy winter clothing; a line of sweat beaded his forehead.

"Oh, my poor baby," she said. "You have no say in any of this, do you?"

Atticus wiggled in his car seat. "No."

She pulled back onto the road, slower this time, and headed to the hardware store. The road was sloppy with melting slush and the fields glistened under the rising autumn sun.

"It gets better," she promised her son, and hoped this was true.

****

A note lay on the counter when she arrived at the store. "Don't mind the mess. Don't touch anything. I'll be in late."

Meredith surveyed the aisles. The store was always a mess, but Crusty had outdone himself this time. Snow shovels lay strewn down the length of one aisle; bags of bird seed stacked like cord wood filled another. A washing machine, dented and scuffed on one side, sat next to the playpen set up for Atticus which currently held a dozen or so boxes labeled "coffee makers."

Annoyed, she took the coffee makers out of the playpen and set Atticus down inside. The ordering system was haphazard at best. The only items that made any sense were the snow shovels. New merchandise appeared frequently but she rarely witnessed their delivery. She imagined trucks lined up in the night to drop off random items. She glared at the snow shovels on the floor, blocking all access to one aisle. What would it hurt to pick them up and stack them neatly?

'*Don't touch anything.*' "Ridiculous."

She gathered up the twenty-two shovels and nested them together in a tidy display by the front door. It didn't take a genius to understand these would be in high demand this time of year. She was proved right when two people, the only customers of the morning, both bought shovels.

"Hoot and holler, what the hell is this?"

Meredith jumped. Crusty's tall figure loomed at the door dividing the bar from the hardware store. He glowered at the shovels and stomped down the aisle where they'd been before she tidied the mess. His head swiveled back and forth, up and down, his gaze raking the shelves. "What did I say? Simple and clear directions. Didn't you read the note?"

She gaped at her angry boss. "The shovels blocked the aisle so I transferred them up front—and sold two of them, by the way."

Crusty growled deep in his throat. "Of course, you did. What else? What else did he buy?"

Her gaze darted around the store. Only one of the customers bought anything else. "A garden gnome," she admitted weakly. "The one bending over, with his pants sort of sagging a bit."

He leaned over the counter toward her, his face red. "He's mooning. Trust the stars, the dirty little gnome'll end up in my front yard, mooning me." He pounded a fist on the counter and she shrank back. She'd never seen her boss so furious. The sweet puppy dog of a man transformed into a raging pit bull over a garden gnome.

"He's a thief," he spat out. "An idiot. And a liar. A…a…" He panted and appeared to notice Meredith's distress at his anger. His tone lowered and he finished, "He's a scourge upon this earth."

Her eyes widened in disbelief so much anger could come from such a silly object. "I didn't know I wasn't supposed to sell it to him," she said. "He was nice."

In fact, the burly man tipped her two dollars even though she told him twice a tip wasn't necessary.

"Oh well," her boss said, his face returning to a normal hue. "I'll just hide it in his wife's vegetable garden in the spring. That'll teach him."

Meredith suppressed a smile at the vision of two grown men sneaking around each other's yards, tormenting each other with a garden gnome. "What did he do?"

"Cheated me out of some land, way back, when I first came out here. I got him back when I bought a truck he wanted. It's not easy being a newcomer in these parts. Got to persevere and be a little tricky." He winked at her, his good humor restored. "You'll learn."

Atticus held his arms out, indicating he wanted to be picked up. "Cuss," Atticus said, the name he'd bestowed on Crusty.

"Your wish is my command," Crusty said and swung Atticus high in the air so the boy could brush the ceiling with his fingertips.

The comment tweaked her memory again for something at Brooke Burns' house...

As she and Curtis left, Brooke just sat there, head held high, perched on her chair like a queen surrounded by courtiers waiting for her next command.

If Caro had been "Cee," then Brooke would have been "Bee." *Queen Bee.*

It struck her in a flash. The beautiful Brooke who worked long hours in the town of Blissful. Not a queen bee at all, but a pretty princess. Brooke Burns must be Mrs. 'Beebee', Jamie's princi-pess. The idea of the woman near her daughter disturbed her. She knew she was overreacting but couldn't stop.

"Do you get over to Blissful much?" she asked as the tall man lifted her son to the ceiling and down, making the toddler squeal in delight. Crusty's eyes twinkled and she knew he was going to offer one of his randy remarks. "The *town* of Blissful."

He appeared hurt at not getting to have his fun. "Sure, from time to time. I used to own a little café over there until I realized my biggest coffee drinkers were fellers sobering up from the night before. More money in getting them drunk, so I sold up and got this place."

"Jamie goes to school over there, you know."

"Not many choices in these parts."

She hesitated. Whatever she said would get back to Honey, and then travel all around the county. She kept her voice steady. "Do you know the principal?"

He chuckled, and then stopped abruptly as a memory hit him. "Poor woman. You heard about her husband. Very sudden."

There was no murder, so there can't be a murderer. Let it go.

Her mouth went dry. Brooke never mentioned she was the principal of Jamie's school. The woman must have known she had a daughter; Brian's murder meant everyone knew everything about her. "I heard about what happened," Meredith said, her voice unsteady. "Tragic."

Crusty thrust Atticus toward her. "Got to get to work next door. Kid here needs a change. Pronto."

She accepted the boy into her arms, her thoughts wandering elsewhere other than dirty diapers.

****

Curtis' truck wasn't at his office. Instead, there was an oversized four-by-four vehicle Meredith noticed at the bar from time to time. Only two people worked in the office: the county sheriff and the city clerk. It wasn't difficult to figure out who else was there. In Hay City, you never knew how someone would react to meeting a stranger, especially if the stranger was a woman recently suspected of murder. She found some people in this remote region to be difficult and others flat-out antagonistic toward her. Hostile or friendly. There was no knowing which of these categories the city clerk would fall under.

She sat in her car for a moment, biting at her lip, trying to decide whether she wanted to go inside to ask when the sheriff would return, then glanced over her shoulder at the kids. "Stay here. I'll be right back."

"I don't like waiting," Jamie complained. "You're always leaving us behind."

Meredith sighed, her mind focused on the coming conversation. "I'll be quick. I promise."

She jumped out of the car before Jamie could protest. There was no one like a five-year-old for offering judgment and guilt.

The two-room city office consisted of little more than a modest lobby with a long counter separating the entry from the other room furnished with three desks. She knew the city shared its office with the county sheriff. The third desk once belonged to an assistant city clerk, a position eliminated in budget cuts. The city didn't bother with a spot for the mayor since he never made an appearance. The third desk was now used as a dumping ground for random files, old mail and dust.

"Help you?"

A man unfolded long legs from under the city clerk's desk. When he stood and walked toward her, she couldn't help but stare. He towered above her, the tallest man she'd ever seen in person, his lean frame making him appear even taller. "Hi," she said, mentally calculating his height. Was it rude to ask how tall?

"Six-eleven," he offered in a cheery voice. "I always like to get that out of the way. No, I never played basketball and, yes, I have to duck under some doorways."

She smiled at him, now noticing the dimples at his cheeks. Thankfully, she categorized him as one of the friendly natives. "I guess you get those questions a lot. I'm Meredith. I live out Road 41."

He nodded as though he already knew. She wasn't surprised; most people she'd met in Hay City already seemed to know everything about her: The newcomer from California, the one suspected of killing her husband. Brian's murder was the crime of the century in these small parts and she'd played a starring role.

"Jonathan Pringle," he said in return. "I'm surprised we haven't met before. I think my kids go to school with your daughter. Jamie, right?"

"Your kids?"

"Rio, my son, he's eight. Graciella's thirteen. They see Jamie on the bus once in a while. I have another one in diapers."

They smiled at each other, in the way of parents with a common bond. There were the shared experiences of sleepless nights, skinned knees and unlimited joy.

"You here on city business?" he asked, hope in his voice. "Need a business permit, have a complaint about someone's cattle grazing on your property, or just in for a chat?"

She remembered her mission. After practically accusing her of murder, would Brooke cause trouble for her daughter at school? "I'm looking for the sheriff, actually."

Jonathan's face fell. "I figured." He glanced toward the window. "He just pulled up outside."

She started. "Oh. I need to go. It was nice meeting you though."

He bobbed his head in acknowledgment. "We should get our kids together sometime." He grabbed a piece of paper and a pen, jotting something down. "And Graciella does some babysitting. Here's my number. Call anytime."

She took the paper and thanked him as she edged to the door, noting the tall man's dimples one more time before turning away. She wanted to talk to Curtis in private. It wouldn't do to talk about the principal in front of another parent, especially in a town where gossip flew from eager tongues to greedy ears.

The door opened and Curtis strode in carrying Atticus with Jamie close behind him. Curtis set the baby down at Meredith's feet. "I found these two outside."

Her face grew warm and she hoped she wasn't blushing. She felt as though she'd been caught at being one of those terrible people who abandon their children in cars. This wasn't a good start. "Oh. I just stopped by. To say hi." She couldn't discuss Brooke in front of Jamie. Flustered, she jammed her hands in her pockets.

Curtis looked between her and Jonathan, who leaned on the counter watching them. "I see you've met Jonathan."

She nodded. "I wanted to talk to you about, um,

Twin Lakes."

He raised his eyebrows at her.

"You're tall," Jamie said, craning her neck to gape at the towering man behind the counter.

"I bet your name is Jamie," he shot back.

Jamie's mouth dropped open. "How did you know?"

He gave a shrug. "You look like a Jamie. Am I right?"

She narrowed her eyes in suspicion but nodded.

He snapped his fingers and smiled broadly at Meredith. "I know what. You should apply for the assistant clerk position here. The job's back in the budget, ten hours a week. Office with a window. And a great boss. Me."

Curtis cleared his throat but didn't speak.

The opportunity for a private conversation about Brooke was slipping away. However, she couldn't ignore the possibility of another job with her finances the way they were. "A job? What would I do?"

He stood up straight, his lean body stretching toward the ceiling. "Mainly help us keep office hours here," he admitted. "Not much work to do, but the sheriff is gone a lot and I'm in and out with my kids. The budget allows for an assistant, and if we don't fill the position, the mayor's going to take the job away."

Meredith glanced at Curtis, registering his set jaw. It annoyed her he knew she needed to earn more money and didn't bother to mention the job. "I work part time over at the hardware store," she hedged.

Jonathan waved one hand in the air dismissively. "Not a problem. We can work a schedule that works. If you apply, I mean, and if the hiring manager," he pointed to himself, "decides to take you on."

The job would solve two of her problems at once, the need to make more money and her lack of a computer. An office job would give her unlimited access to the Internet and the world. Living in Hay City was akin to living on the moon as far as current events went. She'd never been one to follow the news, but an occasional headline would be nice. The only news in these parts was transmitted via gossip and often didn't resemble reality at all.

He snapped his fingers again. "Anyone ever say you look just like that famous actress? The one in all those movies? What's her name? Anyway. You're a dead ringer. Maybe prettier even." He chuckled. "Don't forget, you have my phone number now."

"You're here to talk to me?" Curtis interrupted. He shot a glare at the other man, who rolled his eyes and looked away.

She noted the tense dynamic between the two and tucked the information away, to ask about later. She glanced at Jamie and Atticus, knowing there was only a few minutes before one or the other got antsy. Tucking a strand of hair behind one ear, she smiled an apology at Jonathan and shifted her attention to Curtis and spoke more urgently. "I need to talk to you."

There was silence in the room. Jonathan raised his eyebrows, and then stepped back from the counter. "Hey, Jamie," he offered brightly. "I'm Rio's dad. Want to work the copier machine for me?"

Meredith gave the man a grateful glance as Jamie ran behind the counter. What a relief to have another parent help out. In a moment, the hum and click of the copier filled the room. There was the sound of tearing and she turned to see Atticus ripping the cover off a magazine. She rushed over and snatched the page from his hand.

"You shouldn't be using the copier," Curtis called out above the clacking of the machine. "You're not official here."

"I'm officially unofficial," the other man retorted. "Or am I unofficially official? Doesn't matter. We're pretty casual out here."

Atticus in her arms, she frowned at Jonathan, puzzled.

"I don't really work here," he admitted over the clicking of the copier. "My sister's the city clerk. Stacey's over at Malady having her hair done. She'll be back later."

Curtis made a sound in his throat, his expression turning dark. He touched Meredith's arm and shot an annoyed look at the other man. "Come outside a minute. So we can talk."

She shifted Atticus to her other hip and followed him out the door. She hadn't seen him since going to Brooke's house and worried that broaching the subject of the woman would annoy him.

He spoke grudgingly as soon as the door closed behind them. "Jonathan…Watch out for him."

"He seemed nice. Our kids go to the same school."

"Three kids by three different women and he didn't marry any of them," Curtis said. "I saw how he looked at you just now. Anyway, he doesn't belong in my office, offering people jobs."

A car roared by the lonely two-lane highway bisecting the town's frontage, zipping from one nowhere location to another. Meredith knew by now it didn't matter which direction you traveled, it took a full day to get to a proper city.

"He should have slowed down to town limits," he said, shifting on his feet. "They were going at least seventy."

She waited, hitching Atticus back to her other hip. Curtis glowered after the disappearing car until the vehicle was a dot in the distance. Jonathan raised her hopes for another part-time job and some extra income, but he didn't work there at all. She wondered if there even was a job opening, but it wasn't why she was here.

"Brooke is principal at Jamie's school," she announced, trembling inside as she spoke. If Brooke killed her husband, what else might the woman do?

He raised his eyebrows and studied her face. "You think it's going to be a problem?"

"I didn't make much of an impression. I'm afraid she'll take it out on Jamie." Before he could respond, she continued in a rush. "I've also been thinking. Brooke and Carolyn…Caro, I mean," she corrected herself. "They don't seem like they'd have much in common, to be friends, I mean."

He frowned. "Because one's pretty and the other is…so different?"

She cringed inside to hear him describe Brooke as 'pretty.' "They just seem worlds apart," she said, determined to make Curtis talk about them. "Do you know Caro carries a gun around? In a backpack?"

He gave a brief nod. "Gun permits come through my office. I know everyone who has a concealed weapon in my county. A legal one anyway."

A thought occurred to her. "Does Brooke have a permit?"

He stared at the road ahead and didn't answer.

"You can't tell me?"

"Concealed permits aren't open records in Idaho," he answered after a moment.

It didn't make sense to her people could hide the fact they carried around a deadly weapon. What was it with this place? Everything was upside down. "Wouldn't it make sense for people to know if their neighbor is carrying a gun?" she asked in a frustrated tone.

"Meredith, this is Idaho. People assume their neighbor is carrying a gun. It's how people grew up here; guns are part of the culture."

She fumed inside. If you asked her, Idaho possessed a little too much culture of the wrong kind. "Please tell me the kid behind the deli counter doesn't have a concealed permit or I'm leaving the state right now."

He gave her a puzzled look. "Jeffrey Cole? The kid at the grocery store? What does he have to do with all of this?"

She shook her head, for some reason surprised the kid owned a real name. To her, the petulant teen would always be 'deli boy.' "Nothing."

"Meredith," he said in a soft voice, "you're safe now. Your kids are safe. What happened in Twin Lakes stirred some things up in you. But if anything happens at the school, anything at all, you let me know and I'll step in. I promise."

Hitching Atticus higher, she reached for the door. "If anything happens, it'll be too late."

Chapter Eleven

Honey lined up three cans on a wooden crate before crossing the yard to where Meredith stood. "This is how I learned, years ago. Cans on a crate, right here, first week I was married to Milt. Said he wouldn't stand for a woman who couldn't shoot a charging bear."

The Ruger handgun was heavier than Meredith expected. The weapon was a small lump of cold metal, molded into curves that fit neatly into her hand. The gun wouldn't stop a charging bear; just a way to scare off varmints and small predators, she told herself.

The older woman beamed from ear to ear, thrilled at being called into service and being right once more. "Nothing more potent than a gal holding a gun."

It was a week after she realized Brooke was Jamie's principal, Mrs. 'Beebee.' The discovery unnerved her, although she learned Brooke requested a month or so of bereavement leave. The sleeplessness she always suffered in stressful times returned. She operated on minimal sleep and convinced herself that as long as she kept her eyes closed, this was almost as good as a full night's rest. It was unreasonable to believe Jamie was in any danger from a woman whose husband died of natural causes. When it touched upon her children, though, she didn't care about being reasonable.

Honey tapped her hand. "Lighten up on your grip,

dear. The gun's not trying to run away from you. Don't yank at the trigger; squeeze."

The crack made her inhale sharply. She lowered her hand slowly, still feeling the slap against her palm when she fired. Honey blew out a sigh, releasing a poof of fog into the frozen air. "Okay, let's try again. This time, let's work on our aim a little more."

Her friend chattered and tittered through the lesson, but Meredith was dead serious about learning to shoot. A light misty rain started and stopped and Honey ran back and forth to the front porch to check on Atticus, bundled up in blankets inside a play teepee.

The older woman zipped up her coat as far as it would go, covering the bottom of her chin. "Seen our sheriff lately?"

She shot twice and missed twice. Jamie had told her excitedly Curtis visited the school the previous week. He informed the children about his job, passed around the silver star he liked to wear on his chest, and answered questions until the bell rang for recess—but he didn't call or stop by her house. "Nope," she answered sharply.

"Raise the barrel up even and aim through these notches here." Honey touched her hand. "Are you aiming, dear?"

After forty-five minutes of aiming, shooting, missing, and reloading, her hand was frozen and stinging. The three cans sat on their perch, unblemished.

"You're not a natural, but that's okay. Sometimes the sound of gunshot is all you need to get the point across. But we can do this again. Sooner or later, you're bound to get the hang of it."

Meredith glowered at the cans as a few stray snowflakes drifted down. "I won't give up," she vowed.

****

Rain turned to snow over the next few days, sticking to the ground, piling inch upon inch, and icicles dripped from the eaves. Meredith tugged on her boots and stomped out to the shed, sinking mid-calf into the slush. Ten minutes later, she returned lugging the rabbit hutch up the steps and into the living room. Five tiny, furless creatures wriggled nonstop at Grendel's belly.

Jamie's face scrunched up in horror at the sight. "Mommy, they're so ugly. Where's their fur?"

She studied the newborn rabbits, not sure if they were supposed to have fur at first. Deformed or not, the possibility of having six frozen rabbits in her shed was a worse option. "I don't know. I guess fur comes later." Or maybe these are mutants, she thought. "Let's hope."

Atticus toddled over, examined the cage, and quickly lost interest. He settled down with his building blocks, and carefully laid one on top of the other.

"I'm hungry," Jamie announced, her attention still riveted to the cage. "I'd like waffles."

Meredith's stomach growled, reminding her she hadn't consumed anything other than coffee since she woke. "Not cereal?" She gave an exaggerated expression of shock. Cereal was the household favorite for breakfast.

"I don't think so. Waffles," her daughter ordered again.

One of their few kitchen appliances, aside from a toaster and crock pot, was indeed a waffle iron. It'd been a Christmas gift from Brian one year, but rarely used since his death. "You're right, it does feel like a waffle day," she agreed. "How about some help?"

Jamie patted the top of the cage, obviously torn between waffles and baby rabbits. Hunger won out and, after a lingering backward look, she followed quickly into the kitchen. Jamie stood on a chair at the counter while the ingredients were set out, one by one, in front of her. Meredith handed her a big spoon and cracked eggs into a bowl.

"My teacher is reading *The Cat in the Hat*," the five-year-old chattered, stirring the eggs in a circle. Meredith took up the spoon and whipped the eggs quickly and handed the spoon back to her daughter. "It's my favorite book ever. It's about a bad cat who makes a mess. He cleans everything up again though. What's your favorite book?"

She poured oil into the eggs and measured out the other dry ingredients. "I have lots of favorites. 'War and Peace,' 'Pride and Prejudice,' 'Animal Farm.'"

"'Animal Farm.' What's it about?"

"I don't know. I've never read it."

"Mom," Jamie protested, exasperation in her voice. "A book can't be your favorite if you've never read it."

"All my favorite books are ones I've never read. They're the ones I can look forward to reading."

Her daughter was quiet for a moment, pondering the idea while Meredith plugged in the waffle iron. Jamie poured flour and baking powder into the eggs and stirred the mixture around the bowl. "Do you believe in heaven?"

The topic was a surprise, and she spoke slowly, not wanting to get this wrong for her daughter. "I believe there's something."

"What about for bad people? Do you believe in something for them too?"

They'd never discussed this subject and now, out of the blue, her five-year-old wanted to know if she believed in some version of hell. She sprinkled salt and sugar into the bowl and added a dash of vanilla. "I really don't know. I hope there's something good for everyone. Something better."

"I like it here best," Jamie said, her tone firm. "I like my house and my school and my Laf and my rabbits."

Meredith pointed to herself and her daughter giggled, adding, "And my Mom and Atticus." The girl turned somber, her mirth disappearing. "Daddy's not here anymore. He's not coming back, is he?"

She gave the top of Jamie's head a kiss, breathing in her daughter's shampoo. "No."

"Do you have a daddy?"

She should have expected the question would come someday, the questions about her own parents. Her daughter was growing up. The directness of the words, though, stunned her into silence.

Jamie let the spoon fall into the bowl and it sunk under the waffle batter, vanishing. She turned her face up, eyes wide. "Mom? Is he dead, too?"

It was peculiar how she'd never considered her father might be dead. He'd always been a faceless shadow "out there" somewhere; a stranger to seek one day, despite her mother's warning against seeking him out. "I don't know, sweetie. I never met him."

She poured the waffle mixture into the iron and squeezed the lid shut, batter oozing out from the edges.

"I like it when the stuff squishes out." Jamie

giggled, the topic of dads forgotten.

****

Jamie and Atticus watched the baby rabbits most of the morning, waiting for fur to sprout and trying out names for each of them. Meredith plucked dead rodents out of all three mousetraps and reset them, thinking even dead mice were far cuter than newborn rabbits.

Water seeped into the house from different angles, dripping onto the middle of the stove, the back of the couch, and created an ever widening stain on the ceiling of Jamie's bedroom. She set out pots to collect the drips, then tackled the black mold that returned in the bathroom no matter how much she scrubbed it with bleach. Old wallpaper on one bathroom wall, dark green with pink roses, peeled at its edges. Meredith spent an hour stripping the paper away, finding the glue fused to the wallboard and the result of her efforts was a battered and pocked wall. She turned away, seeking something to do that wouldn't make a situation worse. The house continued to disintegrate faster than she could fix it.

Honey's question about Curtis lingered in her mind. Why didn't he drop by like he used to? Did their relationship have to be all or nothing? She pondered this as she traipsed back out to the shed in search of sandpaper to smooth the mess she'd created to the bathroom wall. The falling snow mutated to half-rain, and she was soaked through when she returned to the house. She toweled off her hair, changed her socks and returned to the bathroom with a handful of used sandpaper, its grit mostly gone.

Meredith sat back on her heels and stared at the destroyed wall, wondering if she'd ruined all chances with Curtis. Her house wasn't the only thing needing repairs. Would she have to be the one who went wooing, and convince him she wouldn't come unglued every time someone died?

A damp smell settled into the house and the wood floors stayed cold no matter how high she turned up the pellet stove. Their home exuded an atmosphere of slow rot in defiance to all her hard work to combat it, despite the new curtains, new paint, and bleach. As much as she tried to love the place back to life, the old house had sat empty and unloved for decades longer.

This is my house, she thought, for better or worse. She'd paid Brian's debt on it and also the property taxes, a concept she still didn't quite understand; why would you continue to pay money on a possession you already purchased, free and clear? Still, they had a roof over their heads, even if it leaked a bit, even if mice nibbled at the woodwork, even if ice formed inside the windows at night. It was the only home she ever lived in and she wasn't going to let go. Even Crusty had a rough start when he moved to Hay City, feuding with a neighbor over land and garden gnomes, but now a business owner with a new love of his own.

As for Curtis…maybe it was time to risk love once more, after all. She could put Jacob and Brooke—and Brian—out of her mind and start fresh.

Life is messy; it's all about how you handle it. Her mother's catchphrase rang out in her head. *One day at a time.* Her own motto kept her afloat. And through it all was Honey's more direct battle cry: *Get a backbone girl.* She wouldn't give up. Never.

She attacked the wall with a fury and rubbed the sandpaper over the surface until it was worn smooth.

****

Jamie clutched her arms tight around her body. "I don't think so."

Meredith eyed the lion costume with dismay. She'd convinced Jamie to use it mostly as pajamas, but it still made an appearance on school mornings from time to time. "It's filthy. You can put it back on as soon as we get home."

"Just today, please. I promise. I double-pinkie promise. Karin says if I break a double-pinkie promise, my toes will fall off."

It was the pleading in her daughter's eyes that softened her resolve. She doubted a double-pinkie promise would matter; her daughter most certainly loved her lion costume more than her toes. With the issue of clothing settled, they headed off to Curtis's house.

She didn't call ahead, telling herself she didn't want to hear he was busy or there was something else he needed to do on his Sunday afternoon. The truth was she wanted to see him, if only for a minute or two.

He lived exactly three-point-six miles from her own house, a seven-minute drive if she drove the speed limit. With the roads sloppy from half-melted snow, the drive took eight-and-a-half minutes, and her heart raced faster as they neared. His home was self-built, a tiny one-bedroom place on a parcel of land adjacent to his parents'. The porch to his house faced a line of tall pines, marking the boundaries of his property. Beyond, there was a view of the Sawtooths, looming high above the trees. Meredith took a breath and then another. The twangs of country music could be heard playing inside and her heart thumped, knowing he was at home.

The door swung open and Curtis stood in his bare feet. "Hey."

"I wanted..." She nodded back toward the car where Jamie waved wildly. "Well, you've been missed so we wanted to invite you on a little snow hike. Jamie wants to go lion hunting."

He smiled and leaned against the doorway. Meredith gazed up at him and her breath caught at the gladness on his face. "Appears like you already caught one."

She glanced back at her daughter and laughed, color rushing to her cheeks. "Honey made the costume for Halloween. My little lion hasn't changed her clothes much since; she even sleeps in it."

He gestured inside. "Trails are pretty messy, but why don't you all come in for a bit. I'm making huckleberry pancakes for a late lunch. Do you suppose lions like huckleberries?"

The easy-going invitation surprised her. Wooing wouldn't be difficult in this case; avoiding broken hearts would be the danger ahead. "Lions definitely like pancakes. And I love huckleberries."

The blare of a car horn caused her to jump and she whirled around to see Jamie in the front seat. She beckoned her children to get out of the car, and the three of them filed into the house and stomped the wetness from their shoes. Meredith took two steps inside the room and stopped by a rack to one side, filled with two pairs of boots and a pair of slippers. She helped her kids off with their shoes and then slipped off her own, noticing with dismay her socks were frayed at the big toes. She felt her face heating up. She'd spent extra time on her hair and clothes. She wore a pale blue sweater that heightened the green flecks in her eyes and left her hair loose and soft at her shoulders. She'd added a tad more makeup than usual, with just a touch of mascara at her lashes, but there'd been no reason to fuss about her old socks.

"Nice place," she offered quickly, hoping he wouldn't notice her feet, and in the next moment as she looked around she meant it.

The tidy room served as living room, dining room and kitchen. As small as the space was, its simplicity was stunning. Dark wide-planked floors, fireplace neatly set with wood, old-fashioned crank windows; the place was sparsely furnished, yet with an eye for clean lines. A skylight high above the dining area carried natural light into the room.

"This is…beautiful," she breathed.

Curtis led them on a tour, clearly proud of his compact house, pointing out various features: the fold-out dining table, extra tall ceilings to add a sense of space, high cabinets for storage, open shelves in the kitchen above a farmhouse sink. He hesitated only for a moment and then beckoned her to the bedroom, where she gasped to see a roll-up garage door set into the back wall.

"Want to see?" he asked and without waiting for an answer, he cranked open the door and the bedroom's entire back wall opened up to a wide deck. Cold air rushed in. "It's great in the summer when there's a breeze. And for watching the stars."

Jamie made him raise and lower his bedroom garage door three times. "You have the best house ever," she exclaimed, eyes shining. "When I grow up, I'm going to have a house just like this one."

"This is amazing," Meredith agreed. "I can't believe you did this all yourself."

Curtis cranked the large wall door closed, locking it firmly against the floor with a thud. "Five hundred and fifty-nine square feet. My original plan called for just five hundred and fifty square feet but I forgot one thing. The extra nine square feet is for my washer/dryer. They're stackable so they need less space."

She shook her head in wonder. She'd never seen such a lovely home, so carefully designed and lovingly crafted. There was something about the meticulous craftsmanship that evoked an emotion in her she couldn't define. This was a man who took care with everything he did, who didn't cut corners.

"You're in the wrong profession," she said. "You should build houses. Or at least design them. I mean, you are really great at this."

"I considered it. Maybe a fallback, if I get voted out as sheriff," he quipped. As he passed by her to go in the other room, he murmured near her ear, "Glad I was missed."

Meredith set the table for four while Jamie poked huckleberries into the sizzling pancakes alongside Curtis, making smiley faces in the batter. "We ate waffles for breakfast but I like pancakes better," she told him.

While they dug into their breakfast-for-lunch, he asked, "How's the class going?"

"Almost done now. I think I'll pass but I don't think I'll be a chemist."

"Did you want to be one?"

She laughed. "This is just the start for me." She

stopped, realizing how true those words were as soon as they were out of her mouth. Starting the class, putting her husband's ashes and memory to rest, fixing up her house; she was launching a new life.

He nodded and appeared to understand her sudden confusion. He gave her a moment.

"You'll need to be careful driving up the mountain now. Most people have four-wheel drive vehicles and can handle the roads. And they'll close the road down pretty soon."

"It was still clear last week," Meredith said. "Even with a little flurry, I didn't have any trouble."

He gave her a stern look. "Things change quick up the road. The mountain can get a couple feet of snow overnight."

"Mom shoots guns with Honey," Jamie chimed in.

There was a long silence before he responded. "You bought a gun?"

She kept her gaze focused on her plate. He knew her fear of guns, and her sudden change of heart might not speak well to her emotional stability. She felt his stare boring into her. "I'm using Honey's. It's just a little target practice, for fun."

"Well," he admitted. "I'm a bit surprised. But it's not a bad idea to know how to use one."

"Predators," she mumbled.

"Lions," Jamie added.

Curtis cleared his throat. "Speaking of Honey," he added, changing the subject. "She invited me over for Thanksgiving dinner and suggested I bring a guest...or three."

Meredith was startled at the invitation. Leave it to her friend to do a little matchmaking behind her back, pushing and arranging and manipulating as usual. It was so natural sitting across from Curtis at his table, her two children on either side. A family. "Thanksgiving?"

"It's about the pilgrims, Mom," Jamie explained, patience in her tone. "And turkey."

One corner of Meredith's lip twisted up. "I'm familiar with it."

Curtis's ears were pink. "A date, then?"

A buzzing from the kitchen counter interrupted before she could answer. Meredith's emotions swirled in different directions. *Is this the moment? Did we just cross the line from friendship to something more?* He was waiting for me to make a move, she realized. To come to him.

"Meredith."

The tone of his voice deepened and his demeanor was somber. She knew the call was work, something he would have to attend to. "What is it? What's happened?"

He took a breath and glanced at her children. "The older priest up at Twin Lakes. Father Karl. It's...just like Jacob. The coroner asked me to go check it out."

Chapter Twelve

Another death in Twin Lakes, but not murder. Definitely not murder, Meredith warned herself even though her brain was screaming otherwise. She rose from the table and forced her hands to keep from fidgeting.

"Kids, we'd better go," she said, barely keeping a quiver from her voice. Death seemed to be lurking too close to her these days.

"I want to go lion hunting," Jamie protested.

Meredith picked up the dishes from the table. She practiced saying the words coolly in her mind before she spoke them out loud. "The sheriff has important work to do. We'll hike another time."

It wasn't fair. Today of all days, the most normal of Sunday afternoons. Why did Father Karl have to up and die? Somehow, she made it to the front door without showing how rattled her nerves were. A million questions flew through her mind, but she swallowed each as they rose to her lips. There were normal questions and obsessive questions, and she'd lost perspective on which was which.

"Thank you for the pancakes," she intoned, keeping her voice flat and her gaze on the floor, not wanting Curtis to see her agitation. "They were delicious."

He walked them to the car and buckled Atticus into

the car seat. He touched Meredith on the arm as she opened her car door. "I'm going to need to talk to you," he said in a low voice. "Everything Jacob might have said to you, in the library."

"He was an old man—Father Karl," she said quickly, agitated at the mention of Jacob. *Stay calm*, she warned herself. "Surely not like Jacob at all."

"Probably not," he agreed right away. "Nothing to worry about. But…"

She waited, her mind filling the gap: Two men from the same church, dead within a short period of time. It wasn't paranoia to link the two together, but she didn't want to be the one to mention it. *Stay calm.*

"…there are some similarities I need to look at," Curtis finished. "It's why the coroner wants me to go as back up."

Lips stiff, she asked, "What similarities?"

"I'll stop by your place when I get back, okay?"

She locked eyes with him as she backed the car out of his driveway, crunching over sloppy snow which was melted in some areas and icy in others. There was a predator on the loose in Twin Lakes and Meredith knew exactly who she was.

****

The snowman tilted slightly to the left in front of her house but stood firm, its base packed firm by two sets of little hands. As she worked alongside her children, her gaze lifted every few minutes to the road. Curtis wouldn't forget his promise to come by. He would have to know she was dying…well, aching to know how the old priest died.

Similarities. The word echoed in her mind.

It was murder, of course. It was obvious as could

be there was a link between the two deaths, the two *murders*; there was no doubt in her mind. Now Curtis would have to agree Jacob's death was suspicious and most likely murder. Now he would have to consider Brooke as a suspect.

I was right all along and not crazy at all.

What she couldn't understand was why Brooke would kill the old priest. What did Jacob and the old priest have in common except for their obvious connection with her?

"Mommy. Pay attention."

She was startled out of her thoughts. Jamie's arms were filled with a pile of clothing to dress the snowman: one of Meredith's dresses, a pair of panties and a bra. After disengaging the underwear from her daughter's hands, she said, "I don't think we need these."

"But she's a girl," Jamie insisted.

"People will figure it out by the dress."

"I saw a man in a dress once. He wore a beard."

She was at a loss how to explain things. "Okay, well…"

She'd heard once you should only explain as much as a child can understand and no more. *What should I say? What are the appropriate words? I don't want to confuse her.* At her feet, Atticus continued to build onto the bottom of the snow-woman, packing handful after handful to the base and occasionally stuffing a fistful of white into his mouth.

"Can Karin and Rio come over to play?" Jamie prattled on. "We'll make snow babies and snow rabbits and…"

She was relieved her five-year-old didn't need her

to say anything more. She'd finally learned most times her daughter simply wanted her mother to be there and listen. She tossed the bra and panties aside and crammed two generous globules onto the chest of their creation and packed more on each side to create hips. Jamie giggled and handed her the dress. They tugged and buttoned the dress best they could around the lumpy figure. Meredith stepped back, admiring their work, and thought a woman—even one made of snow—needed some hair.

"Sheriff," Jamie cried, and Meredith spun around as Curtis's truck rolled into the driveway.

Jamie ran to the truck. "Come see our snow-woman man," the girl called, as he stepped out of his truck. She tugged at his hand and pulled him across the yard.

He examined the curvy figure with a smile. "She's great. Like a princess."

Meredith approached to stand next to him. "Hey."

"Thought you'd want to hear what's happening, up in Twin Lakes," he said, his smile slipping.

She turned to Jamie. "Spaghetti," she said. "Pasta's the perfect thing for our snow-woman's hair. Can you get it from the kitchen?"

The girl ran to the house, her petite boots punching through the soft drifts. They watched her go into the house and then faced each other. "Tell me," she demanded.

Curtis's face was grim. "Father Karl was vomiting, like Jacob, right before he died. We're getting some samples taken, for some type of poisoning. If it comes back positive, we'll have to exhume Jacob's body and have a medical examiner come in to do a full autopsy."

She remembered seeing the old priest once, sweeping the front step of the church as she passed by. He possessed a full head of gray hair slicked back and he stooped slightly as he walked. He wasn't around the day she sought him out in the church, when she hoped to speak to him about Jacob and Brooke. More than ever, she wished she could have talked to him.

"Not a heart attack, like Jacob," she ventured, though inside she felt a chill.

"It could be, of course," he answered. "It would be a pretty big coincidence if they both presented heart attacks in the exact same way. Also, I spoke with the doctor, and she confirmed Father Karl recently had a checkup and everything appeared fine."

Murders were rare in High County. Brian's murder was the county's first in decades. Now, only eight months later, there were two more. Her intuition from the start was Jacob was murdered. And now a priest too. She felt strangely victorious in predicting Jacob was murdered and not dead of a heart attack at all.

"Did you go see Brooke? What does she have to say about this?"

He gave her a warning look. "Don't jump to conclusions. If they both died of poison, it was probably accidental. Other people could be at risk. I need to wait for the toxicology results first."

She shook her head doubtfully. The next words launched themselves out of her mouth before she could stop herself. "Brooke poisoned both of them. She killed Jacob and then killed the priest because …somehow, he knew and she had no choice. You need to arrest her."

Curtis took hold of her hand and blew out a heavy breath. "Slow down. You can't just blurt out everything you're thinking...wild accusations you have no proof about."

Tears sprung to her eyes in frustration. He could be right; she was getting carried away once more. If the men died of poisoning, the deaths were apt to be accidental, not murder. Even as she told herself these things, she didn't believe it at all. Meredith became aware Curtis was still holding her hand and she grew warm. What would she have done if he hadn't believed in her, certain she was innocent? What if he, too, rushed to judgment? She'd even doubted herself, at one point believing she could have killed Brian during a blackout.

Brian. He was buried but he now haunted her; his violent life and death wouldn't release their grip on her. In life, his behavior steadily became abusive and she'd become more isolated than ever. No friends. No family. There'd just been her children as comfort against the darkness closing over her world.

Then they moved to Hay City and she gained everything she ever wanted—a house, friends, security from want. But all this still wasn't enough. She loved her children to the moon and back, but there was more to life. There had to be.

"Meredith?" Curtis wore a puzzled expression. "Are you okay? Where did you go?"

She gave her head a shake. "Just thinking about everything that's happened. My life. You believed in me. I'm more grateful than you can imagine. But...but there's something not right about Brooke. The poison came from somewhere. And Jacob did predict his own murder."

Jamie ran up, holding a fistful of spaghetti. "I have the princess's hair," she cried. "Can I put it on her?"

Meredith turned back to the snow-woman, grateful for the interruption. They spent the next few minutes poking spaghetti around their sculpture's head, giving it blonde spikes that jutted out at all angles. She was distracted, both by the puzzle over possible twin poisonings in Twin Lakes and by the recollection of this kind, sweet man holding her hand. His touch, so gentle and easily offered, awakened a continuous buzzing inside her.

Curtis stood back and examined their work. "This is one crazy lady."

"I think we did a good job," Meredith protested, laughing, and he laughed with her.

"An alien," he proclaimed.

"I don't think so." Jamie spoke firmly, hands on her hips. "She's beautiful, like my princi-pess at school. I like her. I'm going to give Mrs. Beebee one of my bunnies. She's been sick."

The mention of Brooke, or Mrs. Beebee, reminded Meredith the woman would soon return to work as her daughter's school principal. Even if the woman wasn't a murderess, she'd made veiled accusations. Her daughter could suffer for it.

She nodded toward the house. "I need to get my kids out of their wet clothes. Want to come in and warm up?"

Jamie grabbed Curtis's hand. "Come see my baby bunnies. They look like teeny weeny pigs, but they're going to be rabbits. I promise."

Meredith scooped up Atticus, who shoved one more fistful of snow into his mouth. She brushed the rest of the snow off his face. "Your lips are blue."

"Boo," he agreed.

****

Hot cocoa warmed them all. Curtis was more impressed than they were by the baby rabbits, which were called kittens, he informed Jamie. The five-year-old danced about in elation. "Wait 'til I tell Karin I have kittens," she crowed.

Meredith quietly hoped this would forestall her daughter's interest in getting the more common type of kittens, the ones coming from cats. She tucked away this knowledge and figured she could draw it out again to combat her daughter in any future attempt to get more pets.

"What are baby goats called?" Jamie's question set off alarms in Meredith.

She walked up behind them, noting the kittens were still bare of fur, with only their mini elongated ears hinting they were rabbits. "How do you know so much about rabbits?" she interrupted.

He winked at her and tapped his head. "You have no idea how much useless knowledge is trapped up here," he said. "Ask about ancient Sumerian history or how to put up hay. I could go on for hours."

Questions burst forth from Jamie and Meredith was grateful the subject of goats was forgotten. "When will they grow fur? Are they boys or girls? What color will they be? I'll give you one if you want."

He tucked his head down near the hutch to answer the young girl's questions as best he could. Meredith hoped he knew something about poisons and how two grown men could be felled by one.

She shooed her daughter off to play with Atticus so she could question Curtis. "What are you going to do next, if…poison is confirmed in both of them?"

He knelt at the pellet stove in the corner of the room, checked the ashes were cleared, and then he lit the stove. Sometime soon, she'd need to buy more pellets, just one more monthly expense, but it saved on her heating bill. Bills, bills, bills. Her bank account was paltry now, at best, and she'd have to find another job soon. It was ridiculous she'd ever imagined they could make ends meet on a part-time job.

His tone was doubtful. "I...well...I suppose it depends on what kind of poison. Then we'll figure out how they both gained access to it. That's why I want you to tell me more about what Jacob said to you, places he'd been, foods he'd been eating, anything you can remember. If we're dealing with poison, there could be a serious public health risk in Twin Lakes."

There was Brooke, of course, but she held her tongue on that subject. "I tried to ignore him," she confessed. "I probably missed lots of what he said. He mainly talked about his wife."

"Aside from his wife," Curtis prompted. "Anything at all."

"That's the thing. She's all he wanted to talk about. He was afraid of her."

He straightened up, satisfied the pellet stove was churning out heat. "We should know by morning if it's poison and whether Jacob's body will need to be exhumed. If that happens, I'll talk to Brooke; not before. She might have some idea of what Jacob could have taken, and if he'd been talking to Father Karl recently. Exhuming her husband's body...it'll be rough going for her."

Meredith recalled Brooke's elegant figure, her soft voice, and high cheekbones. The woman was forty if she'd been married for twenty years, but she appeared at least ten years younger. She darted a glance at Curtis and was shocked at the sharp jealousy rising within. She gathered their cocoa cups and took them to the kitchen sink, washing and drying them. Finished with her task she whirled about and was startled to find he'd followed her into the kitchen. She bumped against him before she could stop. "Sorry," she apologized. "Tight quarters."

He didn't shift away. She gazed up at him and her breath went shallow. He was unshaven and the rough stubble gave him a rugged appearance. She remembered the first time they met, how she'd thought he was an actor, dressed up and handsome in a Hollywood version of a country sheriff, complete with vest and silver star. Real life sheriffs weren't supposed to look this good.

"You never answered me about Thanksgiving."

His closeness addled her thoughts. His eyes were bright as he gazed down at her; she wanted to edge away so she could get her voice back, but her legs wouldn't obey.

"If you're free," he added.

Of course, she didn't have any plans for the day. There was just her, the kids, and studying. She needed to catch up on her schoolwork, but it was a cinch she'd pass the class; most of her homework assignments were turned in and she'd done well enough on the quizzes. A holiday dinner with friends...*Curtis*...would be nice and then she could consider signing up for a spring class. School was another bill she couldn't afford, but she'd find the money somewhere. It wasn't worth thinking about now.

Right now, there was this big-hearted, gentle, handsome man standing in her house. She gave him a warm smile as an answer.

He edged closer. "Meredith."

She let her body melt into his as he folded his arms around her. His hands, one on the small of her back and the other coming around to rest on one of her shoulder blades, burned through her sweater. She lifted her chin and met his gaze, and then he drew her closer against him. How did she get so lucky?

This is the good part of my life starting.

Chapter Thirteen

Snow fell through the night, piling up on the window edges, on the doorstep, the trees, the long valley, everything in sight. Sipping on her morning coffee, Meredith recalled the frozen landscape when they'd first arrived in Idaho in late February, and how the melt-off didn't occur until well into March. She counted the months ahead on her fingers. Four more months of persistent flurries, with another month of rain beyond. Winter days would be long and dark, filled with long and dark nights. Last night…

The phone rang and she jumped to answer it, nearly upsetting her coffee cup. Crusty's voice boomed through the phone. "Merry morning! Up and at 'em."

"Hi, Crusty. It's early for you."

He chuckled. "Or late. You never know."

Meredith smiled to herself. It was true one never knew with her boss. He was a mystery, with his no-name hardware store located around the side of a dilapidated log structure. A small sign above the door read "Not the bar." The pony-tailed hardware store owner/bartender/postmaster made sure only regulars patronized his bar by a similar sign reading "Not the hardware store." There was no one who worked harder at keeping customers away. The man had to be secretly wealthy and this was his eccentricity; there was no other way he wasn't going bankrupt.

"I need a hand this morning," he continued. "Need you to go down to the hardware store and open up. Take your kids, do some of that college homework of yours. I'll be into open the bar for my regulars around noon."

She hesitated. She was tempted to beg off for the day and take her kids with her up to the mountain library, even though Jamie was home for the holiday week. Gossip must be swirling about the priest's death following so closely after Jacob's. The librarian might pass along a tidbit or two of news about whether it was poison. Surely, no customers would show up at the hardware store on such a snowy day with an emergency need for nails, wind chimes or a four-man raft.

"I'll pay overtime," Crusty added. "All week."

"I suppose I could drop Jamie by Honey's," Meredith conceded. She wasn't in a position to turn down work, especially at overtime pay.

"Take both kids into the store, no problem," he urged. "Honey's busy this morning."

A background giggle came through the phone and it became clear he was with Honey, keeping her busy enough. He was head over heels with the woman.

"I suppose Jamie can help me," Meredith hedged, trying to think how she was going to keep both kids occupied.

"No cleaning," he warned. "No organizing. Just keep an eye out, that's all."

Another giggle sounded, this time closer to the phone.

"All right then," Crusty said. "Gotta run."

The phone clicked and he was gone. She sighed and hung up the phone. There could be no other employer in the world who would let her bring two kids to work, and then forbid her to do anything productive once she got there.

However, there was nothing to be done in Twin Lakes until the autopsy was complete and she had bills to pay. The overtime pay for working Thanksgiving week would be put to good use. She would keep her pre-paid cell phone in her pocket, the one she only used for emergencies. Perhaps Curtis would call with an update as soon as he knew, but she knew this was unlikely. She wasn't part of this investigation. She wasn't a deputy. She was just a nosy single mom with a part–time minimum wage job.

This was a case requiring a suspicious mind, one recognizing how deceitful and monstrous people could be. Curtis lived a quiet life where people discussed the weather and what was for dinner. Meredith came from a much different background. Jacob's death triggered alarm bells in her. She could relate to having fear of one's spouse. She hoped if Brian followed up on his plan to kill her, someone would have penetrated beyond his charming facade.

****

The roads were buried in snow and the car slipped and fishtailed several times as she drove to work. Her breath was shallow and her hands gripped the wheel, traveling atop the unplowed roads. She was certain they would get stuck but the car kept moving forward despite her fears.

"Mom, why do people talk in different languages?"

Meredith leaned over the steering wheel, shoulders tense. "Not now, Jamie."

"*Hola* means 'hi' in Spanish. *Amigo* is friend. *Hola*

amigo is 'hi friend.'" Her daughter bounced in her seat. "I'm learning this in school. I'm going to learn all the Spanish words. I can teach you if you want."

The hardware store appeared in the distance, drawing close. "Hmmm," she muttered, her attention now on the building.

"All my bunnies have names. Pinkie, Patches, Pumpkin, Poodles and Pico." Jamie sang, and then repeated her song four more times. "Pico means small in Spanish."

The best strategy was to acknowledge her daughter or she would repeat herself endlessly. "Okay."

She edged the steering wheel toward the parking lot and brought the car to a stop. She peeled her clenched hands from the wheel, praying the sun or a plow would make the return journey less stressful. Curtis handled driving in the snow up the mountain in such a casual manner and she vowed one day she would be as accomplished.

Jamie ran ahead into the empty store, looping through the aisles and calling out her own inventory as Meredith turned on the lights. "Hi, gloves. Hi, light bulbs. Hi, wooden dinosaur. Hi, big metal things. Hi, aprons. Hi…"

Meredith dropped her schoolbook on the counter with a thud and settled in for the next few hours. She forced herself to concentrate on her homework, stopping every twenty minutes to do something with her kids. Her schoolwork took twice as long this way, but a five-year-old's attention span is short, a nineteen-month old's even shorter, and twenty minutes was stretching it to the limit. Pictures, puzzles, books, etc. were stashed behind the counter for Jamie's visits.

Atticus was more difficult since a toddler can't be convinced to do anything, but Jamie was happy to entertain her little brother. Her daughter contained an endless reservoir of patience for him and called him '*My* Att'cus.'

Last night. There was plenty to think about there. A kiss with Curtis turned into two, then three. She put the children to bed and returned to his arms. They progressed to the couch, first canoodling like teenagers and then…

The banging of the entrance door startled her from the memory. "Where's Crusty? He's late."

The man was on the far side of middle-age with a weighty paunch that threatened the zipper of his jacket. Frown lines marked the edges of his mouth and red veins lined his prominent nose.

Meredith hopped off her stool and blushed as though he could read her mind. She glanced at one of the potato-themed clocks ticking in a corner. "He's opening at noon. Like always. You have ten minutes."

The man eyed the door leading into the bar. "Damn him to the next county and back. He knows I'm coming in. I'll just wait in there."

He edged toward the closed door and she hesitated a fraction of a second before stepping in front of him. "I don't know…" she started, and then stood straight. "I can't let you in."

"Ten minutes. What's the problem?"

She swallowed. Was her job to be a part-time bouncer as well? "You have to wait for Crusty."

His mouth hardened, but he turned away without challenging her further. She watched as he roamed the aisles and hoped her boss wouldn't be late. The potato clock ticked laboriously closer to noon. There was a rattling in the aisles as the man picked up items and set them down again with a clatter.

After a few minutes, he returned to the front of the store. "I know who you are."

Of course, you do.

She fought the urge to roll her eyes. Was there no one within a hundred miles who didn't know she was the widow of a murdered man? "You're the gal who killed her husband."

"No. I'm not," Meredith protested, looking at her children huddled next to an old cassette player with a book on tape reading old nursery rhymes. Her anger at forevermore being identified in the community as a murderer boiled over. "I didn't. You're a rude man."

The door behind the counter opened and Crusty poked his head in. "Hey, Merry. See you met our mayor. Yo there, mate." Her boss directed this toward the mayor. "Hope you're behaving yourself."

The mayor shouldered his way to the door and Crusty let him through. "S'about time."

Meredith shook her head in disbelief as the man walked to the far end of the bar and perched himself atop a stool. "The mayor? He doesn't get my vote."

"That's what everyone says," Crusty said, his shaggy eyebrows swooping down in his forehead. "No one else wants the job either so he wins by default, every year for twelve years now. Any customers?"

She shook her head again, and the large man's eyebrows waggled one way and then the other. He lowered his voice. "I'll just charge the mayor double for all the things he slipped into his pockets. You go on home now."

Crusty shut the door, his long gray ponytail swishing behind him. Meredith heaved a sigh of relief. The peculiar characters roaming Hay City met their match with her boss, especially the city's top official.

A shoplifting barfly mayor. Perfect.

****

They made a date for that evening. The closest restaurant was in Malady, but because the single cafe there opened only for breakfast and lunch, it wasn't an option.

"I'll make dinner," Curtis proposed. "I make a pretty solid lasagna."

"Then I'll put together a salad and French bread," she offered.

Canoodling the night before, at Meredith's house, progressed impatiently forward when it was cut short by a wail from Atticus. They both froze from their position on the couch, waiting to see if her son's fussiness would continue.

"He's going through a phase," she whispered. "He'll settle down in a minute."

But Atticus's cries only grew louder and then Jamie's sleepy voice rose above the squalls. "Mom. Atticus is crying."

"I'm sorry," Meredith said, her heart sinking at the interruption. "I need to check on him."

She returned to the living room with a red-faced Atticus a few minutes later, patting his back as he lay his head on her shoulder. Curtis stood near the door, zipping up his coat. This led to the dinner invitation.

"Think Honey would babysit?" he had asked.

Now, she was at his door, he was opening it and pulling her into his arms. The salad and bread were cast aside on the dining table, set for two and where a single tapered candle burned.

She kicked off her shoes and clothes fell in a trail that led to his bed. She lost track of time as she focused on this man whom she loved whole-heartedly. It was nothing like Brian, nothing like the boy in high school. She almost cried at what she'd been missing all along and what could have been sacrificed to stay in a miserable marriage.

Later, a thought came to her out of the blue, making her gasp as she lay exhausted in Curtis' arms. It wasn't fair she would think of Brian at this moment.

He lifted himself onto an elbow and gazed down at her. "What?"

"Your lasagna," she lied, averting her gaze. "It's ruined."

He grabbed her hand and drew her from the bed. "Lasagna is never ruined," he said. "And I'm starving. Ready for dinner?"

They devoured the food, carving through most of the lasagna and scraping the last of the salad from the bowl. His gaze never left her and his cozy house was warm and safe. The involuntary thought that jolted through her in bed receded to a dark corner of her mind.

Twin Lakes, and all that happened there, was avoided by mutual agreement until they were finished with dinner, but she needed to know. "Just one question," she started.

He answered the question before she voiced the words. "It was a type of poison, but we're not entirely sure what it is. The medical examiner goes up there tomorrow and Jacob's body will be exhumed. We won't know any more until we get a full report."

Meredith nodded, satisfied in the knowledge an investigation was underway. But there was that memory again, bullying its way forward, the one making her gasp in Curtis's bed. *Damn you, Brian.*

The taper burned lower and she was reminded of the lateness of the hour. If only the outside world could be patient and give them more time. Her children needed to be taken home to their own beds.

"Okay, tell me," he demanded as she finally trudged to the front door. "You're upset. If you're having regrets, tell me now."

She faced him, miserable knowing he could see through her so easily. Meredith considered lying and then confessed, "Today's the anniversary of the day I told Brian I was pregnant with Jamie. It's the day he proposed to me."

The first three years of her marriage, this day was circled on her calendar as one of the happiest days of her life. The day was now engraved on her mind as her proverbial fork in the road; she could have decided not to marry Brian and so much pain would have been avoided. Years of her life wasted on someone who only wanted to hurt her.

"This would have been six years for us," she murmured and then rushed to add, "I can't believe I told you, but I want you to know everything about me. Good and bad."

Curtis's face had turned to stone. "Six years for you," he muttered, but she heard the words clearly, the emphasis on 'you.' He was quiet for a moment and she was certain she'd ruined everything.

This day belonged to them and for something good and fresh, not to Brian. She held her breath and waited for his anger for ruining their evening.

"*You* would have been married for six years." He spoke in a quiet voice, not looking at her. "Brian stopped being married a few years earlier. Didn't he?"

Tears welled in her eyes at his hurtful comment. He touched her hand gently. "As long as we're being honest with each other...I'm just saying you deserved someone better. You deserved someone who knew what marriage was all about and wouldn't lie and cheat behind your back. He got you so you're jumping at shadows. You deserve much better."

Her tears welled over and fell down her cheeks. She let them fall without wiping them away. It was the nicest thing anyone ever said to her. He was right, she thought; Brian lied and cheated and Gemma was unlikely to be his first affair.

My husband got himself murdered and I almost ended up in prison for the crime. He left a mess for me to clean up. And, somehow, I feel guilty for all of it.

Her breath caught as she gazed up at Curtis, noticing the nick at the side of his jaw where he'd cut himself shaving and the crinkle lines at the corners of his eyes. Wrinkles from smiling, not from frowning, she noted.

"Here." He reached out and wiped her tears away, then straightened the collar poking up from her sweater. "I guess this is a day for important moments. Can you add me to the list of events?"

Meredith stretched up for a long answering kiss.

****

"They wanted to stay up for you," Honey said as she walked in the door. "I figured they might as well."

Meredith stood frozen inside the doorway, staring

at the scene in her friend's living room. On the living room floor a baby was lying on a blanket, surrounded by stuffed toys and flanked by Meredith's children. Atticus waved a blue stuffed elephant over the baby like the toy was an airplane.

"They don't know who this is," Honey whispered to her, clutching her arm.

"My baba," Atticus said at the same time. "My baba."

She glared at the other woman and her gaze swept the room. "Is she here?" Meredith demanded, eyes narrowed.

Honey shook her head, her expression all innocence. "Gemma dropped him off for the night," she confessed. "What am I supposed to do, turn away my great grand baby? Anyway, look how sweet all of them are together. They play together so nicely."

Her countenance was grim. Gemma's baby. Brian's baby. Dead or alive, every which way she turned, Brian was still there mocking her. "Jamie. Atticus. Time to go home."

"No," Atticus announced clearly. "My baba."

Meredith's breath came fast as she pushed from her mind the fact they were half-brothers. "Not your baba. Time to go."

Atticus screwed up his face to cry, though her daughter rose calmly.

Honey's hands fluttered. "The three of them get along so well," she protested. "No harm done."

Meredith refused to meet her friend's eyes. There had been so much harm done in her life already. Jamie tugged a whimpering Atticus up off the floor and walked him to the door. "I want to go home," the young girl announced. "I'm tired. Babies are too much work."

Honey's chuckle was a little too loud, covering the tension. Meredith didn't break a smile at Jamie's adult pronouncement. She swung a kicking Atticus up on one hip and shot the other woman another disapproving glare before something occurred to her.

"Thank you for watching the kids," she said, her tone stilted and formal. "This isn't the first time, is it? That they've all been here together."

Her friend shook her head and then gave a sheepish shrug. "They're just children. They entertain each other so well. I didn't see the harm."

Meredith gripped her daughter's hand and led her out the door.

She vowed never to return.

Chapter Fourteen

As she'd learned in her life too many times, vows were made to be broken. Three days later, Curtis gripped her elbow and steered her through Honey's front door.

"My baba," shouted Atticus.

In the corner of the living room, Crusty set the baby down in his rocker and tucked a blanket around him. Atticus barreled headlong across the room on his chubby legs to the rocker, with Jamie following. They sat next to the baby, cooing and touching his hands while Meredith stood rigid with eyes narrowed.

She couldn't stop staring at Gemma who stood at the tall stone fireplace next to Egan, who wore a satisfied smile. Finally, shaking off Curtis' hand, she turned to Honey. "What's all this?"

"Come help me in the kitchen, dear." The older woman disappeared around the corner, calling out as she went, "The potatoes need mashing. Gemma, why don't you keep an eye on the kids."

"Did you know?" Meredith spoke low to Curtis. He shook his head, looking miserable.

It was ridiculous that the possibility of others being invited to this Thanksgiving dinner never crossed her mind. She should have realized the woman would invite her own granddaughter and would want her new great-grandson there, too.

She noted Egan's arm draped loosely over Gemma's shoulders and wondered how their reunion came about, and how he'd gotten past Honey's earnest dislike of him. Gemma, too, didn't appear to mind Egan's affection. Any lingering grief she might have suffered over Brian's death was vanished. The girl, with a newborn babe at her feet, had moved on. *Of course, I have too*, she realized with a jolt.

She followed Honey into the kitchen. "We're not staying." Her friend handed over the potato masher and pointed at a steaming pot. "Give it a go, will you?"

She obeyed without thinking, heaving the masher into the soft white cubes, and took some solace in squashing them. On the counter behind her, her friend picked up a carving knife and attacked a massive turkey, slicing chunks of meat off the bone. "We really aren't staying."

Arching one brow, Honey set down her knife and opened the refrigerator. "What about your kids? You'd deprive them of my delicious Thanksgiving dinner out of spite? That's not like you." She set the butter and milk next to the potatoes. "Add a lot of butter. The whole cube will do. Keep mashing, no chunks. I like my potatoes rich and creamy."

Meredith plopped the cube of butter into the pot and splashed in some milk. *What am I doing? Brian's girlfriend and baby are in the other room.* She set down the masher and turned to face the other woman, who was back at work on the turkey. "What were you thinking? How could you do this?"

Honey turned, holding the carving knife in front of her. Meredith glanced down at sharp, heavy blade, and considered that her friend was capable of just about anything. "All families have problems." Honey waved the massive knife in the air dismissively. "But they'll still sit down together at Thanksgiving and enjoy a meal together. Don't spoil this for your children."

Her children would have a fit if she made them leave. They wouldn't understand and she couldn't explain it to them. There was nothing back at her house to cook for a Thanksgiving meal and the grocery store was closed for the holiday. Honey trapped her into having Thanksgiving dinner with Gemma and the…child. Brian's baby. "They aren't my family."

Her friend sighed and hefted the platter piled high with turkey, giving her a firm look. "Oh yes we are. We all are. You may as well get used to it."

Honey carried the turkey to the dining room. "Dinner," she announced cheerfully. "Everyone, come find a place at the table."

****

Meredith didn't speak during dinner. She kept her gaze glued on her plate and fiddled with her fork even as Jamie kept up a steady chatter. Curtis contributed a polite amount of conversation and Gemma, at the far end of the table, focused on the baby. Crusty, Egan and Honey discussed land prices while Jamie and Atticus just ate and ate.

"I love Thanksgiving," her daughter announced through a mouthful of turkey while cranberry sauce rimmed her mouth. Everyone laughed except Meredith, who was determined not to enjoy one minute at a table where Gemma sat.

"Too," added Atticus. "More."

She wiped at Jamie's mouth, then lifted Atticus from the table. "If you eat any more, you'll blow up."

"Bl'up," he agreed. "Bl'up, bl'up."

"Just wait 'til you taste my sweet pumpkin pie, little one," Honey offered.

The five-year-old eyed the turkey slices still left on the large platter. "Can I take some turkey home instead? We don't get to eat meat at home anymore."

"Jamie." Meredith's tone was warning and her face reddened. "Don't be rude."

Honey tsked, though her expression was pleased. "I'll make up a package for all of you. There's more than plenty left over."

Egan stood and stretched, rubbing his stomach. "Why do all you gals always want to be vegetarians? I don't get it."

Her lips went thin. "We're not trying to go vegetarian."

She stopped. Why should she explain to everyone how meat was pricey and she needed to cut back on expenses? She made sure her growing children consumed plenty of protein; no one in her house was starving or being deprived. There was no reason to share her financial problems with anyone. In any case, eating more fruit and vegetables was healthy.

"I'd never go vegetarian." Gemma smiled up at Egan as she spoke, twisting the ends of her hair, and he gave her an approving nod in return.

Meredith stacked plates and marched off to the kitchen. The turkey sat like a lump in her stomach, weighted down by mashed potatoes and green bean casserole. She parked herself at the sink and sunk her arms up to their elbows in dishwater. The clatter of dishes meant she was saved from having to talk to anyone. She scrubbed, rinsed, and stacked, taking her rage out on the cranberry and gravy stained plates piled high around her.

Honey was at her shoulder, her voice low. "Here's a secret. Mushrooms. Chopped fine. In the stuffing."

She swung around, thinking of the moist delectable stuffing. "What?"

Honey gave a broad smile. "Surprised you, huh? No one ever guesses. It adds a nutty flavor and a little texture. Plus, there's good protein in mushrooms. Chop 'em fine, add them to just about anything and no one knows. Just a thought if you're cutting back on meat with those growing kids of yours."

Meredith wrinkled her nose in distaste. "I don't like mushrooms."

"You never knew what you were eating though, did you? They're easy to sneak in without anyone knowing the difference."

Honey settled in next to her, drying the dishes and then bustling around to tuck them away in cupboards. Without any warning, the woman launched into what happened in Twin Lakes. "I read somewhere it isn't unusual to have deaths go in threes. I just can't get it out of my mind, a person dying right there in a confessional as though he were struck down for his sins. And then a priest too."

"And Brian," Meredith added in a low voice.

"Or..." Honey drew out the word and then fell silent.

Meredith withdrew her hands from the dishwater and yanked out the sink stopper. "Or what?"

"Hard to know whether your husband was the first, or Jacob was the first in a run of three," Honey mused. "There's either one more or we're done, depending on how you count. Course, this is all speculation and superstition. Doesn't mean another death is on the horizon."

"I'm not superstitious," she responded, although this wasn't entirely true. Hadn't she felt haunted by Brian?

"I wouldn't be surprised if that lazy Jacob Burns got himself murdered," Honey prattled on, scrubbing at her stove top. "Letting his wife be the breadwinner with an important job, growing his hair over his ears and down his neck, at his age. He was asking for something bad to happen."

Sometimes it was difficult to know when Honey was serious or just provoking a reaction. Meredith grabbed a dishtowel and began drying the silverware. "You don't murder someone for being laid off."

Honey's face was hidden as she hunched over the stove, still scrubbing. "There's lots of reasons for killing someone. You may well have considered something similar yourself," she said, making Meredith glance around to make sure they were alone. "We all have those thoughts, but thank goodness most times, they go away. Some people get those thoughts and can't get them out of their mind; so, they do it."

From the first time she'd met her, it seemed Honey could see inside her mind. Brian debased her, abused her and cheated on her. In the months leading up to his murder, fantasies about killing him filled her mind. After his murder, she worried, somehow, she killed him while under the influence of sleeping pills. In the months since, she convinced herself she never would have actually killed him. But who could say for certain what was down the other fork in the road?

"Murder's a pretty big step to take, regardless."

Honey shrugged. "You never know what's in someone else's mind." She spoke lightly, and assessed her now spotless stove, wiping an invisible speck off the top.

Once more, she wondered if her friend had anything to do with Brian's murder. Had Honey persuaded someone else to kill Brian to protect her granddaughter? Meredith glanced behind her to where Honey was gathering more items from the dining table and whispering something to Gemma.

Gemma would have known if Brian carried a gun in his car. She could have told Honey about his whereabouts, and Honey could have shared this information with someone unstable enough to commit murder.

What if, what if, what if, she thought. In the end, someone else pulled the trigger. He was in prison. Wasn't this enough?

As though conjured by these thoughts, Gemma lugged in the final dishes and sidled up next to her at the sink. A scent of flowers and ginger filled the kitchen. "This is just as difficult for me, you know," the girl said with a pout. "Don't act like it's all on you."

Meredith gritted her teeth in frustration. Would this Thanksgiving never be over? "Don't talk to me."

"Gram said having you all over was the neighborly thing to do, since you don't have a family." Gemma said the words lightly but the words hit home as intended. "I understand you never had a father at all."

She whirled to face her. It hadn't occurred to her Brian would have told this girl the personal details of her life. The alcoholic mother and absent father, her nomadic existence, and how grateful she was when Brian gave her the first stability she'd ever known. It was galling to have Gemma view her with pity. A smirk crept into the girl's face as Meredith visibly fought to control her emotions. If her friend was manipulative, this granddaughter of hers was cunning.

Honey stopped behind them, holding a turkey baster and handful of silverware. "Gemma was so grateful you sent her money, to pay Brian's debt on the house. Weren't you, dear?"

The girl paused and to Meredith's surprise, obediently replied, "Yes, Gram."

"It's not so easy to find a buyer way out here. Especially for a house so run-down. Meredith has done wonders. We really like having you here. Don't we, dear?"

The girl sounded chastened. "Yes, Gram." She skulked off to the living room to join the others.

"She has some growing up to do." Honey sighed. "Teen age years are such a worry."

Meredith darted a look at Honey, then turned back to the sink to hide her expression. *Teen age.* "How old is she?"

"Nineteen, last week, and thinks she knows everything."

She swallowed thickly. "She was barely seventeen then? When Brian started up with her?"

Honey shook her head in disgust. "Men preying on underage girls. He wouldn't have stopped, you know."

She'd known the girl was young...but how could Brian do such a thing. He'd been thirty-two then, nearly twice his teen age girlfriend's age. Just when Meredith believed she was on the road to recovery from that part of her life, the life she had with Brian and then his murder, something arose to drag her straight back into the old murky pit.

She toweled off the final dishes and dried her hands. Her stomach churned and rolled. "Thank you for a wonderful dinner, Honey. It's time for us to go."

****

They finally got out the door, but not until Honey wrapped up a dessert tray to go, along with a large foil package full of turkey and stuffing. Jamie carried the foil container to Curtis' truck, nose tucked close to the packet, her expression one of supreme contentment. The topic of baby goats wasn't broached, at least not in her hearing, and Jamie seemed to have forgotten all about them.

The tension in Meredith's body didn't ease until Curtis pulled up in her own driveway and she'd unloaded her daughter and Atticus from his truck. It felt good to be back at home, this house she'd hated in the beginning. The run-down place became a home at some point in the past eight or nine months. Despite the peeling kitchen linoleum, the lime green toilet, the leaking roof. Even the landscape, once viewed as empty, was in continual flux with the seasons and movement of wildlife.

She stood at the driver's side of the truck, not yet ready to say goodbye. They'd hardly had a chance to speak to each other at the Thanksgiving dinner. He helped her on and off with her coat, and they sat platonically next to each other at Honey's table. After the night before, she could hardly stand not touching him. She wanted nothing more than to lead him into her house to her bedroom, but there were her children to consider.

"Thank you. I couldn't have survived today without you."

Curtis made a sound of frustration. "Honey is a stubborn woman," he said. "You handled the situation as good as anyone could have."

Jamie and Atticus disappeared through the front door of the house. *This is the best moment of the day. This moment alone with Curtis and with my kids safe at home. Don't get greedy for more.*

She couldn't help herself. "Stay for a bit? We can eat Honey's pumpkin pie."

Curtis's answering smile warmed her to the core and she felt ridiculously happy.

****

Curtis lingered after pie, waiting while she tucked Jamie and Atticus into bed. Her daughter popped up twice, first wanting a glass of water and then complained she wasn't sleepy. When she was finally settled and all was quiet, Meredith set their cups on the kitchen table with a sigh.

He wasted no time in drawing her into his arms for a long moment. The aggravations of Honey and Gemma slipped away, her fears about bills disappeared, and the specter of death pursuing her ceased to exist. There was only Curtis and his warmth, the tugging of his fingers to lift her sweater and his lips covering hers.

"Mommy?" Jamie stood in the kitchen doorway.

They broke away from each other. Meredith stumbled backward against the table and an excuse bubbled to her lips, but no words emerged. Heat rose to her face. She needed to talk to her daughter about Curtis and his role in their lives. What if starting something new was too soon after Brian's death? The girl had adored her father.

"It's snowing in my bedroom."

Meredith noticed for the first time Jamie's hair was wet and she shivered. "What?"

Curtis headed down the hallway with Meredith a half step behind. From the doorway to her daughter's room, they stared as flakes drifted down through a gaping hole where the roof opened up. A soggy wood shingle swung loosely above the torn ceiling that surrendered to expose the darkening sky.

The good part of my life is going to have to wait a bit longer. My house is tumbling down.

Julie Howard

Part Three

Some say "accidents happen."
Others say there's no such thing as an accident.

Chapter Fifteen

"I can patch the roof after the storm passes. I guess I didn't catch all the bad shingles up there this summer." Curtis' doubtful tone betrayed his words.

They stared at the hole above them, watching as large flakes fluttered down to melt on the carpet, the bed, the dresser. Pieces of ceiling, soggy insulation, mouse droppings and disintegrating wood shingles were in the middle of the floor. Meredith rubbed her arms against the icy chill and was thankful her five-year-old hadn't been below the roof when it collapsed. She scooted Jamie to the bathroom to towel off her hair and then settled her in her own bed for the night.

Years of rot and neglect were catching up to her roof with moisture from snows and rains seeping farther inside every year. She pictured water dripping through the shingles and puddling in the attic space above their heads, turning her ceiling into mush. There had to be bigger problems brewing than one or two roof shingles. More of the ceiling would come down, either piece by piece or in one swift grand finale.

"The problem's bigger than just a few shingles. I can't afford a new roof. Or a new ceiling. Or any of the rest of it. This house is falling apart faster than I can deal with it." She spat out the words in frustration. "I just need a bulldozer. But I can't afford that either."

Curtis bowed his head. Meredith waited for him to

contradict her, to protest the roof was a minor repair and the rest of the house solid. The seconds ticked away before he answered, staring at the soiled carpet. "You know, demolition's not a bad idea."

She stared at him, aghast. "You expect me to knock down the only house we have? Then what? Pitch a tent? Build an igloo?"

He chewed his lip. "This house was built piecemeal from scraps and then left to rot over the years. My parents have a trailer I'm sure you could use. You could park it on your property."

Tears sprang to her eyes. This was the only house she ever lived in. She'd swallowed her pride and paid Gemma the money Brian had cheated her out of for the deed to the house. She fought to stay there, in spite of everything, to give her children a secure home. She hung curtains and painted walls, scrubbed years of grime off the floors, and washed windows. No one knew how much having a home of her own meant to her. How could she have it destroyed? Not to mention living in a trailer with two young children through an Idaho winter was unthinkable.

"This is my house," she whispered.

"Meredith. I'll build you a new one. A better one."

She gaped at him, watching as he grew more animated as the idea took hold in his mind.

His gaze roamed around the room, assessing. "I've been playing around with plans for another house. Bigger. Better than mine. High ceilings with open beams, cedar closets, a real cook's kitchen. I can do construction on weekends and evenings. You can help."

"What are you talking about? I can't afford...I couldn't let..."

Curtis broke in. "You can't afford to keep this house the way it is. You have to do something. I can use some of the materials from this house, maybe. The windows. Some of the wood planks from the floor." He stopped there and grabbed her hand. "Meredith, let me do this. Let me build a house for you."

His eyes were bright and he was excited about the idea of building a house, any house at all. Of course, he knew she couldn't afford to pay much of anything; she scarcely had enough money to live and keep up with bills. She paid Gemma for the house, all the money she could afford, and now it was falling down on their heads. No wonder the girl let the house go for a pittance. How could she let Curtis do something so big, so impressive for her? It was impossible. Her mind swirled and she forced herself to focus on one thing: the snow coming into Jamie's bedroom. She would take her problems one step at a time, just as her meditation book advised.

She turned away from him so he wouldn't see her face. "I need to cover the hole."

She felt his excitement ebbing into disappointment. They stood there for a moment, each glum in their own way. He gazed at the broken ceiling. "I can get up there with a tarp, keep the damp out for now. It's not safe in here tonight. Not until the roof is fixed."

She nodded. "Jamie can move into Atticus's room." She paused and flickered a glance at him. "I'll think about your offer. Okay?"

As he studied her face, his lips made a slight curve. "Okay."

****

She stared at the ceiling above her bed for hours

that night, next to a kicking Jamie, wondering if the entire roof was going to come down on them while they slept. Every once in a while, she rose and walked through the house searching for any trace of collapse or water stains. Could it be possible Curtis had no idea how destitute she was? He had a stable well-paying job, family backing and minimal expenses. Perhaps he took it for granted when you needed money, ready funds just appeared from somewhere.

She read a storybook as a child where a woman had been given three wishes. There were likely more important wishes requested and granted, but Meredith only remembered one: a purse that never emptied of gold coins. A magic wallet would be my wish right now, she thought.

Even if Curtis labored for free, she couldn't buy an entire house worth of materials. The wood, walls, a roof. There were two options: stay or go. If they stayed, she needed a full-time job and a way to repair the existing roof. She needed enough money to keep repairing problems continuing to crop up from this old house. It would be a constant drain, a money pit.

If they relocated again, as she should have after Brian's death, she could put the house up for sale as-is. Someone else might buy the place for the land and have the money to knock the house down and start over. She would be free to look elsewhere for a job that would cover expenses. For a moment, this possibility gave her hope, a way to make things work for her children.

In a flash, she was back in Curtis's arms and the memory was painful. It was a glimpse of what could have been, but no longer. She couldn't let another man take over her life and liberty, not after Brian.

It was becoming clear she wasn't destined to stay in Hay City. The world kept laying down signposts telling her to leave ever since she arrived. Brian's murder. Gemma's baby. Lack of a real job. A disintegrating house. Some people had an easier life than others. Her road had been difficult since the beginning, but she'd gotten tougher. She was young, healthy, and determined. Lots of people were just starting out at age twenty-four, launching successful careers and lives. There were plenty of people who thrived without a college degree. This wasn't the end, just a new beginning, she encouraged herself. This was the road she was meant to travel.

There's no reason I can't start over again. It's a big world.

****

There were some people who wouldn't take no for an answer.

Honey stood at the door holding up a cloth-covered plate. "You can't stay mad forever."

Meredith grimaced at her, debating for a second whether she actually could.

"Oh, but it's cold out here." Honey lifted her shoulders in an exaggerated shiver. "Bitter."

She opened the door wider, stepping to one side, and the woman hurried inside.

Honey pressed the plate into Meredith's hands and shucked off her coat. "You have no idea what's been brewing over at my place. Chaos." Noting the rabbit hutch, she gave a nod. "Seems like you have a growing family, too." She bustled into the kitchen and rummaged for four plates, paused, and then put two back. "Let's the two of us have a chat until the kids discover we're here eating sweet potato pie. I over planned for Thanksgiving and had to put three more pies in the freezer. Heavens knows what I was thinking."

Meredith quietly put a kettle on the stove for tea, sensing her friend had something on her mind. The woman always did. She set out mugs and tea, and waited.

"Egan." Honey huffed out his name. "He wants to marry my Gemma. She said yes, just as quick as you can blink your eye. Heaven help us all."

Meredith swallowed. Just six months earlier, Gemma revealed her plans to marry Brian. The two would have made a perfect pair: deceitful, greedy, opportunists. She felt sorry for Egan. Less than a month ago, he didn't even know where to find the girl and now they were engaged? For all his rough edges, he was probably a nice country boy underneath his unkempt beard.

"She's marrying Egan? Does she even like him?"

The other woman's tone was clipped, annoyed. "My granddaughter likes a man around admiring her. And turns out the young fellow got on at the mine at a good salary. She likes that, too. Anyway, he offered to adopt the baby. Thought you should know."

The kettle began to whistle, the pitch high and screeching, and Meredith poured the water and dropped tea bags into the mugs, grateful for the interruption. She'd been nursing a hope that Gemma would go somewhere else far away, removing Brian's baby from their lives. "Where would they live?"

"Not with me; I set them straight on that one, right away. They can go live with Egan's land-grubbing family, and my granddaughter can learn another hard lesson in life."

Honey's lips pursed together, waiting. Meredith set the steaming mugs on the table, refusing to ask any questions about the apparent bad blood between the families. The other woman waited and when no reply came, heaved a sigh at being thwarted in gossiping about Egan's family. She switched gears and her dumpling face lit up. "What does our sheriff think about what happened in Twin Lakes? Poison? Those men could have gotten themselves into something foolish, eating something gone spoiled. Some men just aren't too fussy. Warm mayonnaise, half-cooked chicken, old eggs."

Meredith was glad the subject was changed. She would far rather talk about death than about Gemma. "Curtis said the ground is frozen and they need to get more equipment up the mountain to exhume Jacob's body."

Her friend raised her eyebrows. "They say poison's a woman's weapon."

"He isn't calling it a crime." Meredith couldn't help adding, "Yet."

"Murder begets murder. One, two, three," Honey said in a whisper, leaning forward.

The woman's eyes shone at this tidbit of gossip, the specter of a corpse exposed from its resting place and speculation about murder. Jamie rushed into the kitchen, demanding pie and cutting off the conversation. Atticus joined them and the next fifteen minutes was filled with chatter about rabbits as they wolfed down their pie.

"Will your baby goats sleep in your living room in

the winter?" Jamie asked after scraping her plate clean.

"Oh no. I have a heater out in the barn for all the animals. They're cozy all winter long. But no little kids until the spring. Kids are what we call baby goats."

The young girl smiled to herself and Meredith knew her daughter would launch a spring offensive to get a baby goat. Her kids scampered off to play in Atticus's room.

Honey carved off a second piece of pie for herself and Meredith refilled their mugs. Whatever the difficulties with her friend, it felt good to sit and share her distress with someone. "My roof's coming down," she shared. "There's a hole in Jamie's room covered with a tarp."

Honey nodded as though she wasn't surprised at all. "Life is two steps forward, one back."

Meredith studied her tea, wondering if the older woman had always been full of aphorisms and folksy sayings. If an apocalyptic event occurred, Honey probably would have comforting words to say about that too. Right now, she needed solid advice and comfort, not empty words.

"I don't think I'm getting the full two steps forward," she said, certain she was due a little sympathy. Everything was going wrong at a time when it all should be going right. She found herself unburdening herself of her most recent problems; her collapsing house, her financial crisis, her need for a job. Any remaining frustrations she had with her friend thawed the more she talked. It was soothing to talk to someone who enjoyed listening to one's troubles.

"You can't expect to get them all at one time," Honey explained with a shrug. "At some points in our lives, it's five or six steps back and then, all in a rush, seven or eight or ten steps forward. You'll see." Honey served herself another slice of pie.

"I hope someone up there is keeping track for me."

The woman gave her a stern look. "I made a mess of my life a ways back. You know, I had a thing for bad boys back in my day. I didn't like being told what to do and, my goodness, there was this one boy in school who broke all the rules. Of course, he had to be the boy for me." She shook her head, her expression grim at the memory of her teenaged self. "I was pregnant my senior year of high school and proud of it, stupid girl that I was."

Meredith tried to imagine a teenage Honey and could only picture a round full-hipped girl with large shoulders who wouldn't let anyone boss her around.

"I lost that one but was pregnant again inside of six months. You'd think we'd have learned a lesson. Ha, not a chance. We ran off, got married and...Shorty..." She spat out the name... "built us this house. Judith, Gemma's mother, was born."

Honey leaned forward on the table and her voice lowered to a hiss. "You know what happens to bad boys when they grow up? They become bad men. There were no steps forward for me back then, none at all. I was pregnant again when he set fire to the house. Miscarried."

She paused in her story, lost in its telling. A bad marriage. A violent end. Two babies gone. She leaned back again, her voice softening. "I was all prepared to tell you about Gemma and your husband, the first time I came to your house to visit. But then I saw your little ones and the bruises on you and saw myself all over again. History was repeating itself, right here in the same house, and I knew what was coming next. You deserved better."

Meredith sat frozen in her seat. The doubts she had about the woman being involved in Brian's murder were always at the forefront. "Honey," she started, but her tongue thickened in her mouth. How do you ask a friend, your best friend, whether she was behind the murder of your husband? Would she ever be able to put the suspicion to rest?

Honey brightened. "Milt arrived just in time. He was a friend of the family. Tall and big like me. He just swept me off my feet. Some people might call it a boomerang romance, but it sure bounced me into the right arms. I never had a bad day with my sweet Milt." She wiped at a tear and stood, scraping back her chair from the table, indicating their chat was over.

"You just get your chin up, girl," she said. "Your time is now. A hole in your roof? Heavens. It's not the end of the world."

Chapter Sixteen

Meredith woke with eyes swollen from crying and lack of sleep. She stared in the mirror and touched several newly developed lines on her face. Fine wrinkles now etched the corners of her eyes, a former crease in her forehead was a canyon and the corners of her mouth took on the appearance of craters.

I'm twenty-four and feel like I've lived a lifetime already. Her mouth sagged downward as she studied her reflection. *Chin up, girl.* Honey's down home sayings were cheery but they didn't pay the bills.

One day at a time. The mantra didn't cheer her. The day in front of her was impossible. Her roof was collapsing and the chemistry final exam was tomorrow. Studying was the last thing she wanted to do. What was the point anyway there was no likelihood now she'd ever be able to afford another class?

Life is messy. It's how you handle it that counts.

Her mother's words didn't help either. Of course, life was messy. She'd learned this well enough.

She recalled a middle-aged woman who'd worked at the Wild West Motel, one of the many such places she'd lived in as a child. The woman, with hard shiny eyes boring into whoever walked by, had a constant bitter attitude, always negative in outlook no matter what the topic.

"Good morning," Meredith's mother would sing

out as they passed.

Not today it isn't," the woman would say each time, her mouth cemented into a constant scowl.

Her mother secretly nicknamed her the wicked witch of the Wild West and they laughed together over the name.

That'll be me. Bitter and mean. The wicked witch of Hay City. She scowled into the mirror and then turned away quickly. Her impression of the woman from the motel was a little too precise.

****

Deli boy coughed delicately into his hand, then wiped it against his apron. "You've probably noticed I've been gone awhile."

"No." Meredith skipped the deli counter on most of her shopping trips now. Cutting her weekly half pound of deli turkey and ham not only saved her the aggravation of seeing the offensive kid, but also cut her grocery bill. A pound of hamburger, at half the cost of deli meats, could be stretched into a meatloaf dinner, spaghetti sauce and several days of meatloaf sandwiches. Jamie complained and clamored for her favorite turkey, but Meredith remained firm. They would have deli turkey for sandwiches once a month, as a treat.

Probably unhappy at not being missed, deli boy's tone turned indignant. "I've been really sick."

He waited. She paused and then obliged him with the smallest amount of sympathy she could muster. "Too bad."

"I could've died." He raised his eyebrows at her, indicating he expected alarm. "But I didn't."

"So I see."

He glared at her and her lack of dismay. She marveled at his belief she would care, after all they'd been through together, all his barbs and nastiness. Deli boy was a blight upon Hay City, corrosive and evil, in her opinion.

"It wasn't my fault, picking a destroying angel," he continued, determined to tell his death-defying story. "They look a lot like button mushrooms. Tricky buggers."

Despite herself, Meredith was drawn in by the unusual name. "Destroying angel?"

Deli boy straightened up, happy to have finally piqued her curiosity and having the opportunity to exhibit authority on the subject. "They're just like those mushrooms in your cart there; hard to tell the difference unless you're really paying attention. I was focusing on the chanterelles, the money mushrooms, but picked a few buttons along the way. Darned if I didn't slip in a destroying angel. Could've been lights out for me, forever."

He thumped his skinny chest. "Good thing I'm tough. Barfed them up right away. Got most of the poison out of my system quick. Still, I'd have to say it was touch and go there for a while."

She frowned, glancing down at the mushrooms in her cart. There was a very good reason she'd avoided mushrooms all her life; slimy, disgusting, and poisonous as well. This was the first time she ever decided to buy some, thinking she could chop them fine and add them to meals to add a bit of meaty texture and extra nutrients, as Honey suggested.

A strange idea occurred to her. As much as she disdained talking to the noxious teen, she had to ask.

"These poisonous mushrooms…you just found them out in a field somewhere?"

He gave her a withering glance. "Forested area. That's all I'll tell you. I don't give away my hunting grounds for chanterelles. I make some good money picking them every year."

"The destroying angels. Do they make you throw up?"

"Like the dickens." He opened his mouth and mimicked throwing up on the deli case.

"Poison," she whispered.

He nodded. "Killers."

Meredith remembered Jacob saying something about Brooke going for long walks. Would she have picked destroying angels along the way? It would have been easy enough to slip a few poisonous mushrooms into a meal. Poor unsuspecting Jacob and Father Karl. They would have eaten the mushrooms, thinking they were the ordinary everyday button kind, the type you see in grocery stores everywhere. She needed to tell Curtis. She didn't know why Brooke killed her husband and the priest, but now she knew how.

"Hey, you getting your turkey and ham? Half pound of each, right?"

She stared down at the mushrooms in her cart and swallowed. The fact deli-boy finally remembered her order, the same order every time since they'd moved to Hay City, didn't give her a sense of victory. There were more important things to think about.

"Just the turkey, quarter-pound only today." She turned to Jamie. "Hey kiddo. Stay here a moment and get the turkey, okay?"

Jamie appeared pleased with the responsibility.

"I'm in charge of Atticus, too?"

She nodded, grabbed the bag of disgusting fungi out of the cart and strode off to the produce department. She had a return to make.

****

She was breathless as she told Curtis about deliboy's close call. She blurted out the story as soon as she entered his office.

He raised his eyebrows in question. "Jeffrey Cole? Mushrooms?"

"He called them destroying angels, but I'm sure there are lots of poisonous mushrooms out there," Meredith rushed on. "Listen, Jeffrey was out picking mushrooms right about the time Jacob died. There must have been these mushrooms everywhere."

Curtis rose from his desk and approached the counter where Meredith stood. He rubbed his neck in thought. "A storm's coming in. The equipment for Jacob's exhumation won't go up until the weather passes. Until we can get a full autopsy done, we won't know if he died from anything other than a heart attack. In the meantime, I'm waiting on a detailed report on Father Karl's death. I'll give them a call about possible mushroom poisoning though."

She huffed in exasperation. "Why does this take so long?" The concern lurking under the surface boiled over. "Brooke will go back to work soon. To Jamie's school. You need to do something."

His expression hardened somewhat at her suggestion he wasn't fulfilling his duties. "There's been no proof of murder. No witnesses to anything suspicious."

"Jacob told me…" she broke in, then bit her lip.

They'd been through all this before.

"Meredith." He squeezed her hand. "Do you understand what I'm telling you? It doesn't matter what I believe; my job is to collect solid evidence. If there's no evidence, or no confession, no prosecutor will touch the case. In Twin Lakes, there's no proof of murder."

"Yet."

He nodded in acknowledgment. "I'm frustrated, too, by this waiting. I need to know exactly what we're dealing with." His voice softened, a gentling. "Have a little more faith in people."

She withdrew her hand; she wasn't in a mood to be comforted. She needed to know Jamie was safe and no more people would die. She wanted Curtis to be as mistrustful as her. "You're too nice to be a sheriff. Too worried about doing the right thing."

What was meant to be a criticism emerged as a compliment. She struggled to find something more pointed to say. Adjectives flowed through her mind, but they all came back to Curtis's gentle nature, his continuing belief in the goodness of the people around him. Sheriffs weren't supposed to be so good-looking, so generous, so kind, offering to build houses for people they met less than a year ago. They were supposed to be embittered by life, quick to recognize the wicked impulses of those around them.

Making an exasperated sound, Meredith turned and stomped out. He would be shocked when Brooke was finally hauled to justice. He would become bitter and mean soon enough. *Like me.* Consoled by the thought, she headed to Honey's house for another lesson in marksmanship.

****

She lay in bed the next morning debating whether to drive to Twin Lakes and take her final exam. The roads would be slick and unpredictable, but she was proud of how well she could drive in the icy weather after such a short time. Just a few simple rules and it was easy: Drive slower, turn the wheel in the direction of a slide, and don't panic. Why didn't they post these rules on roads in snow country?

There was no point in taking the final test if she wasn't going to keep taking classes. She couldn't take classes if she didn't have money to pay for them. And she didn't have the money if her house was falling down. Why did it always come back to money? Would she be as obsessed with it as Brian and Gemma?

I'm going to move forward in my life and not let anything stop me.

She wavered for a moment. Words were easy to say; doing was another thing. It didn't hurt that she wanted a chance to see Brooke again. If Curtis wouldn't talk to Jacob's wife about the mushrooms, then she would just have to take charge. He would thank her after Brooke confessed.

Meredith tugged the covers up to her chin, the morning chill more insistent than usual and making her reluctant to budge out of bed. She knew Honey would be willing to watch her kids while she drove to Twin Lakes. Even if the woman was a bit devilish, Honey was accommodating and helpful when one was in a pinch. She was learning it took a healthy amount of forgiveness to get along with people in Hay City.

The afternoon before, Honey was surprised at her request for more target practice. "This may be more of a springtime activity," she suggested. "There's more than a foot of snow on the ground and more coming, I hear."

Meredith jutted out her chin. "I don't mind going out by myself. The cold won't bother me."

"I don't think you're quite ready to be turned loose on your own. Let me get my woolens on and we'll give it a go for twenty minutes."

They settled Jamie and Atticus in front of the TV with a snack and blankets, and Meredith plugged away, trying aimlessly to hit a cardboard box. Even with the larger target, she missed every time. She knew she would eventually get the hang of it. Reloading came easier now, and she was certain her aim would improve with a few more lessons.

A giggle and a thump startled her out of her daydreaming. There was something about the giggle's pitch that made her rise out of bed. There were good giggles and the type children gave when they were doing something they shouldn't. This was definitely the second type.

She headed to her kids' room, the one they now shared since Jamie's ceiling collapsed, and realized with a jolt the door to her daughter's old room was open. A cold breeze flowed through the house and she strode forward faster. The roof was unstable and dangerous in there. Jamie knew she was supposed to stay out.

"Mommy." Her daughter's voice was delighted as she saw Meredith at the doorway of her room. "See what we did."

Meredith gaped at the sight before her in dismay. The tarp blew off the hole above at some point in the night and snow piled into the room. The carpet was a frozen blanket of white. Her children must have arisen early because in the middle of the room, below the hole, they'd built a snowman.

Chapter Seventeen

Seeing a snowman in her house spurred Meredith into action. She needed to get out of her house for the day. Let the storms blow through the roof and fill the house chin deep. What difference did it make? There was no point in taking the final exam, of course. She knew this but not taking the test would require too much explaining to everyone. It was easier to take it, pass or fail, and then she could put college behind her. She could focus on the present and future needs of herself and her children.

The rumble of a snowplow echoed as the heavy vehicle worked its way down her road from the main road and back. At least one person in this county did their job, she thought with relief. That's what she believed until they drove down the road and she found the plow driver once again created a narrow and winding snake path. She turned the steering wheel one way and then the other, creeping along the cleared tracks and wondering why on earth someone would continue to plow the road to her house in such a strange manner. The driver must be drunk or half asleep and surely inept. It was strange her road was the only one plowed in such a crazy, serpentine pattern.

She delivered Jamie to the school bus stop in time and dropped Atticus off with Honey.

"You sure you don't want to stay here and use my

computer?" Honey asked. "It's a bad day to go up."

Meredith stood at the doorway, not even stepping inside. "I need to check out a book at the library," she lied smoothly. "I'll be careful, I promise."

"Just don't drive like you shoot."

She didn't ask if Gemma's baby was going to be there, too; what did this matter either? If Gemma was marrying Egan and staying, there'd be no avoiding baby Brian. If Meredith took her children and left, they'd never see Gemma's baby again.

White blanketed the road up the mountain and no tire marks were on the road for her to follow. Fresh crust collapsed under her car's tires and she kept as close to the mountainside as she dared, worrying about hitting a buried rock or shrub at the edge of the road. Better to hit a rock than plummet over the side of the cliff, she assured herself. Progress was slow but her confidence grew the farther she drove. By the time she was three-quarters the way up the mountain she wondered why she'd been so apprehensive about driving. She slowed her car to a crawl as she made the sharp curves, turned her wheel into skids whenever the tires slipped, and kept moving forward.

When she passed the "Road Closed For Winter" sign, she felt like a real Idahoan. Rugged and self-sufficient. She'd traveled this road numerous times and an extra dusting wasn't going to stop her. The librarian would be impressed by her tenacity, though Meredith didn't know exactly why she craved this approval. Just this one last time up the road and it could snow to the treetops. For now, she could manage. Nothing was going to stop her.

The library's parking lot was empty and Twin

Lakes' roads were free of tire marks. No one else possessed the nerve, as she did, to drive in the soft snow. One set of footprints led down the street to the library's front doors and she was assured of a quiet room during her final exam.

Leona sat behind the counter, another thick book on her lap. "What are you doing here?" She didn't appear pleased to have company.

Meredith was annoyed at the chilly reception. The woman acted as though this was a private residence and not a public office, funded by taxpayers. "You're open? I have some work to do."

The librarian glared at her. "You drove up the mountain, in these conditions, with a storm coming in? Just what we expect of you lowlanders though; every year someone gives the roads a try and slides off the side of the mountain. Never fails."

"The roads weren't bad at all. I didn't slide much."

"Just takes once." Leona returned to the book on her lap, one of a popular children's series about dragons and werewolves.

Meredith hesitated, wanting to jolt the woman out of her peevishness, but couldn't think of anything to say. Dismissed, she turned her focus to taking her final exam. The room stayed empty of any other patrons over the following two hours and she labored in silence. Once started, the test questions became a personal challenge to overcome, a representation of other challenges yet to be met. The test was difficult but by the time the last question was answered, she felt she'd done well enough to pass the course. Even if her grade didn't matter, there was no point in doing a poor job.

Papers packed up and the chemistry book closed

for the last time, her fingers hovered over the keyboard for a moment. Then, in the search field she typed in: "destroying angel." Hundreds of websites popped up on the subject of the *white Amanita*, otherwise known as the destroying angel for its wicked deadliness.

"Infamously deadly," one site read. "Among the most toxic known mushrooms," read another. "Affects all living tissue."

Pictures of the all-white mushroom showed them bulbous in their youth and appearing more like button mushrooms as they matured. At full growth, the tops opened outward and displayed white gills underneath, reminding her of angels spreading their wings. There was a certain beauty in the pictures, which only accentuated her growing horror as she read on.

Adding to their lethal-ness was the fact symptoms tended not to appear until toxins were already absorbed, causing irreparable damage to internal organs and spiraling the unlucky person toward coma and death. Vomiting, she read with a jolt, was a primary symptom. Survival came only to the most fortunate. Appropriately named indeed, she thought.

She sat back in her chair, thankful she always avoided eating any mushrooms if she could help it. Her heart thumped in her chest as she stretched her arms forward and typed in "heart attack symptoms." Over and over, results showed nausea and vomiting as one possible symptom. Just one symptom among many, she read. There were so many questions crowding her mind. Someone in Twin Lakes had answers. She logged off the computer.

"I saw you going into the church that day," Leona said as Meredith headed to the exit.

She heard an accusation in the librarian's tone and waited for more.

"There wasn't trouble here until you showed up. Now Jacob's gone and our priest too. I don't know if I like you in my library."

Being cursed wasn't anything Meredith hadn't already considered. Bad luck clung to her. As hard as she tried to change her life, unfortunate events continued to crop up. The librarian's eyes were wide, with a touch of concern at the edge of her expression.

She's afraid of me, Meredith realized. "None of this is my fault," she said.

Leona looked doubtful and Meredith plunged out the library doors, wanting to get away from the woman's critical stare. "Good luck going back down," the librarian called after her.

Her satisfaction at finishing her test was ruined. She breathed in the frigid air and glanced around the snow-covered streets. There wouldn't be another reason to return to the library until spring and there was no reason at all to make peace with this churlish woman.

Flakes drifted in slow spirals, adding to the depth piled up already. Steel gray clouds drifted across the darkening sky and she felt a twinge of uneasiness that a bigger storm was building. Just takes once, Leona said. One slide would carry her off the edge of the mountain to her death. It was a spiteful thing to say, to fill her head with doubts. She'd gotten up the mountain; she would get down again.

Her old car with the dented door and spider-webbed crack on the windshield slumped in the parking lot. The timeworn sedan appeared better under the clean coating of white and she decided it could sit there a little longer. Brooke's house was a short walk away and the church, with Father Michael, not much farther. It wouldn't hurt to stop by and ask some questions. First and foremost would be when Brooke was returning to work.

The slush was deeper and wetter in Twin Lakes and twice she slipped and nearly fell. By the time she arrived at Brooke's door, she was out of breath. Her feet were frozen and the bottom half of her jeans were soaked through.

"Mary." Brooke didn't seem surprised to see her, standing at the doorstep on a snowy day. Jacob was dead and buried, but the evidence of his wife's crime would soon be unearthed in the exhumation. Brooke's calm demeanor made her all the more determined to shake the woman's cool.

"It's Meredith."

"Yes, you're right." Brooke said the words as though she were praising Meredith for knowing her own name, like a child in one of her classrooms.

"I was just…" She almost said she was just passing by, but this was ridiculous, considering Twin Lakes was miles up a snow-covered road from her home in Hay City. "…at the library and thought, maybe, we could talk."

Brooke's calm exterior stayed unruffled. She opened the door wider and let Meredith enter. This time, she didn't lead her into the living room or offer coffee. Brooke stood in the entry, coldness in her expression and stance, and waited.

She hoped the woman didn't notice her nervousness. It occurred to her there was a reason investigators worked in pairs when confronting a potentially dangerous suspect. "You never explained about the car…the brakes were never fixed."

"You never explained how this is your business," Brooke retorted, the demure woman from the previous visit gone. "They're digging up my husband, you know."

"I'm sorry," she said, although she wasn't sorry at all. "I met him and was worried about him and the things he said. When he died…"

The house was silent. Water puddled on the floor beneath Meredith's boots. She breathed in a pleasant scent of cinnamon and pumpkin and noticed a small artificial Christmas tree set up on a table, tinsel dripping from the branches. A twinge of anxiety went through her about the coming holiday and shopping to do with money she didn't have. She wondered at how Brooke still wanted to celebrate Christmas right after her husband died. In her own home, the holiday would need to be downplayed. It would evoke so many memories in Jamie—and herself.

Brooke shifted on her feet. "Jacob was prone to exaggeration. The brakes needed replacing but they weren't dangerous. With just me working right now, paying for repairs wasn't in our budget. I'm not surprised Jacob said those things to you. He was having a tough time, having so much time and nothing to do."

The explanation sounded reasonable, but still didn't explain Jacob's fears about his wife.

"He said…" Meredith started, but Brooke interrupted.

"I know, I know." She put a hand up to cover her eyes, but the move appeared contrived. She lowered her hand. "He was fired from his job, for that kind of irrational behavior, the things he'd say. Even to complete strangers."

Meredith glanced at the window and where a fresh shower of white spilled from the sky. The drive down the mountain would be more challenging and she hoped her own car's brakes were up to the task. She needed to leave but, even more, needed to hear what Brooke had to say. The confidence which grew in her after Brian died was gone. Jacob's death unnerved her and she needed to put it right, as though doing so would put her own life back on course.

"He was taking medication for depression as well as anxiety," Brooke added. "One rare side effect of the medication is heart arrhythmia leading to heart attack. The doctor knew all this. The sheriff too. I guess you believe you should know all about us too. People love gossip, don't they?"

The remark hit home. "I'm not here for gossip," Meredith protested. "It's just, he needed someone to listen to him, and I didn't do a good job. I feel like I let him down."

Brooke gave her an assessing look. "This isn't your business. You should go home."

Doubt flooded her mind. Jacob suffered some type of mental anguish and could have inflated his wife's actions and motivations. She put a hand on the doorknob; there was nothing more to say.

Brooke didn't budge. "Tell Jamie I'll be back at school soon. Your daughter's gotten the whole school calling me the princi-pess. She's a sweet girl."

The door opened with a whisper and she was back in the snow in a flash. Brooke stood at the doorway, an ice queen unfazed by the cold. The door swung shut.

Heavy, wet flakes plopped onto her hair as she trudged back to her car. Her apprehension grew about the stealthy storm descending on the mountain, blunting her vision. She blinked snowflakes away. Getting down the mountain was going to take all her concentration and new found winter driving skills. She wasn't feeling quite as confident now.

Brooke's words echoed in her mind and Meredith considered whether the words were a threat. *I'll be back at school soon.*

****

Anxiety grew into alarm as her car inched downhill, swimming more than driving through the sloppy roads. A few times, the tires spun uselessly before finding traction once more. Still, Twin Lakes fell farther behind and as her car rounded each bend in the mountain, she celebrated a little victory. The "Road Closed" sign was still somewhere ahead and this became her goal. *If I can make it to the sign, it'll be okay.* Both hands clenched the steering wheel and her body was taut. Despite the cold radiating through the windows, dampness grew under her arms as her tension increased. She eased the brakes around curves and tried to keep the car at a steady, slow pace even as gravity pulled it down the hill faster. *I'll be back at school soon.* Brooke's words nagged and distracted her.

A strange odor, of burning and something acrid, crept into the cabin of the car and Meredith wondered if this was the last trip her car would ever make. How much more punishment would this old heap handle? It shouldn't have lasted this long, with the screeching noises and smoke plumes upon starting. Maybe Brian was right, she thought. *Maybe I'll have this car for a* very long time.

Her husband was exultant upon presenting her with the car, dents and all. She recalled the day, early in the spring, with snow still heavy on the ground and Brian still alive. Her mind flew back to that moment, picturing her husband, vibrant and hot-tempered. So many secrets emerged out since then. She felt like Pandora would have, opening a box and unleashing evil into the world. Everything might have been different if she never found those boxes, filled with money and pictures, spilling out his secret life. *I'll be back at school soon,* resounded in her mind. She recalled the librarian's words: *There wasn't trouble here until you showed up.*

The sensation of gliding snapped her back to the present with a start. Before her was a curve in the road and the car tires were sliding, not rolling, toward the cliff's edge. In panic, she pressed hard on the brakes and focused on the precipice rushing toward her. Turning into the slide meant she'd aim directly toward death. Survival instinct took over and she swiveled the steering wheel furiously away from the drop off. The action propelled the car even quicker toward the edge and Meredith closed her eyes. *Stupid, stupid, stupid. My last thoughts on earth.*

With a crunch, the car stopped, jolting into a snow bank at the mountain's rim. A rushing filled her ears and her heart thumped a wild rhythm as she came to terms with the fact she was still alive. Around her, snow fell in thick flakes. She watched them gather on the windshield as her breath slowed. Alive. She was alive.

When she was ready, she shifted into reverse. The tires spun and the engine whined in protest. The car didn't budge as she stomped the gas pedal to the floor. The vehicle settled deeper and an angry plume of dark smoke rose from the exhaust. She shoved the door open and stepped out into knee-deep drifts to see her tires buried to their tops in the snow.

She looked up the road and then down, and finally reached in the car to turn the key off. No one else was foolish enough to drive into a storm. She calculated it was five miles to Twin Lakes, too far a distance to hike up the mountain in the snow. There was no question of walking down the mountain, it being miles farther to Hay City.

This is how people die. They get stuck and if they don't freeze to death, a hungry bear comes along.

She climbed back into the car and slammed the door, closing out those possible deaths, and debating two unpleasant options. Stay and starve, or go and freeze. She was a foolish lowlander, indeed, to cross a "Road Closed" sign.

The vibrations struck her before the sound, alerting her to an approaching vehicle. By the time the snowmobile appeared around the bend, Meredith stood in the middle of the road. She waved her arms as though her car could possibly be missed. The vehicle slowed and then stopped. The rider sat for a moment, bundled in ski pants, heavy jacket, face mask and cap.

The voice under the mask was female. "Seems like you're in a pickle."

"I don't know what happened," Meredith said, her tone filled with relief. "My car just started sliding."

"Guess you didn't notice the storm. Or the sign down the road."

She didn't care about being chastised. She

wouldn't freeze, starve or be eaten by a bear. "What do I do now?" How do I get my car out?"

The woman took off her cap, then her mask. Meredith winced. Caro Reynolds sat on her machine appearing pleased with the situation before her.

"Most people carry a shovel in their car this time of year. Otherwise, they call the sheriff. He has a tow line on his truck." She waited a beat before adding, "You don't have a shovel, do you?"

Meredith shook her head. "I..." The next few words came even harder. "I didn't carry my phone today. I didn't think..."

Caro chuckled and gazed up the road. "You didn't think; bet that happens to you a lot. It's a bit of a hike then." She settled her mask back over her face and adjusted the eye holes.

"No. Wait!" Caro couldn't possibly leave her stranded. Just because...because...well, she implied Brooke killed her own husband. "Do you have a phone with you?"

Caro hesitated, and then dug deep into a pocket and produced a cell phone. Meredith high-stepped through the snow and took it from Caro's hand, half afraid the woman would snatch the phone back at the last second. She watched Caro nervously while she dialed Curtis's number. It rang and rang. Her toes were numb in her boots and her pants were soaked up to her knees. Finally, on the sixth ring, there was a click as the line connected.

There was a long pause and someone breathed hard into the receiver. Curtis sounded impatient. "Yep."

"I'm sorry," she said. "I interrupted something."

In the background something clanked, a sound of

metal on metal. A male voice in the background said something indistinct. His tone softened. "Meredith. This isn't your number."

The words spilled from her in a rush. "It's Caro's phone. Curtis, I did something really foolish. I'm up near Twin Lakes, a few miles past the closure sign. My car's stuck. Can you help me?"

He didn't pause or ask any questions. "I can be there in an hour."

"You're busy." Her throat closed up at his forgiving nature, how he set aside their past meeting so quickly. She'd been so awful, her impatience flaring and running out her mouth before she could temper her words.

"Just wrapping up a project. All done now. Are you safe? Warm?"

"I'm okay. Fine."

Caro made an impatient sound and held her hand out for the phone. Meredith said a quick goodbye and handed the phone over. Caro pocketed it and settled her cap tighter over her ears. She revved the engine and, with one last disapproving shake of her head, rumbled away without another word.

****

There was no doubt Curtis rescued people stuck in the snow a time or two. He expertly hooked her car to a winch at the back of his truck and towed her free in no time. Not once did he say anything about her driving up the mountain and crossing the road closure sign. He hopped out of his truck to face her.

While she waited for him, Meredith brushed her hair and retied it into a ponytail, then into a braid and then brushed it all back out again. People had always called her pretty, but mirrors never agreed. There were only the flaws reflected. Eyes too big, face too thin, features never adding up to a reasonable whole. Her mother always called her "quietly unique."

What the heck did that mean? She'd rather be a classic beauty, sultry and curvy. Staring back at her in the rear view mirror were her anxious eyes and nose reddened by the cold, and she gave up on making herself presentable.

Now she stood in the middle of the road, soaked to her knees and shivering. "I'm sorry."

He smiled at her and the tension loosened inside her. "You do seem to get into messes. Better get going. I'll follow you home."

"It's okay. I'm sure I can make it from here."

The day had been a disaster. Jamie and Atticus would have to stay at Honey's until her nerves recovered, and she'd put on dry socks and jeans. She wanted nothing more than to go home, even if it was collapsing. Inside her home, there were no seasons, no mountains, and no countries. The crumbling place was her safe haven from the world.

His words were gentle but firm, brooking no debate. "Go on now. I'll follow you."

****

She was almost to her driveway when she noticed the boxy white structure set up between the house and shed. She pulled up close and remained in her car staring as Curtis parked behind her.

"C'mon." He was at her door, twisting at the handle, opening it. In a daze, she climbed out of her car and followed him to the door of a large travel trailer. The ground underneath was cleared and the trailer leveled on concrete blocks.

"You did this? For us? While I was gone?"

"You need a sturdy roof over your head."

"This is what you were doing when I called earlier? Even after how I behaved yesterday in your office."

He nodded and handed her a key as he motioned her inside. "Take a look around. I lived in here for more than a year while I built my house. It's roomier than it seems."

She stepped up and peered inside, her thoughts swirling. Did he do this out of charity or friendship, concern or…? She glanced at him and then toured through the compact interior.

"It'll be close quarters but you'll have your house right next door if you need space during the day. Sleeping here will give you peace of mind during the nights. The space gets pretty warm and cozy; you'll be fine through the winter."

She knew he was waiting for her to say something. *He offered to build a house for me. He brought this trailer here.* Meredith opened cabinets to stall for time. The tiny space contained everything she and her children would need. Jamie would love sleeping in the top bunk and Atticus would be safe in the bed below. There was a larger bed in the back, separated off by a door that would give her privacy. The trailer even possessed a compact kitchen and dining area, complete with refrigerator, microwave, and sink. A miniature bathroom, the size of a closet, consisted of toilet and sink. The trailer was an entire house compressed into the smallest possible space.

Curtis stood silently and waited for her response. She ran a hand through her tangled hair. The trailer would solve her problems short term. It would keep her children safe at night. He did this for them. For *her*.

She turned and stepped into his arms and raised up her face. He didn't hesitate; they were alone and there were no interruptions.

Chapter Eighteen

Curtis settled his shirt back over his head and shoulders and followed it by a sweater. She lay back on the trailer's bed, the blankets heaped in confusion to one side. The front end of the storm made itself known with a whistling wind knocking against one wall.

"I don't think I can move," she said lazily.

He stretched out a hand and pulled her up. "If you stay there much longer, I'll have to undress again."

"Please," she quipped, but started the process of finding her clothes and dressing. Her children needed to be picked up and she needed to figure out something for dinner.

He grabbed her and drew her close. "It was the purple paint in your hair."

"Purple paint?"

"When you painted Jamie's room last spring, to cover up the monster she imagined on the wall," he recalled. "I couldn't stop thinking about it. And you."

"Then? With everything going on?"

She didn't want to raise the subject of Brian, not at that moment, but the words slipped out. She'd been the prime murder suspect and was confused about Curtis's intentions. Running away was in the back of her mind then. She might have left at that point and never looked back, striving to erase Hay City and all that happened there from her memory. It would have been easier then, before this sheriff became so ingrained in her life, before the tire swing and Grendel, and Jamie starting school.

His expression was serious. "I saw how hard you were trying, how difficult everything was for you. I thought, here's a woman who doesn't give up, no matter what. She has grit."

Grit. Meredith turned the word over in her mind and decided she liked it. *I'm strong, someone with grit. He likes this part of me.* She decided to impress him further. "I saw Brooke today. She admitted she didn't fix the brakes on Jacob's car; she lied to him." Meredith lifted her head, working to deliver a pose of a woman with grit. Jacob could still have suffered a fatal side effect from his medication. Or he might have been accidentally poisoned. But her inner voice still whispered murder.

Curtis shifted away, breaking their connection, his expression darkening. "You did what?"

"I was in Twin Lakes anyway, to take my final exam. Brooke said Jacob died from his medication and being mentally unstable; that it all led up to a heart attack."

"You went back?" The anger in his tone startled her. "Why would you do such a thing?"

At first, she shrank at his tone, then stiffened her spine. "She told me she's going back to work soon. She could be dangerous. I don't wear a silver star, but I have every right to go see her."

He took a deep breath. "This is a delicate situation. We'll have results back before Brooke returns to school; after that, I can move forward. Until then, all we have on record is Jacob died of a heart attack and

Father Karl ingested some unknown substance. I need some kind of evidence for proof of murder, if any murders even occurred. I promise I won't let anything happen to Jamie."

She was close to tears. "You can't promise something like that. How can Jacob's body be exhumed when they can't get a backhoe up the mountain?"

His jaw worked; he gave a firm nod. "We'll get the equipment up the mountain, one way or another, if I have to drag it up there myself."

She gave him a weak smile. To her, the case was as simple as A-B-C. A: Jacob predicted his wife was going to kill him. B: Jacob was dead. C…well, there wasn't even the need for a C. Open-and-shut case. Simple. But for a murder case, you needed to prove murder, and that started with the body.

"This takes so long," she groused.

"An investigation isn't like the movies; it's a process," he agreed, and then added in a rueful tone: "I'm new to this and I need to do it by the book. I need to do this right. If I get ahead of the evidence…if there is evidence…I could ruin a case for a prosecutor."

Meredith saw how the confession hurt him. He wanted to do the right thing. Her expression softened. Curtis kissed her once and she leaned in for an encore. Then the wind swept through the trailer and he was gone. She put a hand up to her mouth and brushed a finger across her lips. She could still feel his mouth on hers, the contours of his body and his arms holding her.

A small worry nibbled at the edge of her mind. Brooke's grief had been convincing and a priest was vouching for her. Jacob plainly suffered some type of mental breakdown so his outpouring of marital woes could have been wildly exaggerated. Had she stood in the living room of a grieving widow and accused her of murder? Now that she'd prodded Curtis forward, doubts assailed her. His way of getting evidence first was probably better, she acknowledged.

She peered out the square patch of window in the trailer. Curtis's truck arrowed straight to the main road, cutting through the snow despite its depths and ignoring the plow's erratic curves. He carved a new path, straightening out the trail for her. Meredith realized she'd gotten something completely wrong. It wasn't that he didn't care about whether there was a murder in Twin Lakes; it was he cared too much. He didn't want to get anything wrong. She needed to trust him.

But Curtis didn't believe people could be wicked and vengeful.

I do.

****

"*Drive A Bulldozer! Wield A Hammer! Knock It Down!*"

She stared at the laminated sign stuck on the grocery store's single gas pump. Below the words was a picture of a grayish stubby house, windows dark and dreary, frozen onto an empty landscape. She drew closer to examine the sign. Her house. It appeared worse than ever. In the photo, the sad, little house appeared to be sagging in the middle as though the ground underneath was weary of holding it up. Her garden huddled under a bed of white, the trees bare of leaves, and the old rusted metal shed at the side hinted at toxic materials within. None of her hard work over the summer months was evident. Somehow, the house appeared even worse than when she first saw it. This was a house crying out to be torn down.

But it's my house. Who put up this sign?

Meredith glanced around, but she was alone in the freezing parking lot. Long shadows stretched over the valley, reminding her how lengthy a day it'd been. It seemed ages since the morning when she'd vowed: *I'm going to advance in my life and not let anything stop me.*

She returned her attention to the sign and wiped the front clean so she could read the print below the photograph. Below the picture were the words: "Pay twenty dollars for ten minutes for the opportunity to knock down walls. Just one hundred dollars for ten minutes driving a bulldozer. Let's demolish this wreck and raise money for a brand-new home."

She caught her breath as she read the last line: "Contact Honey for more information about buying salvage items from the demolition."

Honey did this. She's tearing down my home and turning me into a charity case.

She snatched the poster off the pump and folded the paper over and over. She marched inside to pay for her gas. Then she would pick up her kids and, once and for all, tell Honey to stay the hell out of her life.

****

Deli-boy grinned at her from the cash register. "My family's donating the use of our 'dozer. To knock your place down. I'm in charge. Can't wait."

Meredith glared at him as she handed over money for the fuel. If there were anything worse than having her house destroyed, it would be having deli-boy at the helm.

"Vroom, vroom." He made revving noises; pushed

and pulled his arms forward and back as though he were shifting gears. "Course, demolition won't be until the spring melt-off. You shoulda done this over the summer."

She gritted her teeth and strode out of the store, avoiding the gaze of other shoppers. Heat rose in her cheeks. She'd been the kid in school in the free-lunch line. She'd been the kid in thrift store clothes, the motel rat, a charity case. The familiar shame of being different and less than others returned to her.

Honey broadcast her neediness to the entire town and invited the public to witness her humiliation. Her own mother never resorted to begging, even when they were homeless themselves. Anyway, the house just had a hole in its roof. So what if a little bit of snow and water got inside? She'd mop up the mess in the spring, open the windows and let everything dry out. Scrub out the mold, patch the hole and repaint Jamie's room. It wouldn't be too difficult. Bit by bit, she'd get ahead of the damage.

Meredith lifted her head and wrenched open her car door. *I'm a woman with grit. I'm a woman with grit. I'm a woman with grit.*

The words echoed in her mind all the way to Honey's house.

****

Jonathan Pringle answered the door. She took a step back in surprise.

He waved her in the door with a grin. "Honey's out back, checking on the goats with Jamie and Rio. She got them earlier than I expected. That leaves just us chickens in the house."

Meredith glanced around the living room at the

remnants of a craft project involving tissue paper, glue sticks, sparkles, crayons, and tape. A fire burned in the fireplace, making the room cozy and warm. "I didn't know you knew Honey. Where's Atticus?"

He nodded toward the bedrooms. "Snoozing. The older kids wore him out. Actually, Rio's worn out too. Only ones still going strong are Jamie and Honey."

"So, uh, how did you say you knew Honey?"

He gestured to her coat. "Everyone knows her. Let me help you out of that."

The last thing she wanted to do was stay for a chat but it seemed she had little choice. She shrugged off her coat and stamped the rest of the snow off her boots onto the entry rug. Jonathan loomed over her, with the top of her head barely reaching his shoulders.

"There's hot cocoa in the kitchen," he said. "I'll pour you a cup while I figure out how I know Honey."

She followed him, puzzled by the strange statement. How would you not know how you knew someone? He poured them each a cup of steaming cocoa and then sprinkled mini marshmallows on top. Jonathan smiled at her, unleashing the deep dimple in his cheek. "Let me see if I can get this right. My stepdad was second cousin to Milt, Honey's late husband. Maybe third cousin. Something like that. I used to come over and play with the piglets. Guess she sold them all now, to go into this goat business." He shook his head in mock disapproval. "If you ask me, pigs are cuter. And smarter."

A banging sounded at the back door; sounds of thunder rumbled down the hallway. Jamie and Rio burst into the kitchen. Her daughter's cheeks were flushed red underneath the gray knit cap tugged down over her ears. "Mom! Can I have some goats?" Panting, she ripped off the cap, wide and sparkling. Rio stood quietly next to his father, paying close attention to Jamie, admiration shining in his eyes.

Meredith knew the request would come and she was ready for battle. "Not in a million years."

"They're awesome. I bet Honey would give me a baby." The young girl faced the kitchen doorway as Honey appeared, huge in her puffy coat. "Right, Honey?"

Meredith glared at the woman, daring her to give Jamie encouragement.

"Raising goats is not for sissies." Honey said, her tone light. She studied Meredith's face and unsnapped her coat, tugging it off. "You look all in, dear. How'd the final test go?"

She shrugged. "I stopped to get gas on my way here." They stared at each other and understanding dawned in Honey's face. Jonathan glanced from one to the other, puzzled.

"I'm not a sissy," her daughter chimed in. "Mom, I'm not a sissy."

"You certainly aren't," Jonathan answered.

Meredith stood, her voice firm. She faced the other woman and ticked off her orders on the fingers of one hand. "No goats. No bulldozers. No posters. No more."

Exhaustion swept through her body. Between taking the final, confronting Brooke, dealing with impassible roads and a stuck car, sparring with Curtis over Brooke's possible guilt, and now this latest stunt from Honey...today had been one impossibly long day. "Get your things, Jamie."

She strode down the hall to wake Atticus. It was

time to go home, whatever it looked like.

****

Jonathan walked them to the car, carrying Atticus, his long legs lifting easily through the snow. Darkness swallowed the valley although it wasn't yet five o'clock. The porch light danced eerie shadows across the yard.

"We built a snowman in our house." Jamie's voice was full of pride and glee, as she hopped behind the long-legged man to land in each of his footprints. "Want to come see him?"

Jonathan gave the young girl a dimpled smile. "You betcha. Another time though."

Jamie climbed into the backseat and helped Atticus snap into the car seat. Jonathan stood by the driver side door, his hand on the handle, keeping it from closing. He leaned down, his expression earnest. "This is weird, but I thought I'd just say it anyway."

Meredith cringed inside, worried he was going to invite her out on a date. She recalled Curtis's warning about the man collecting baby mamas around the valley. He lowered his voice. "I have a message from Caro. From Twin Lakes."

This was the last thing she expected him to say. "What?"

"She was here to see me this morning. Drove her snowmobile all the way down the hill." A cold wind gusted into the compartment of the car. "She babysat me as a kid. I used to have quite a thing for her. It was years and years ago, but you never get over those things, you know? Actually, we had a moment or two about seven, maybe eight years back. Wasn't all I thought it'd be."

"I'm freezing," Meredith said, a violent chill going through her.

His tone turned businesslike. "Right. She wants you to leave Brooke alone. That's all. I'm only passing the message along. I'm just the messenger, always the go-between around here." He paused and glanced back at the snug house where smoke rose from the chimney. Jonathan leaned closer, so oppressively she shrank from him. He was practically in the car now, his mouth near her shoulder. "You get people riled up in this community, divide them into sides. Like what happened in the spring, you know."

She couldn't believe he would talk about Brian in front of Jamie. "We need to go. It's getting cold in here."

Jonathan ignored her. "I have something to say to you. It's about time you hear this."

Meredith glanced over at Honey's house and was startled to see a movement at the window. Was Honey watching them? Her skin prickled with nerves. She twisted in her seat. "Hang on a minute, kiddos. I'll be right back."

He retreated a step as she climbed out of the car. She slammed the door behind her, furious and uneasy. Why couldn't everyone put Brian's murder behind them, as she was trying to do? Regardless of the circumstances, people must know this was a painful subject. "Say whatever it is you have to say."

She was sure he would accuse her of Brian's murder. The entire county already judged her and found her guilty, despite the evidence. As friendly as he'd been at the start, Jonathan was no different. People in Hay City were hateful, just plain hateful. She wasn't prepared for his next words.

"Gemma came to me first. I'm the town notary and she wanted me to notarize documents signing her house over to Brian. This was before you made an appearance, before Gemma knew she was pregnant." His demeanor was changed, no longer looming. Instead, his shoulders slumped and the corners of his mouth turned down. "One wrist was sprained and there were bruises up her arm."

She stood frozen, not feeling the biting wind kicking up around them. Instead, the memory of Brian's hands around her neck flashed through her mind.

"We all saw the guy come around from time to time. He'd come in town and Gemma would have some kind of 'accident.' He'd disappear and she'd be okay again. Everyone knew what was going on. Then the guy shows up with a wife…you…and two kids in tow. We don't like that kind of thing around here."

Everyone knew right from the start, she thought. Everyone but me. "It's not your business," she whispered, her voice hoarse and trembling.

"But it was," he said. "I was the messenger then too." He nodded toward the house. "I let Honey know about the house; somebody needed to know. Then Gemma gets pregnant and starts talking about marrying this brute. Honey asked me to talk with Shorty, about how he could gain redemption for his sins. She knows how to push people's buttons. I think she just wanted Shorty to scare Brian off, though she wasn't too upset afterward, the way everything turned out."

Meredith was stunned. "You…and Honey…You did this."

He shook his head vehemently. "Shorty did it. I

never said to kill Brian. Honey never did either. Shorty picked up the gun. He made the decision. He pulled the trigger. I've thought long and hard about the whole situation. My conscience is clean."

The world spun around. In a daze, she glanced at the car toward her children, Atticus calm in his car seat in back and Jamie now in the front seat pretending to drive. Her gaze traveled across the drive to Honey's cozy house, now fully lit in the darkness. Her intuition about the woman was right. She shivered violently.

"Why are you telling me this? Why now?"

His jaw tightened and he jammed his hands into the pockets of his jeans. "There's justice and then there's country justice. Kind of the old saying, 'What goes around, comes around.' Up in Twin Lakes? It'll settle out. It's none of your business."

"You think it's murder, too?" The accusation popped out of her mouth before she could stop it.

His expression went blank, and he didn't answer.

"What do you know?" she asked.

"I never said murder." He strode away, toward the house and called over his shoulder. "I just said this is none of your business."

Meredith recalled Brooke's reference to Jamie, anger rising again in her chest. "As much as yours," she called out.

What if her daughter was in danger? All the children at the school were in danger. She gave a furious look toward Honey's house. These people exacted their own brand of justice on her husband. Whatever their intention, the result was the same. Brian was dead. And Honey…she was at the center.

She turned and yanked open the car door. Jamie

took one look at her face and scrambled into the back next to Atticus. Meredith gripped the steering wheel until her knuckles were white all the way home. Brooke, Caro, Honey, Jonathan…all guilty in her mind. They were guilty of something, she just didn't know what.

Jonathan's words echoed in her mind: *There's justice and then there's country justice.*

Chapter Nineteen

It wasn't as though Honey pulled the trigger that killed Brian. It could be argued that Honey *was* the trigger by her interference.

Unsure of what to do, Meredith wrestled with these two separate ideas. No one asked or coerced Shorty to kill Brian. Hadn't she complained to Honey about her marriage and how she felt trapped? Her complaints were nothing but a cry for help and Honey stepped in. Then, a series of events, tangled up in one another and led to her husband's brutal end. If she were honest, life was better without him.

I'm as bad as them. I'd be a hypocrite to say otherwise.

These thoughts delayed her immediate impulse to rush to Curtis with fresh accusations about people in his county. There was also the possibility he'd only say she was meddling once again, jumping at shadows and believing the worst in the people around her. It was easier to keep her mind a blank and block the emotions threatening to overwhelm her. This is how people have mental breakdowns, she thought. Maybe I'm already in the middle of one and don't know it, she considered.

And then there was Jacob. There was something wrong in Twin Lakes. Even Jonathan hinted at it with his cryptic remark that country justice would settle things out. Caro knew something too and wanted to keep outsiders away.

Meredith focused on the present, feeding herself and her kids, taking Jamie to the bus stop and working her shift at the hardware store. She reminded herself Brooke wasn't at school to threaten her daughter, while on leave for mourning. With her class over, she didn't need Honey to watch Atticus. The house couldn't be repaired until the spring and there was money enough to get them through the next few months. There was no reason she couldn't ignore all her problems. For now. Avoidance was a successful strategy for her in the past, most of the time.

The bus was late arriving at the store parking lot a few days after Jonathan's confession, just late enough that Meredith was starting to worry. Winter swept through the valley this last week of school before the holidays and roads were treacherous. Sliding off the road near Twin Lakes eroded her confidence about her own winter driving skills. She decided Jamie was safer in a big vehicle driven by a well-trained professional who was used to driving on county roads under all conditions.

Three other cars lined up next to her vehicle; other parents also waiting for their children to arrive. She recognized none of them and returned her attention to the road where the bus would eventually appear. She was startled when her passenger door swung open and a woman climbed in next to her, a heavy scent of laundry soap filling the car as she closed the door.

"Hey there. I've been wanting to meet you forever." The woman flashed an enormous smile, teeth slightly crooked in her mouth.

"Um, hi."

She introduced herself as though Meredith should have already known who she was. "I'm Stacey. Jonathan's sis. I work at the city office, if you can call what I do work. And you're Meredith—the Meredith everyone talks about 'round here. You might as well be famous."

Stacey spoke in a rush, her voice breathy and eyes wide, scanning Meredith from head to toe. She turned in her seat where Atticus in his car seat stared back at her. "And this must be Atticus, Jamie's little brother. Hi-ya little fella." She scooted back around. "We should get together for coffee. I'm free pretty much most of the time."

Meredith gaped at her. Long, manicured nails were a direct contrast to her bowl haircut. She topped her sweatpants with a sequined bomber jacket. The only makeup she wore was a beauty mark at the side of her mouth. From head to toe, she was a mismatch, a woman still seeking her own definition.

She didn't want anything to do with Jonathan's sister, yet another Hay City person to be wary of. She worked up an excuse. "I…I work part-time…"

"…at the hardware store." Stacey interrupted, finishing the sentence. "I know. Doesn't matter. We'll get together in the morning, when Jamie's in school. But make it after eleven; I'm a late sleeper. Can't help myself, I've always been a night owl."

Meredith glanced down the road, her brow furrowed. The invitation was nice on the surface; in any other situation, it would be good to expand her circle of friends. Especially since Honey was crossed off her list. Right now, though, she was worried about her daughter. She wondered if the woman had a cell phone to call the school about the missing bus.

"I'm a working girl too. City clerk. You already know all about me, I'm sure. My little brother…" Stacey gave a strange giggle. "…I call him little even though he's a giant…he's always happy to fill in for me. No big deal. I'm picking up Rio today. We help each other out. What else is family for?"

Meredith barely heard the woman's chatter, her worry rising as the minutes ticked by. "Do you think something happened to the bus? Should we call the school? They're late by forty-five minutes, almost an hour now."

Stacey waved her hand in dismissal and chatted on like a woman starved for conversation. "Oh, the bus'll show up. You can come by my place if you want. Though I should warn you, I'm not the most finicky housekeeper. My dad lives with me, too, but he mostly stays in his room watching porn now he has a pension from the mine. Whatever. I don't care, as long as he keeps the volume down. We live in the house that looks like a barn, back behind the coroner's office."

A rectangular yellow shadow appeared on the horizon, moving slowly toward them. Her heart leaped. "There it is," she said in relief.

The other woman glanced toward the road with disinterest and then raised her eyebrows. "So. Tomorrow then? Jonathan can fill in for me at work."

Finally, anxiety over Jamie's bus quieted, she made a quick decision. "Sure. Okay," she agreed. It seemed easier to get out of work at the hardware store than to say no to this woman.

Stacey heaved a sigh and opened the car door. "Thank God. This town is dead. I want to hear all about

California. I'm going there someday, soon as I get some money saved and..."

The car door slammed shut mid-sentence and the woman climbed into her car, one nearly as old and decrepit as Meredith's. The bus rumbled into the parking lot and its door whooshed open. A moment later, her daughter was next to her, full of chatter about school and the holiday party planned in the classroom. Meredith barely heard her, her mind on Stacey. The woman was a study in contrasts and appeared to be sincere in her wish to be friends. And a friendly chat would be a nice distraction from her own melancholy musings. Did the woman know about her brother's ideas about country justice? As Meredith pulled out of the parking lot, she realized there was only one way to find out.

Anyway, the next day also marked another milestone in her life. *I'll be twenty-five.*

****

"Happy birthday, I guess." Deli boy slouched against the case of cold cuts, a bottle of window cleaner in one hand and a dirty rag in the other. His tone was devoid of good wishes.

She stopped in her tracks. She didn't intend to buy any of her usual turkey and ham on this shopping trip. This was just a quick stop to pick up a coffee cake or donuts on the way to Stacey's house, not wanting to show up empty-handed. It was too bad the baked goods were next to the deli counter.

"How did you know?"

"Giant Jonathan. You just missed him. You guys together now?"

"Not likely." The last thing she wanted was to be

linked with the man. Not before their last conversation and certainly not now. Not ever. But how would Jonathan know today was her birthday?

Deli boy squirted the cleaner at his case and over spray landed on the roast chicken inside. "Probably good. You have enough kids already."

She glared at him.

"So, what are you?" he continued, wiping the glass in bored circles. "Like thirty, thirty-five?"

Suspicious he was trying to provoke a response, it needed to be corrected before he started rumors she was pushing forty. Besides, her vanity was tweaked. "Twenty-five."

His mouth dropped open. "Really? You have a lot of wrinkles."

She gritted her teeth and shoved the cart past him. It wasn't true; deli boy would say anything to get under her skin. For some reason, he'd made her his special target. Twenty-five wasn't old. Neither was thirty-five, not exactly, but she'd rather not be mistaken for a thirty-something just yet. *What if someone mistakes me for Atticus's grandmother instead of his mother?*

She swerved her cart into the cosmetics aisle and browsed moisturizers. Aloe, glycerin, silicone and...she peered closer to make sure she was reading this right...even urea. Urine?

Deli boy was at her shoulder, a smug expression on his face as he eyed the shelves. "Need help?"

"Not from you. Thanks." She turned to go, furious he caught her out, seeking ways to smooth her wrinkles.

"Wait."

"What?"

His egg-shaped Adam's apple twitched under a

skinny neck. "You're selling baby rabbits? Any left?"

Meredith considered whether there could be any land mines connected to his question and decided it was safe to answer. "A few."

"I wouldn't mind having one."

That morning before heading to the bus stop, they frantically searched for the nearly-month-old rabbits, loosed from the cage by Jamie. The juveniles were hopping fuzz-balls with large almond-eyes and soft ears laid back on their shoulders. Once freed, they scattered throughout the trailer, crawling under the bed, behind the refrigerator and in a crevice by the stove. Meredith grabbed a broom and poked and scooted them into Jamie's hands. Once again, they'd made it just in time for the bus, honking to keep it from leaving her kindergartner behind.

"They'll be ready to go by New Year's," she said, then considering whom she was talking to, added, "Payment in advance."

His face was eager and boyish. "Fifteen dollars, right?"

She nodded and he fumbled under his apron for his wallet, and plucked out three five-dollar bills, limp and strangely damp.

"You aren't going to do anything…weird…with it, are you?" Her daughter would never forgive her if someone ate one of Grendel's offspring.

He looked at her with disgust. "I'm not a monster." Deli boy stomped away, toward his counter. "Why would you say that?"

She tucked the moist bills into her coat pocket. One down, she thought. Four to go.

****

Stacey started talking the moment she opened the door. She snatched the bag of cookies from Meredith's hand and waved her and Atticus inside. "Rio is so excited about getting one of Jamie's rabbits. He talked about it all yesterday. I guess Jonathan said yes. Rio's mom is less than excited, but she'll come around. Come on in."

The woman gestured into the converted barn, leading the way to a couch piled with folded laundry and magazines. Meredith set Atticus down and started the process of stripping him of the layers of clothes he wore—hat, gloves, coat, and sweater. There was nowhere to put their winter gear so she stacked their belongings at the side of the couch.

Stacey, wearing faded jeans and an "I Love Kittens" sweatshirt, snatched up papers and books from a chair and plopped down. "Just throw the stuff on the floor. I warned you the place would be messy, didn't I?"

Meredith hesitated and then carefully set a stack of magazines on the floor. Stacey selected a cookie from the bag and then handed the bag over.

"Who would ever think to have cookies for breakfast?" The woman's eyebrows rose in approval. "People out here always do the same old thing, like doughnuts or bagels. It takes a newcomer to inject some fresh ideas. That's why I want to go to California—to get out of this rut."

She decided not to disclose that the store doughnuts were stale, and cookies weren't an innovative California breakfast. The woman appeared too impressed.

"These are my favorite. Nothing better in the world

than chocolate chip, although I can't eat too much of them or I'll never get a husband. Hard enough out here." Stacey took a bite of her cookie and chewed vigorously, dropping crumbs to the carpet.

Meredith handed Atticus a cookie and settled him on her lap. "Have you ever been married?"

She selected a cookie and looked around for a place to set the bag. The table at her side was overwhelmed with tiny figurines and the floor was littered with bulging shopping bags. Folded men's underwear and t-shirts were on the couch to her side. Not seeing a bare surface, she kept the cookie sack tucked at her side.

The woman waggled her ring-less fingers. "Marriage doesn't run in my family. You've met my brother, Jonathan, right? He sets a bad example for the men around here."

Meredith nibbled her cookie so she wouldn't have to comment.

Stacey summed up the men in Hay City. "Too young, too old, too poor, too married. Slim pickings. One of these days, soon as I can afford to live on my own, I'm leaving. Now…" The woman leaned forward. "…tell me about California."

She did her best to entertain her host with descriptions of long stretches of beach, streets on end lined with stores and restaurants, blue skies, and warm winters. Stacey ate two more cookies, her jaws slowing as she listened in rapt attention. Meredith noticed the beauty mark on the woman's cheek had disappeared.

"I knew it," she crowed. "I ask everyone who's been there and they all say the same thing so the stories must be true. Sounds like heaven."

"I was starting to think the same thing about Hay City," Meredith said, surprising herself. "Big mountains, quiet nights. We get deer grazing in our backyard. I've never seen so much open space."

"But it's so borrrrring here." The other woman stretched out the word and rolled her eyes. "I suppose maybe not for you. You've been up in Twin Lakes with those poisoning deaths. What's the story up there, anyway?"

Meredith was instantly on alert. Stacey said "poisoning deaths." Plural. "The last I heard, they were waiting to exhume Jacob Burns' body."

Stacey waved a hand. "Done and done. Jonathan filled me in. He heard our sheriff talking on the phone. Once they knew they were looking for poison, they found it straight away."

Meredith wanted to jump off the sofa and race to Curtis's office. She wanted to…to do something, anything, but what?

"Guess the sheriff is asking all sorts of questions now," the other woman went on. "People up there are getting pretty upset."

"You know more than I do," she said flatly, more than a little annoyed Curtis didn't tell her this news. "Did you hear what kind of poison?"

Atticus wiggled off her lap to the floor and began exploring the room. She monitored him out of the corner of her eye, thinking the place was anything but childproof.

"Jonathan didn't find out," Stacey said with a laugh. "The sheriff caught him listening and kicked him out of the office."

There was a crash and Atticus squealed. Christmas

ornaments rolled across the floor, pouring out of a large plastic bag underneath a table.

She jumped up and grabbed the ornaments, checking for damage as she gathered them into a pile. "Oh, I'm sorry."

The other woman rose and grabbed another cookie before returning to her seat. "No biggie. I have lots of those old things. Just stuff them back in the sack."

Meredith finished cleaning up the mess and then settled back on the sofa, this time holding firm onto Atticus. She handed him another cookie, paused, and took another one for herself as well. While they all chewed, she wondered what else the other woman knew. Stacey eyed the cookie bag pointedly and she handed it over.

"Sooo..." This came through a mouthful of cookie. "What's the story on you and the sheriff?"

She reddened. "We're friends."

"Really good friends, I hear." Stacey's tone was matter-of-fact. "That's okay. When you and I are better acquainted, you'll tell me everything. We'll do this again soon, okay?"

She stood, feeling slightly nauseated. At some point, they'd eaten all dozen cookies.

They walked to the door. "I'm so glad we're going to be friends," Stacey pronounced. "At least until I get out to California."

They agreed to get together again and Meredith promised to buy more cookies, which elicited another crooked smile. During the slushy drive home, Meredith realized she enjoyed talking with the mixed-up Stacey. And she learned one key piece of news: Both men in Twin Falls died of poison.

****

Curtis didn't answer his phone and wasn't in his office all afternoon. Her mood darkened as she considered he was avoiding her but lifted when she realized he was probably in Twin Falls seeking evidence. As she tucked Jamie into bed that night, her daughter suddenly sat up. "I have an important question to ask."

Meredith sat back, waiting.

"Can I have an inner net for Christmas? Karin has one. So does Rio. Everyone in my class does."

She smiled. "What do you know about the internet?"

"If you have one, you can watch movies all the time and learn a bunch of stuff. Karin says all the books in the world are in one. But I don't think so." Her daughter sounded doubtful. "It would have to be bigger than our whole house."

Meredith didn't know how to describe the internet so a five-year-old would understand so she didn't attempt it. "We'll try." She gave Jamie a hug. "You know I'm trying really hard, right?"

"Mommy, are we poor?"

She gazed down at her daughter, her heart twisting. When she was a child, at times homeless, the question never occurred to her. The teasing over her thrift store clothes and poor kids' lunch didn't start until middle school.

"I suppose to some people we are. To people with more than us, we're poor. There are lots of people who have much, much less. To them, we're rich."

"Rio doesn't have any rabbits," Jamie said, considering. "Or a little brother. We have two houses too; our big house and our trailer."

Meredith smiled. Two houses. She'd never considered their state of affairs that way. "We have lots, don't we?"

The girl scooted under her blankets, laying back down. "Rio's dad says he can have one of Grendel's babies."

She settled the blankets around Jamie and smoothed her curly hair. Her daughter closed her eyes. The world was so simple when you were young. The older you got, the more complicated things were. At least another one of those blasted rabbits was spoken for. *Two rabbits gone. Three to go.*

Happy birthday to me.

Chapter Twenty

Meredith broke a path in the drifts between the trailer and the front door to the house and shed. That night, the depths grew alarmingly and Meredith shoveled and stomped down the path once again. Her fear was Atticus or Jamie would trudge off the path and fall through into a soft spot. To prevent this, she spent time packing down the sides of the trail into solid walls, now too high for her children to easily scale.

The rumble of the snow plow made her turn and wave. Without the road and driveway plowed, they'd be stuck for sure. She'd been meaning to ask someone why her road was plowed in such a strange serpentine manner, zig-zagged from her driveway to the main highway. The only reason she could fathom was it was meant to slow traffic to avoid accidents.

Deli boy. Her eyes widened as she saw him in the driver's seat, frowning as he steered one direction and then the other, weaving the plow toward her. The crazy plowing pattern wasn't a favor, it was a curse.

"Hey!" she shouted out once, and then realized he wouldn't be able to hear her over the powerful engine. Even if he could, it was unlikely anything would change. Not even anticipation of a baby bunny softened his evil heart.

Deli boy kept his gaze on the road and the plow's controls, even as Meredith stood in her doorway. He pushed snow out of her driveway and turned the machine around and back down the serpentine path.

Meredith stomped back into the trailer to get Jamie off to school and herself to work.

****

The hardware store was quiet. A rare customer came in to buy snow shovels and ice melt and, most days, the mailman was her only visitor. The official start of winter was still a couple of weeks away, but no one spoke of this as autumn any longer. An Idaho winter ate at the edges of autumn and spring, lengthening its intemperate season by at least another month on each end. Weather slowed deliveries and the two-lane highway running past Hay City saw few vehicles pass by. She felt guilty at taking a paycheck for doing so much nothing.

Boots stamping at the entry of the hardware store startled Meredith from her spot on the floor, where she helped Atticus stack blocks. A man stood at the door, pants tucked into heavy work boots and a cap covering his ears. "Hey, where do you want it?"

She scrambled to her feet. Crusty didn't tell her to expect anything or anyone. This was the most excitement there'd been at the hardware store in weeks. Through the open door behind the man, she could see an unmarked delivery truck idling in the parking lot. "What is it?"

"Hell if I know. Boxes. Twenty-five of them." He gave the store a critical eye. "They ain't gonna fit."

Meredith hesitated only for a moment. The hardware store was her responsibility. It wasn't as though her boss possessed a system for arranging the store anyway. Items were shoved into every corner and up to the ceiling. "Just carry them all in; we'll find a place for them."

He shrugged and the door banged close. Twenty-five boxes full of things to shelve sounded like heaven after months of little to do except sit and stare at the cluttered aisles. Crusty left her in charge, calling earlier and, with glee in his tone, told her he'd slept in and would arrive late. In the background, Honey voice hummed a tune.

The door thumped open and the deliveryman was back, wheeling a dolly piled high with boxes. Meredith rushed forward and pointed down one aisle. "Um, over there. At the back."

The boxes, dented in places, torn in others, appeared as though they'd been used for other products in several previous shipments. More boxes followed. They filled the back of the store, a couple containers small as a shoebox, and a half dozen in old refrigerator boxes. A trail of wet footprints and dolly tracks led through the store, from the door down the aisles.

The last box, a wooden crate, was the biggest of all and accompanied into the store with grunts and cursing. The oversized crate was scooted off the dolly by the door with a scowl. Breathing heavily, the man shoved a clipboard in Meredith's face. "Sign here."

Her hand trembled as she signed, nervous now she'd allowed the motley assortment into Crusty's domain, turning his hardware store into a used-goods warehouse. The deliveryman strode toward the exit. "What's in all these?" she called toward him.

He didn't turn. "You ordered them, lady." The door slammed behind him.

Meredith gazed dejectedly at the old boxes, sure

now there could be nothing exciting inside. It struck her the delivery could have been meant for someone else, for how could the contents possibly fit inside the store? What if she'd accepted delivery of old clothes and broken TVs headed for a thrift shop? She wished now she'd opened a couple while the truck was still there.

Hands on hips, she made the decision to open a box or two. "There's only one way to find out," she muttered. Best case, she could start shelving some of the goods. Worst case, she could reseal the boxes and wait for her boss to arrive.

Armed with a box cutter, she started with the smallest box, surprisingly heavy for its size. Nested inside was cabinet hardware, beautiful brushed nickel handles and knobs. It was a strange order to make in the middle of winter, dragging a truck out along dangerous roads to a lonely outpost. Meredith sliced the box cutter down the side of one refrigerator box and nearly choked. The box was full of insulation, the type sandwiched between walls of houses and in attics, secured in tight rolls of plastic wrap. The items appeared to be a special order for someone working on their house, a project for the coming icy months. Either that or Crusty was stocking up early for a spring sale.

She went next to the enormous crate left by the door, first testing its substantial weight, and then tried to peek between the wooden slats. Before she could stop herself, Meredith grabbed a hammer in her hands and was tugging at one of the slats.

"Holy cow, he's done it now."

The hardware store was a jumble of goods, but this had to be a first. Inside the box was a full-sized jetted bathtub. There was no way a bathtub was going to fit in one of the hardware store's aisles, let alone on one of the shelves. Perhaps the tub would sit where it was by the door as a showcase item, a conversation piece for customers as they entered.

"Mama." Atticus stood at her side. "Ah-ble."

Meredith set the hammer on top of the box and picked up her toddler. "Ready for some apples? Please?"

"Pease."

She hugged him and returned to the counter where a snack bag was packed with apple slices, juice, and peanut butter sandwiches. A thud on the other side of the wall made her aware of Crusty's arrival in the bar, finally roused from Honey's cozy home. Apples and juice in hand, she settled Atticus in the playpen to enjoy his snack.

Meredith never ventured into the bar, having an aversion to drink and drinking. Having grown up with an alcoholic mother, she worried about having the propensity to follow a similar fate. It was easier to stay away and never find out. The morning's strange shipment of goods was so unusual, however, she overcame her qualms and opened the connecting door into the bar and peered inside.

"Happy days are here again," her boss burst out upon seeing her. "Oh, happy, happy days."

Meredith stepped into the darkened room. A long wooden bar dominated the space, its top smooth and worn by the hands of its many customers. Sweet and malty odors were mixed with stale cigarettes. Peanut shells littered corners of the floor, speaking to Crusty's usual style of housekeeping.

"Ever have a day when everything goes right?" He

waved her closer to the bar where he was putting glasses away. "When even your toes are sitting up and taking notice?"

Meredith nodded even though she didn't know what he was talking about. It was a good time to let him know about the shipment; if the delivery was a mistake, her boss was in too good a mood to fire her.

"I'm thinking about getting one of those rabbits of Jamie's," he said as he gazed around the room. "Kind of a mascot sort of thing. Let him roam around the bar, live here full time. I hear they can be house-trained, mostly."

She doubted this was a good idea, a rabbit hopping below unsteady feet, likely being fed everything from beef jerky to pork rinds. This was her boss, though, and the rabbits were growing fast. It meant three down, two to go. Changing the subject, she said, "Your beard's nice today."

He stroked the gray hair covering his neck and dipping to mid-chest. "Honey gave me a trim last night. I'll tell you what, cutting a few hairs didn't diminish this grizzled Samson's powers."

"Delivery," Meredith sputtered, not wanting to hear any more along those lines. "Big delivery next store."

"Ah." he said. "Aha. He showed up this morning, did he?" Crusty reddened then just as quick recovered. "Best take a look." He was at the hardware store door in an instant, his long legs covering the distance in a few long strides, ponytail swishing behind. "Hey captain," he greeted Atticus, and gave a low whistle as he took in the multitude of boxes crowding the store. "Yup. Yessiree. Quite a sight."

"There's a bathtub in the one by the door," Meredith offered, hoping he'd explain. "I took a peek." She added, joking, "It's like you ordered a whole house."

Crusty went still. There was no way, of course, he'd ordered an entire house. No one would place such an order through a small hardware store. No one would pack items in used refrigerator boxes and ship them through the snow. The timing was striking. Only one person was talking about building a house in this small town.

"Crusty?" Her voice hardened. "Where'd all this come from? Who's it for?"

When he fidgeted, her suspicion was confirmed. "No," she said. "Send the stuff back."

He looked miserable but she felt no guilt at ruining his perfect day. He was head over heels with the wrong woman; a conniving, meddling woman who wanted to build her a new house. She weighed the possibility the man knew the depths of Honey's character, the dark side of the sweet, convivial woman. Perhaps, though, her role in Brian's murder was innocent, a conversation rippling into something harsher than was meant to be.

He cleared his throat. "I can't. Anyway, it's not returnable."

"Crusty." Her voice rose and Atticus dropped his juice container in alarm. "I can't pay for this. Not even part of it. Why doesn't anyone listen?"

Atticus stood in the playpen, his face scrunched up in worry and ready to cry. "Mama."

Her boss spoke in a rush. "You don't need to think about all that. Honey's in charge and no one says no to her. It won't cost you a dime. I know people who know people who come across things. They owed me a favor."

Meredith studied the stained and battered boxes in suspicion. Her on-again, off-again friend had some explaining to do, as always. Curtis too, for he was certainly involved. And now Crusty was in on this crazy plan as well, mixing her up in some nefarious dealings with people who "come across things."

His tone was earnest, begging. "You have to let her do this."

"No. I don't."

"It's okay to let people help you, Meredith. Sometimes it's a favor to them." Her boss's eyes watered; he blinked twice and cleared his throat. "Makes them feel useful."

She didn't know what to say. It never occurred to her that in the act of accepting help from others she'd be doing them a favor in return. "This is an entire house," she whispered. "No one does this."

His face lit up, eyes twinkling. "It's why this is so exciting. No one ever gets a chance to do something like this. You've gotten the whole town talking; hell, the whole county. Neighbors who haven't spoken to each other in years are forming work crews and joining design committees. We haven't had this much excitement since an avalanche slid down the eastern mountain in '02, wiped out Bailey's onion shed and two prize bulls. Hay City could use this, Merry."

Crusty lifted his wild shaggy eyebrows and waited for her response. Even Atticus was quiet, gazing up into her face. In the preceding six months, she'd focused on people who didn't like her. How had she passed over all the people who were talking about doing a house-wrecking and house-raising for her in the spring? How had she not seen the welcoming smiles and waves of those willing to accept a stranger in their community? Meredith was so used to the harsh circumstances of her life, the positives faded into the background.

Sounds just like me, she thought.

"Anyway," he continued, "it's not the whole house. Just a few odds and ends."

"Why does Honey do so much for me?" Meredith asked. "I don't understand."

He gave a soft chuckle and then turned serious. "She sees herself in you. No one helped her when she needed help the most. This community turned a blind eye during her first marriage, even while her husband was beating her half to death. Honey's a survivor and so are you. You're both tough women; pretty similar, actually."

This was an alarming idea, that she was like Honey. There were wonderful parts to her friend. She was warm, neighborly, and capable. There were also some unpleasant attributes: meddling and gossipy for a start. Meredith didn't want to consider she was a mini-Honey in the making.

"Don't I have any say in this?" There was a hint of concession in her tone, surprising even to herself. It was impossible to accept so much. Impossible.

Crusty gave her an appraising look. "Sometimes you have to make a choice whether you're part of a place or not. Some people never get the option. Choice is the gift, not the house. Don't take this for granted."

Meredith regarded the containers, an avalanche of ill-gotten gains, in the light of ambiguity in her life. Love and hate, friendship and conflict; even villainy

and virtue, all rolled up together. Could she choose?
****

Puzzles, books, games, and budgeting consumed the evening as a fresh storm rocked the small trailer, with still no news from Curtis for the second straight day. Her irritation with him grew. A hammering at the door startled her so bad the breath caught in her throat.

Curtis stood at the door, the frigid wind blowing in from behind him and filling the trailer with icy daggers. "I was ordered to pick you up and take you to Honey's for cheese pie."

"Come in. Hurry." Meredith opened the door wider and he stepped inside the trailer and glanced around. At the dining table, Jamie worked a puzzle of the United States. Atticus sat on his bunk with a book and a bag of fish shaped crackers.

"Hi, Sheriff," Jamie said without looking up. "I'm busy."

"I see. Where's Idaho?"

Jamie jabbed her finger down in an Idaho-shaped gap. "Somebody took it. But it'd go right here."

"Cheese pie?" Meredith asked. He was freshly shaven and smelled of soap and mint, a nick on his throat still covered with a dab of tissue. She bit her lip, torn between crying "Tell me what's going on," and being angry he hadn't called her. She wanted to touch his face, his arms, his chest. She wondered if he'd missed her as much.

He faced her, his expression neutral. "Goat cheese pie. That's what Honey said. I'm supposed to get you over there."

"Curtis," she started. "I tried calling you."

"I've been tied up with the medical examiner and

the doctor and taking calls from most of Twin Lakes' population," he said with a grimace. "Yesterday, they tried to get the backhoe down the mountain and it slid over the edge. Almost flipped over the fellow hauling it, as well. The guy's uncle is a state senator, who called me to ask whose stupid idea it was to haul heavy equipment into back country this time of year."

Meredith's mouth rounded into an "oh," and Jamie stared as his voice grew tenser. Atticus toddled over to Curtis and hugged his leg. He glanced down and patted the boy's head. A rabbit darted past their feet and Meredith scrambled to grab it. She caught the critter by a hind leg and picked it up. "This guy's been on the run since last night." She set it in the cage and latched the door. "Jamie keeps letting them out."

"They don't want to be in a cage," her daughter complained.

Curtis raised his eyebrows at her. "Meredith? I would have called, but it's been crazy. And Brooke…"

She darted him a warning glance. Brooke was the school principal and, whatever was happening, she couldn't discuss the woman in front of her daughter. "Catch me up later," she said quickly and grabbed for their coats, deciding going was easier than staying. "Goat cheese pie is from goat's milk, not from the goat. Let's bundle up and get going."

"I'm not eating a cheese goat," Jamie protested.

"No." Atticus said, sounding happy to add his opinion. "No go."

"Sometimes we have to do things…" Meredith started, and her daughter finished the sentence along with her, "we don't want to do."

She glanced around her trailer, so snug and warm,

and didn't want to leave. The shortened days made her want to do nothing except curl up with a cup of tea and a big book, long enough to last the winter. But somehow Honey, the mastermind of Brian's murder and the upcoming destruction of her house, always got her way.

If Honey wanted them to eat goat cheese pie in a blizzard, they'd eat goat cheese pie. It gave her an opportunity to snatch a moment away from her kids, so she could hear what was happening in Twin Lakes.

****

Crusty was in the kitchen, an apron tied around his waist, the ties barely reaching around the back. He did a little dance and curtsy when they entered, making Jamie laugh and Meredith crack a smile despite herself. Curtis gave him a short nod and headed to the living room to warm his hands by the fire.

Honey appeared, wearing a matching apron. "People do cozy a house up. Isn't this nice, having everyone together?"

No one answered as a gusting wind blew ice pellets against the house, rattling the windows. Honey beckoned them to sit near the fire. Meredith glanced at her and quickly averted her gaze. "Crusty and I'll serve up the pie. You just sit and be comfy."

Jamie glanced at the door, the edges of her mouth turning down. "Honey, is the wind going to blow your house down?"

Honey gave her lively laugh. "It wouldn't dare," she said. "The wind can huff and puff all it wants."

Curtis touched Meredith's elbow and nodded toward the couch by the fireplace. She settled in next to him, thankful to have him at her side. Jamie and Atticus sat cross-legged on the floor near the fireplace.

"Accidental or murder?" Meredith mumbled out of one side of her mouth toward Curtis.

He gave a small shake of his head as Crusty carried in the plates, wedges of something white on top. Meredith accepted hers with trepidation and didn't mind waiting for others to be served. She met Curtis's eye and they smiled in mutual understanding, knowing there was no choice but to eat everything on their plates, down to the last crumb. His gaze held hers for a moment and Meredith's heart thudded.

Honey's tone was cheerful. "You're all my guinea pigs. I added a little extra sugar to counter the tang of goat, and I think it works fine."

Crusty stared at his plate with something akin to alarm. He sat down, took a deep breath, and swallowed his pie in two leviathan bites. He nodded at the rest of them to do the same. "Delicious. I'll take another piece." Crusty returned to the kitchen for seconds before anyone else took a single bite.

Honey beamed and her gaze swept the room, triumphant.

Jamie looked up at her with a solemn expression. "I don't like cheese pie."

Honey set a plate down in front of the girl, who glared at the white wedge of pie. "You've never tasted mine. Take a bite."

Meredith took a tentative bite, nibbling at the cheesy white substance. "It's cheesecake," she said.

Honey laughed. "I guess you could call it that. Cheesecake, cheese pie—all the same."

"It's yummy." Meredith dug in, and with that pronouncement, Curtis and Jamie started in on their slices too, finishing them quickly. Only Atticus refused his pie, thrusting the fork away each time Jamie tried to give him a bite. The five of them polished off the entire pie.

****

Meredith was trying to figure out how to get Curtis to herself for a few minutes away from everyone, when Honey asked, "How are things up the mountain? Getting everything cleared up?"

She tensed and bit her lip to keep herself from speaking out. She played with her fork, rearranging remnants of the graham cracker crust around on the plate.

Curtis kept a casual expression. "Nothing to worry about."

Honey leaned forward. "But poison, right?"

He glanced at Meredith, who studied her plate. "Poisonous mushrooms," he agreed, making Meredith startle at the news. She'd been right. "It appears both men ingested the same thing."

"Exactly what I've been trying to tell her," Crusty said in a congenial tone. "People have to die sometime, of something. Poison's as good a reason as any."

Honey scanned from Curtis' impassive expression to Meredith's stony face and gave up on getting any confidential information divulged. Jamie took leaps across the room, counting out loud how many hops it took to go from wall to wall. Atticus ran after her. The sound of sleet pelting the windows and roof made Meredith wonder if they'd get stuck on the way home. She stood suddenly, unable to wait one more moment.

"Curtis, can you help me with something?" she asked, wildly casting about for a reason to get him alone. "My, uh, thing broke."

Blushing, she headed down the hall, not glancing behind to see if he followed her into the bathroom. A half-second later, he was next to her. He shut the door and twisted the lock.

"Your thing?" he asked, a smile in his eyes and lips twitching. He clasped her into his arms and kissed her until she gasped for breath.

"Tell me what's going on," she whispered. "What about Brooke? Why haven't you called me?"

He didn't let go of her. "I don't want you involved in this. The medical examiner is going to list the deaths as accidental; there's nothing to show otherwise."

"But Jacob said..." she protested.

"He apparently didn't voice those concerns to anyone else. This is a dead end for me. Everyone I talked to only has good things to say about Brooke and they describe Jacob as being unbalanced. There's absolutely nothing to show any motive from anyone to kill an old priest. A medical examiner's report, the whole town vouching for Brooke's character. Half the town picks mushrooms in the fall. They agree it's easy to slip up if you don't pay attention."

Meredith deflated at the news. Her instincts led her astray, heightened by her own recent trauma. She wanted it to be murder, but everything spoke against this. One couldn't *choose* murder to be true; it either was or wasn't. The bright side was Jamie's principal wasn't a murderer after all. She could put this behind her and be comforted that her daughter would remain safe at school. All would be well.

He gave a weary sigh. "People up there aren't happy with you, or me. The accident with the equipment and all my questioning—Leona's starting a petition to get me recalled as sheriff."

She stared at him, horrified at the series of events she'd set into action. A mini-Honey meddling and disrupting other people's lives. Curtis's life aspiration was to be like his grandfather, who was trusted and respected during a long career as sheriff of High County. "Recalled? Oh no. They can't possibly."

"People out here tend to circle the wagons when one of their own is threatened," he said. "If there's any retaliation, I'll deal with it, not you or Jamie. No target shooting needed, okay?"

Meredith shook her head, sick over what she was hearing. "Curtis, I'm so sorry."

He took a lock of her hair between his fingers and rubbed it thoughtfully. "I'm not sorry. It was the right thing to do. Anyway, a recall is likely to blow over by the time the snow melts."

There was a tap on the door. "If you've gotten your 'thing' fixed, come have some tea," Honey called through the door.

Meredith had an image of Honey standing outside, her ear pressed to the door, trying to listen in. "Just about done," she called back.

"Not quite," Curtis said, and drew her close again.

****

"So, what are you doing about separating out those rabbits of yours?" Honey asked when they returned to the living room.

Meredith stared straight at her for the first time since walking in the door. Honey met her eye calmly. It was impressive how confident the woman was, how she plowed ahead not caring how she disrupted lives. *I'm not like her,* she swore to herself. "You mean giving them away?"

Honey shook her head, a serious expression on her face. "Dearie, they need to be separated. Little boys from little girls. They multiply."

Meredith stared at her in horror. There was limited space in the trailer for just one cage, let alone two or more. Already, the cramped living quarters had taken on a distinct odor of a den of rabbits.

Honey smiled at her sweetly. "You'd best transfer them here so I can put them out in my barn. They'll be warm and dry until homes are found."

Meredith didn't want to accept but was more afraid of the growing rabbits breeding. "They're Jamie's," she said weakly. "She might not like moving them."

Her daughter started rolling somersaults down the hall, chased by a squealing Atticus.

"Let her stomp around a bit, blow off some steam," Honey said. "She'll be fine once she sees how happy they are hanging out with the chickens. In any case, I wanted to wish you a belated happy birthday."

"Thank you," Meredith answered quietly. "How'd you know? How does everyone know?"

"Jonathan. He knows a lot of things, spending time in the city office with all those records."

Curtis sat up straight, his jaw tense. "He doesn't work for the city. He shouldn't be there at all, snooping around."

Honey shrugged. "Talk to the mayor. Jonathan's his godson."

Meredith recalled the previous spring when Curtis made a copy of her driver's license after he took her fingerprints. "He's peeking at more than just city records," she noted, giving Curtis a pointed look. His face grew dark as the realization dawned on him.

Honey's tone was airy. "It takes a while to settle in to country living. Eveything's a little more relaxed out here. I imagine it's different than what you're used to."

"I'll see to Jonathan, don't you worry," Curtis broke in. "I've had enough of his coming and going, regardless of his relations. If he's getting into my files…"

Honey broke in smoothly. "There isn't one person on the face of the earth that isn't unscrupulous in one way or another. Anyway, he's not a bad fellow, just likes to feel needed. Probably his way of getting to know you. He likes the ladies."

Curtis shifted in his seat, moving slightly closer to Meredith. Heat from his thigh burned into hers. A fresh gust of wind sent a high-pitched squeal around the chimney. Atticus toddled over to Meredith and laid his head against her, his forehead sweaty with activity.

"We need to go," she said, picking Atticus up. He immediately dropped his head against her shoulder and stuck a thumb in his mouth. They crowded around the entry, preparing themselves to leave the warmth of shelter for an ice storm.

"We never got around to plans for your house," Honey cried out in disappointment.

Meredith lifted her chin. "There are no plans, other than some repair work in the spring."

Curtis helped Meredith on with her coat, lifting her hair off her neck to settle the coat on her shoulders. His fingers brushed her skin, sending a tingling down her spine. She ducked her head, afraid to look up at him and expose the yearning in her eyes for all to see.

"I won't say another word about it," Honey promised, eyes crinkling at the corners, and then echoed the refrain Meredith was becoming familiar with: "Not until the snow melts."

Meredith bit back her instinctive reply. Crusty's words about Honey returned to her, how no one helped her back when she needed help the most. Honey knew what it was like to have a bad husband, to have her home yanked out from under her and she'd fought her way back. Being given a choice is a gift, her boss had said. Meredith's resolve weakened.

"Thank you for the pie," was all she ended up saying as they walked out the door.

Chapter Twenty-One

The storm left the long valley buried in an expanse of alabaster. Icicles dripped like shards from the eaves, and the tall pine behind Meredith's house accumulated pillows of white on its branches. A winter's gloom settled in with low clouds hanging over the tops of the surrounding peaks while dawn awakened late and dim.

There would be no school and no leaving the home front on this day. Meredith checked on the growing rabbits, their hutch tucked under the dining table, grateful they would soon be moving to Honey's barn. Her anger toward Honey had morphed into a deep, hopeless frustration; the woman was unstoppable. Yet there was something so sweet and genuine about her as well, it was impossible to want to stop her either. In any case, getting the rabbits out of the trailer was an offer Meredith wasn't about to refuse.

She tugged on her boots, heaved on her coat and geared up for the task of shoveling a pathway to the house. Even though they possessed everything they needed in the trailer, Meredith routinely checked the house for further damage. There was no stopping the erosion of the roof in Jamie's bedroom; once started, it continued to cave in piece by piece. After hauling her daughter's furniture and belongings into the hallway, Meredith avoided the room altogether.

The latest concern was a growing stain in the

corner of the kitchen ceiling. It was as if, once started, the rotting away of her home accelerated its pace. Against her will, the case seemed to be building toward knocking the house down and starting over. Room by room, piece by piece, this one was disintegrating. All she could do was watch it happen, put buckets under any new drips and lock the door again behind her.

Except for days like today, when her kids needed space to run unhindered by coats, and she needed a change of scenery. Poisonous mushrooms…just as she predicted…were at the root of the deaths in Twin Lakes. For the first night in a week, Brian didn't appear in her dreams. It was as if being right about something banished his critical voice.

The first step out the trailer's door sunk her thigh high into the drifts. Her house appeared to be miles away, ten thousand shovels full of snow or more in the distance. She debated whether they really needed to access the house at all. The place could moulder and sink into the ground for all she cared. But staying cooped inside and stuck with two energetic children wasn't an option. They all would need more space to roam. She gripped the shovel and dug in.

Over the past months, muscles had toned on her already lean frame. Walking, gardening, and fixing up the house took a different type of strength than what was needed when she was an apartment dweller. Being a homeowner, especially of a fixer-upper, was a daily workout all its own. Shoveling snow, however, was on a whole new level. Her arms and back ached from lifting and twisting, but she soldiered on. A third of the way to the house, Meredith stopped and dropped the shovel.

She stripped off her thin gloves and considered the blisters rubbed open on her palms. Around her was the deepest silence she'd ever experienced, all sounds muted by the snow below and clouds above. Everything was still except a narrow column of smoke from a distant chimney. She marched back to the trailer. "Everyone out," she ordered.

Bundled into their winter gear, just their round faces showing, Jamie and Atticus spilled out of the trailer armed with hand shovels. Meredith wielded her own shovel again and angled a thin line straight for the house. She tasked her children with widening the path behind her.

Is it terrible to make a toddler shovel snow? Or is this what people called character building?

In truth, Atticus didn't help much with his plastic shovel and pail, meant more for playtime at the beach than child labor. He squatted and dug a hole for awhile. Jamie, though, chopped and hacked away.

"Mom, phone."

Meredith stopped and listened. Across the yard, her old-fashioned land line phone rang, its long spiral cord tethering the handset to a wall inside the house. "They'll have to wait until we're dug out."

The phone rang on for another minute before the ringing stopped. Few people called since she knew only a handful of people, so the call was probably from a salesman. It couldn't be Curtis, Honey or Crusty since they knew she stayed nights in the trailer. The more she considered it, though, the more she worried. What if one of her friends was hurt from the powerful overnight storm? What if they were checking on her and she wasn't answering?

"Mom, phone again."

"I hear it." Meredith stopped to rest, the jangling of the phone cutting into her nerves. There was nothing like an unanswered phone to build anxiety. She judged clearing the span to the house would take them another half hour and her arms were rebelling. A series of powerful running leaps could have carried her there, but traversing the deep drifts would have soaked her pants. Besides, she was too tired to leap. "Whoever it is will have to wait."

She sat down on the flat scoop of her snow shovel and took deep breaths. Jamie continued to shovel, undaunted by the fact the drifts reached her waist. Meredith pondered her daughter's stouthearted energy and why someone would call on this snowy morning.

"I'm going back to the trailer for a minute," she finally decided. "Be right back."

Three living people had the number for her emergency cell phone, the pre-paid phone she used only in a crisis. They were her entire circle of friends. Honey, Crusty and Curtis, even if they got on her nerves from time to time, they were the best friends she'd ever known. Even if, on occasion, she swore she never wanted to see them again. One thing was for certain: if she was ever in trouble, these were friends who would never let her down. If something important arose, they would try her cell phone as well.

Just as Meredith touched the handle on the trailer, her cell phone rang from the charger inside. She yanked open the door and lunged for her phone. "What happened?"

It was Curtis, sounding anxious. "Meredith."

A car accident. A house fire. Curtis injured and in

the hospital. Images flashed through her mind. "What is it? Are you okay?"

"I'm fine. Where are you? Why haven't you been answering your phone? Is everyone okay over there?"

"We're out shoveling, halfway between the house and trailer."

She heard him exhale a breath. "I was worried. When you didn't answer. No one answered."

"We're okay." There was a pause. "Curtis?"

His voice sounded anguished. "There's been another poisoning in Twin Lakes."

Meredith gasped. This one couldn't be accidental, not after the community was warned about mixing up their mushrooms. A new poisoning would be deliberate. Meredith had no doubt who was behind this latest one. "Who did she poison this time? Who else did she kill?"

"Carolyn. Caro. She was found unconscious in a puddle of vomit. She's in the hospital but isn't expected to make it."

I knew it. I was right all along. Feeling victorious in the face of Caro's imminent death was terrible, but Meredith couldn't help it. The people of Twin Lakes protected their own and they'd circled their wagons around a murderer.

Curtis surprised her with an order. "You have to come with me."

"What? Where? The snow's too deep to go anywhere."

"I have a plow on my truck," he said. "We need to get to the hospital in Mountain Home to talk to Carolyn before…if she's still…if she can talk. She's the only one who can say for certain where the poison came from. Brooke…" Meredith heard him swallow. "Brooke is the link between all three. I need you there to be a second set of ears for me."

His distress and frustration were obvious. He'd been led by the rules of hard evidence and found nothing to pursue. He wanted to believe good of a very bad person and now someone else would die because of it. He wanted to do the right thing so badly that he ended up doing the wrong thing. This could be the event to change him from believing in the good nature of people. Why had she ever wanted him to turn sour and suspicious? Her heart ached for him.

"Of course, I'll go."

****

Honey brightened upon seeing them and hearing there was another poisoning. "I'll watch the kids. You two go on and take care of business. You'll let me know all the details when you get back."

Meredith was amazed as always at the woman's cheerful attitude in the face of any calamity, seizing any opportunity to be at the forefront of gossip. She was equally amazed Curtis wanted her along on his trip to the hospital. His jaw was tight and gaze distant when he picked her up and he said little with her children in the truck.

Honey shooed Jamie and Atticus inside her house and walked onto her own freshly shoveled porch to see Meredith and Curtis on their way.

"Thank you for this." Meredith placed one hand on Curtis's arm as she turned to say goodbye to Honey.

Honey straightened her shoulders. "We take care of each other out here."

****

Caro was unconscious when they arrived at the

hospital, alone in the room except for the sound of beeping machines. Solution bags hung from poles stood guard next to her bed, dripping steady beats into chambers which led into the clear plastic tubes running into her arm. A tube snaked into her mouth and emitted a rhythmic hiss. Heavy bags weighed beneath her eyes and her skin had taken on a gray cast. The only sign she lived was the steady blip of the heart monitor.

Meredith stood at the door, and memories flooded her from when her mother died of alcohol poisoning all those years ago. It occurred to her that her mother would have been younger than Caro when she died and the thought depressed her. At the time, her mother seemed a million years old, her face sunken and lined, her body wasted to a skeleton's frame from years of drinking her daily meals. There'd been so much desperation packed into the hours her mother lingered in the space between life and death. When it was over, Meredith didn't feel the relief of a foregone conclusion; she was a child losing her mother and her only lifeline.

"Carolyn." Curtis spoke in a hushed voice. "Caro."

There was no response from the bed and no flicker of Caro's eyelids to indicate an awareness they were in the room.

A nurse appeared at Meredith's shoulder. "We're trying to locate next of kin."

Meredith glanced from the nurse to Caro's bed. "Is she going to…can she talk?"

The nurse eyed her. "Are you related?"

Curtis turned and pointed to the star pinned to his chest to announce his official status. Then his expression lightened. "Mary? Mary Marks?"

"Curtis Barnaby. I haven't seen you in forever. I

heard you ran for sheriff. Good for you. How're your parents and sister?"

He worked up a friendly smile for the nurse. "They're all fine. How about you?"

Meredith looked between them, annoyed by the idle chitchat over a dying woman's bed. Crucial business was at hand. "Excuse me. The woman lying in bed here, stuck full of tubes. Can she talk?"

Nurse Marks kept her gaze on Curtis. "Your associate? We have privacy laws about this kind of thing."

He gave a short nod, his expression growing somber once again. "My associate," he agreed.

The nurse turned her attention to Meredith. "She's in complete organ failure. We're trying to find next-of-kin." The nurse warmed up to her subject. "This type of poisonous mushroom, once it's well into the system, works quietly and fast. They air-lifted her here but it was much too late. The poison's destroyed her liver and now has progressed onto her other organs. There's no reversing the damage at this point. The next step is heart failure."

"She's…"

"…going to die." The nurse finished Meredith's sentence. "Soon."

Curtis' shoulders sagged. Meredith knew the news landed hard upon him—a third death in his county, on his watch.

Nurse Marks gestured down the corridor. "Her friends are in the chapel. You might want to talk to them."

"Her friends?" Meredith asked.

"Well, a friend and her priest."

Meredith's eyes widened. The murderess was in the hospital.

Curtis edged to her side and gripped her by one elbow, squeezing lightly as though to warn her not to say anything more. "Say hello to your family for me," he said quickly to Nurse Marks, as they hurried from the room.

Father Michael emerged from the chapel as they approached. His expression grave, he startled when he saw them and then stood firmly in front of the door. "She's praying for her friend. Please respect her time."

Meredith made a scoffing noise. "Her friend?"

"I'm afraid I have to insist this time." Curtis said gravely.

Father Michael's eyes misted. "I beg you. Please leave her alone. She's a good person, faultless in all this…this mess. No sin that isn't being punished." He bit his lip and abruptly strode away from them.

Meredith and Curtis traded glances. She dashed after the priest and Curtis followed. "You know something." It was just short of an accusation.

He stopped and his shoulders slumped. "I don't know why all this happened. Or why God would let such a good woman suffer."

Meredith had a feeling he wasn't talking about Caro. "You have to tell us what you know. What did Brooke do?"

His eyebrows raised and he let out a huff. "Brooke did nothing. I told you she's faultless. I can't say more. Confession is a sacrament." He glanced down the corridor toward Caro's room.

Meredith squared her shoulders. Now was the time to shake out the truth. Caro, Brooke, and Father

Michael—there was some sort of strange threesome here she didn't understand, a relationship going beyond one of friendship and prayer.

"I'll tell you what happened then," Meredith said, her voice steady and sure. "Brooke poisoned her husband because she was tired of him. She poisoned Father Karl too because…because…for some reason. Then Caro found out, so Brooke poisoned her, too."

Curtis shot her a warning look. "Meredith…"

Father Michael stared at her in horror. "Absolutely not. Absolutely not. That's not what happened at all."

Brooke's soft voice floated to them from the door of the chapel where she'd just emerged. "I'll tell them. What difference does it make now?"

They swung around as one and stared at her. Even disheveled, Brooke was lovely. Her dark hair framed her heart-shaped face and swept against her shoulders. It was clear she'd dressed hurriedly, sliding on a pair of jeans accentuating her curvy figure, topped by an oversized T-shirt that must have been Jacob's. The sight infuriated Meredith. How dare she wear her dead husband's clothes. What a cold-hearted killer Brooke must be.

"Yes," Meredith demanded. "Tell us everything."

Father Michael shook his head, but the motion wasn't a refusal. It was a sad movement, a defeat.

Brooke lifted her gaze to the priest, and something unsaid passed between them. "Caro told me what she confessed to you. I'm not breaking a sacrament by telling."

She turned to Curtis, ignoring Meredith. "Caro and I grew up together. We've always been best friends. When we were teenagers, I helped her through her mother's death and she helped me through acne and dating. When we grew up, I helped her through a divorce and she's been with me through..." Brooke hesitated only slightly. "...Jacob's instability."

Father Michael put a comforting hand on Brooke's shoulder.

"Caro would cook for us during the week," she continued. "Jacob's cooking was terrible; too much salt or not enough, raw or overcooked. He couldn't concentrate on recipes anymore so he'd put strange things in our meals, like strawberry jam on fish and hot pepper in pancakes." She gazed down the corridor toward Caro's room. "Caro, though, is wonderful in the kitchen. She offered to help and would make enough for several meals and we'd freeze individual meals so I'd have them when I got home from work late."

She paused and her voice dropped to nearly a whisper. "It was the soup. I didn't know or I wouldn't have taken it to the church, for Father Karl to have at Thanksgiving. I knew he'd be alone and I wanted him to have something. It was the soup." Brooke gave a dry-eyed sob. "I didn't know."

Curtis spoke gently. "You're saying Caro put something in the soup?"

"It was an accident. I'm sure of it." The words burst from Brooke and she looked up, defying Curtis to disagree. She gave Meredith an angry glance. "Caro told me it was an accident. She picked some mushrooms on a hike and put them in the soup she made for us. Jacob ate the soup that Saturday night when I was late coming home from a shopping trip in Boise. After he died, I didn't eat much at all and the soup just sat in the freezer. So, I took some to Father

Karl. After he died too, and poison was discovered, Caro figured out what happened. She was in torment afterward."

Meredith listened to the story with doubt. The story was possible; there was no one to vouch for Brooke's story. There was no one except her to confirm Caro was at fault. Except for a priest who was unwilling to talk. She glanced at Curtis and recognized sympathy in his face. *You're too good and trusting,* she thought.

"We only have your word on this," Meredith said. "Caro's dying and Father Michael's not talking." She glared at Father Michael who appeared deep in thought.

"I cannot break the holy sacrament of the confessional. I can tell you though…" he studied the floor tiles… "I've never known Brooke to tell a lie."

"Still sounds fishy to me," Meredith muttered.

"If the deaths of Jacob and Father Karl were accidental, as you say, then what happened to Caro?" Curtis asked.

Brooke didn't speak for a moment and Father Karl turned and walked down the hall. She waited until he was out of earshot. "Caro was devastated over what happened. Two people dead. One was my husband and the other her priest." Brooke glared at Meredith. "Then, people showed up at my door making accusations. Can you imagine how she felt?"

Meredith's mouth gaped at the accusation she somehow played a role in Caro's death. Brooke choked out her next words. "She went on a hike and picked more of those mushrooms. They found pieces in Caro's stomach when they pumped it."

Hospital monitors beeped and nurses' shoes pattered on the tiles. Curtis gazed down the hallway toward Father Michael with a frown. Meredith held her breath, her mind racing to pick apart Brooke's story. No witnesses, she realized. There was no one to back up Brooke's story except Father Michael.

Curtis touched Brooke's shoulder. "You should be with her now."

****

Caro died hours later. After a hurried conference call with the Twin Falls doctor and the High County coroner, Curtis agreed the death would be ruled a suicide. Meredith wasn't convinced. The deaths hinged on Brooke's hospital hallway testimony and Father Michael's support of her. Hadn't Jacob and Brooke been having marriage problems? Hadn't Jacob worried his wife wanted to kill him? Caro never woke up to confirm she purposely ingested the destroying angels. It rankled her Brooke slipped in a veiled accusation of her own, suggesting Meredith was partially at fault for Caro's death.

She sat next to Curtis on a second chair they'd set onto his back deck, snow cleared away, a blanket over their laps and ski caps settled over their ears. Their hands were bare of gloves despite the sub-freezing temperature, but Meredith didn't feel the chill. Curtis laced his fingers through hers and drew them up to his lips. He kissed her fingertips before lowering their interlaced hands again. Meredith's heart raced at the touch.

Curtis gazed out over the yard where Jamie ferried Atticus along on a sled, shouting out she was a sled dog. "My grandfather always said the job of sheriff was twofold: to keep people safe and to make them feel safe."

Meredith waited. Three people were dead; they hadn't been safe at all.

"He said if people feel safe, a sheriff has a job for life," he added, his voice low.

She squeezed his hand, unable to believe Curtis would knowingly let a murderer go free in order to keep the illusion there was no crime in his county. But she heard him convincing himself he made the right decision.

"Murder's the last thing I want to consider when someone dies," he said, his voice coming stronger now. "Most people are good, hard-working, and generous."

Atticus tumbled off the sled and Jamie stopped to help him up. The two of them started barking in unison and ran back and forth across the snow.

"Sometimes they do. Commit murder," Meredith said, thinking of Brian.

Curtis gave her hand a gentle squeeze in return, just enough so she knew he was aware of her thoughts. She gazed at him and was glad he was such a kind-hearted person, even if a murderess would go free. Life was complicated and murky, full of half-truths and uncomfortable decisions.

Being given a choice is the gift, she reminded herself. In some instances, choosing was difficult; where to live or whether someone was a true friend, or even between a murder and an accident.

Meredith knew one thing though: If she needed to make a choice of who to trust in the end, she'd choose Curtis.

Chapter Twenty-Two

The buzz about the three poisoning deaths in Twin Lakes lasted exactly ten days. Then Stacey was fired from her job as city clerk. Down in the long valley, this was even bigger news. Getting fired took formidable negligence in this tiny, far-flung town, where new employees were so difficult to find. After a year of spotty attendance and sending her snooping brother to work in her place, Jonathan's sister was sent packing by the city council.

The news put deli-boy into more of a funk than usual. He'd been raised to a bit of local celebrity after the poisoning deaths since people learned he also ingested destroying angels and lived. His heroic recovery faded in comparison to such fresh controversy closer to home. Proximity always multiplied interest. Leona's bitter attempt for a recall petition of Curtis failed to get enough signatures throughout the county. People were only interested in talking about the latest scandal.

Honey, of course, prodded Meredith to apply for Stacey's job. Meredith was stunned Honey would think she could fill such an important city role. "I'm not qualified in any way," she protested.

With everything going on, she'd only been back to visit Stacey once more, right after the woman was fired, and the two hours flew by. This time, the woman sported purple eyeliner and talked about losing her virginity in junior high school to her best friend. "He's a big shot in California now, making up stuff for the internet," she said. "I'm going to visit him some day. I bet he'd give me a job."

Stacey acted unconcerned about being fired, but Meredith wondered if the woman's attitude was just a show of bravado. There weren't many full-time jobs in Hay City and the surrounding towns.

Meredith turned her attention back to the present and to Honey. "I don't know why you think I can do these things. I suppose I don't even know what a city clerk does."

Her friend laughed. "Not much in Hay City. They'll probably just hire an assistant clerk position anyway to save money. They mostly need a warm body sitting at a desk. You'd have lots of time to learn the job."

"If I can get the job, that is."

Honey raised one high arching eyebrow. "Out here, dear, it's who you know. And you know me. You get your application in and let me handle the rest."

Meredith was doubtful, but desperately wanted the job. A full-time job would offer her family security and maybe even enable her to start saving a bit here and there. Hopefully, Stacey wouldn't hold it against her. She recollected Jonathan and his veiled threats with distaste and hoped he wouldn't automatically be awarded the position.

Honey waved that idea away. "Don't worry. Jonathan doesn't want a full-time job where he has to show up five days a week. Heavens, who does these days? Let me talk to the mayor; he's an old friend. I know the city council folk too. I'll put a word in."

Meredith didn't protest anymore. Trying to stop Honey was like stepping in front of a freight train.

****

"It's okay," Crusty said, though his downcast expression was in contrast to his words. "Although I've pretty much gotten used to you now."

Meredith gazed around the hardware store from her spot at the counter. There was only the rare customer who patronized the store, and then their purchases were usually paltry. Crusty didn't need her there at all. In the past, customers made their selection and then gone in the bar to pay, having a beer before they headed home again to finish their project.

"I don't have the job, just put in an application and thought you should know. I'm not leaving yet. It's a long shot, but this would be full time."

Her boss chuckled as though she were being foolish. "The mayor'll be here in a bit. I'll put in a word."

She smiled her gratitude. Having friends support her was a new occurrence in her life and this bolstered her determination to stay in Hay City. The downside to friends was they poked their noses into your life, an annoyance that would take some getting used to. Still, she would be heartbroken if she needed to get a job in another city and start all over somewhere else.

Then there was Curtis. Meredith's stomach clenched at the possibility of leaving him. Moving to Boise where there was a better chance to find a job able to support her and her kids would put them hours apart. Whatever was happening between them wouldn't survive such a separation.

She'd even started to consider letting him build a house for her, if that's what it took. Living in a borrowed trailer was a temporary situation, meant to get them through the winter, until something could be done with the house. Daily, the snow piled up on the roof, and the water damage was spreading, seeping down the walls and rotting the core. Come spring, either the house would have to be repaired or, more likely, fall down on its own.

"Morning, Merry." The postman stomped off his boots and hauled his mail sack to the counter. Because the hardware store doubled as the local post office, mail for the more far-flung homes was left there for citizens to collect. He unloaded his bag onto the counter. "Couple of important looking missives for you this morning."

Meredith smiled to herself. Patrick the postman enjoyed finding new words for the letters he delivered. Communiques, dispatches, epistles; her vocabulary regarding letters was growing. "If they're bills, take them away. I have plenty enough already."

"I can't do that," he said sternly. "This is the U.S. Mail. I'm required by law to make every effort to deliver each bulletin, whether junk mail or postcard."

There was no joking with the man when it came to the serious business of mail. "Of course. Just leave everything on the counter. I'll get it sorted from here."

The daily delivery was a godsend as the chore gave her at least ten minutes of work during her four-hour shift. Meredith would sort the delivery and tuck each household's mail into cubbies below the counter. Some people only showed up once a month for their mail, traveling in from their god-knows-where off-grid survivalist home and appearing ragged, rough, and barely surviving.

"Guess you've heard the news from Twin Lakes." The postman peeked at her out of the corner of his eye, satisfied by her puzzled expression. "Father Michael was shifted to a new parish in North Dakota. Two new priests in Twin Lakes already. Talk of the town. And there's more."

Meredith waited, letting the news wash over her. Patrick enjoyed his job of spreading county gossip just as much as he enjoyed delivering the mail. "Brooke Burns put her house up for sale, moving out. Not surprising, considering all she's been through. Her leaving is a loss for the community though. I always enjoy the lovely ladies of High County." Patrick gave Meredith a nod, letting her know he included her in the description.

She waited, frozen, somehow already knowing what he'd say next. Patrick chuckled and headed for the door. "She's going to North Dakota, too." He paused. "Guess they're sort of a couple, you know? Father Michael and Brooke. Too bad priests can't marry. They'd make a handsome twosome."

The door slammed behind him, punished by a whipping December wind. Meredith recalled her concerns over the strange threesome of Father Michael, Brooke, and Caro. What if it always was a twosome? What if there were three extraneous people staring over their shoulders: Caro, Jacob, and Father Karl? Every impulse told her to run to Curtis and tell him of this new development and share her fresh suspicions. It wasn't so far-fetched to believe an unsanctified love was a motive for murder.

She bit her lip, teetering between her suspicions and letting the subject go. I don't want Curtis to be like me, she thought, always believing the worst in people. Maybe it wasn't strange at all for a bereaved widow, one who recently lost her best friend, to follow the person best equipped to offer comfort.

Curtis would never believe this new theory of murder, anyway. He wanted to think the best in people. Certainly, if ever there were a good place to commit a murder, High County would be the spot, with a sheriff who took the presumption of innocence to a whole new level.

Crusty's words echoed in her head about needing to choose one's loyalties. Choice. A weighty gift to be given.

I'm sorry, Jacob, if I'm wrong, but I'm going to trust the sheriff.

Meredith forced her attention to the two letters addressed to her, nervous over their contents. Both were thin but ever since the postman set them on the counter, they had grown in her mind. She had an inkling of what was inside by their return addresses. First, she took care of the daily mail, tucking each letter in the rightful cubby, and glanced at her own letters from time to time.

The first was from the state college where she'd taken the online chemistry course. Inside there'd be her final grade. Meredith opened this one first and avoided the other envelope for the moment. She scanned the brief notice inside letting her know her grade was a B-minus. The so-so grade didn't bother her. There wasn't money for spring classes; college would have to wait a little longer. Someday, the timing would be right for a college career; for now, she'd roll with the punches.

Life is messy, she recalled her mother always saying; *it's all in how you handle it.* She folded the letter and tucked the plain white sheet back in the envelope. She held it just for a moment, glancing at the garbage can, before sliding the envelope into her handbag.

Meredith peered at the other letter on the counter. This one was in a white business-sized envelope with a return address from Fifteen Palms, Florida. She shivered. The grandmother she'd never met lived in Fifteen Palms.

Jamie and Atticus were occupied with a book on tape, using a real old-fashioned cassette machine operating on ribbon tape cassettes. Crusty presented a handful of cassettes to Jamie when they walked in the door that morning, saying he found them at the top of one of the back shelves. The cassettes contained nursery rhymes and fairy tales, and her children were captivated by the device all morning. Jamie kept stopping the machine, letting Atticus pop out the cassette and reinsert it. Her two children peered through the plastic window and where the tape spun round and round, mesmerized by the rotations. The machine was a godsend since school was on holiday break for three weeks, a horrifying amount of time for a single working mother living in a small trailer.

Fifteen Palms. The name evoked bad memories from the times as a child when she futilely sought her grandmother's help. No help ever arrived, even as Meredith's mother wasted away. What kind of woman would shun her daughter and granddaughter at a time of their greatest need?

Meredith picked up the letter and examined the

return address once more. Holt, Holt & Bailey Law Offices. The envelope was light, containing a single piece of paper. Even before she opened the envelope, Meredith knew her grandmother must be dead. There would be no meeting her now, the cold woman who threw her daughter out of her house without further consideration.

Brian would have ripped the envelope open in a flash, eager to hear of a long-overdue inheritance. Her grandmother was wealthy and her husband often fantasized aloud about her death and a possible inheritance to come. He spent millions in his mind, buying houses at the beach, fast cars, and annual tickets to the Super Bowl. Brian never stopped believing someday he would be a rich man, one way or another. Meredith edged a finger under the flap and peeled back the paper to uncover the letter inside. Heavy black type showed on creamy woven paper, expensive and imposing with the firm's logo at the top in bold script.

"Dear Mrs. Lowe," the letter read. *"It is my sad duty to inform you that your grandmother passed from this world a week ago. My firm has represented your grandmother's affairs for many decades and is now handling her estate.*

"I personally remember your mother and have fond memories of her as a child. I understand your mother has also passed on and I offer my sincere condolences to you."

She gasped softly at the mention of her mother and tears sprang to her eyes. She had no connection to anyone who knew her mother, and there'd been no one to share the depth of her loss when her mother died. The unexpected mention by someone who once knew her was both gratifying and painful. She wiped at her tears. The notice that her grandmother died left her cold inside; she'd never met the woman.

"I am writing to you now under your grandmother's instructions upon her death. You should know up front the bulk of her estate has been left toward building a new hospital wing in her name here in Fifteen Palms, Florida. Most of the remainder goes to various charities she supported over the years. She was a fine and generous woman."

Meredith's hand trembled with rage. Her grandmother was anything but generous to her own family. Apparently, the woman enjoyed being kind to strangers more than to her daughter and granddaughter. Now, a hospital wing would bear her name as a testament of generosity. Meredith's fingers itched to crumple the paper and throw it away. Only curiosity spurred her forward. There must be some reason the lawyer was writing to her other than letting her know her grandmother died.

"However, two items have been left for you and they are in the care of my firm. One is a small package your grandmother sealed before leaving in my possession. The other is a letter she requested I read to you in person and then destroy with you as a witness. Because of this unique request, I have to ask you to come see me at my office.

Ms. Lowe, this is a strange request made stranger because of your estranged relationship with my client. I understand the reluctance you may have to go to the trouble of travel for what will be a paltry inheritance. However, I have read the letter. It clarifies issues surrounding your parentage, although your mother may have shared her own skewed version of events."

Her vision blurred for a moment. *Your parentage.* Her grandmother knew her father's identity and perhaps why her mother never wanted them to meet. Her mother refused to tell her his name or anything about him other than to say she was better off not knowing him. Whatever terrible thing he did, wasn't it better to know? She read the last paragraph.

"Your grandmother was an impatient person, even in death. She instructed my firm to destroy this letter six weeks after her death if you do not appear. We certainly understand, however, if you would prefer to have this letter destroyed and the package mailed to your current address. In fact, in my opinion, this may be the most preferable option.

If you decide to come to Fifteen Palms, a small sum has been provided for your travel costs. Let my office know and the funds will be made available.

You have my condolences. Sincerely..."

The hand holding the letter lowered to her side and Meredith dropped it to the floor. She walked out the door and into a thick snowfall, the enormous flakes blanketing the gray sky and landscape. Icy pellets stung her face and blew into her eyes, and the biting cold took her breath away.

Florida, with a warm winter sun, couldn't have been farther away at this moment. Her wretched grandmother, indifferent to her in life, surely wouldn't solicit familial healing in death. There could be nothing good out of going to Florida.

Still. The letter would tell her who her father was, and perhaps what shattered her mother's life so completely. There was only so much ambiguity a person could handle.

Meredith wavered. She'd survived twenty-five years without a father and perhaps life was best left that way. Her mother refused to tell her who he was; wouldn't she be dishonoring her mother by learning his identity now? Choices.

She scooped up a handful of snow and squeezed tight, compacting the soft fluff into a solid sphere of ice, and hurled it across the parking lot.

If nothing else, she'd learned there was no escaping the past. Her disastrous marriage, baby Brian, Gemma; there was nothing to do except find a place for these things in her life and mind, and progress forward. A new confidence surged up in her. She knew now she was strong enough to handle the misfortunes and heartaches of her life. She could go to college, have a job, a house, and friends. She could choose to belong to this community, let them tear down her house and help Curtis build a new one.

If I wanted, I could do anything. I'm a woman with grit. No one's stopping me except me.

Jamie was at the door behind her, her tone scolding. "Mom. Get out of the cold."

Meredith turned around, her decision already made. She would face the past her mother couldn't; there was nothing so bad she couldn't survive it. The past year proved this to her. The lawyer's letter was dated December fifteenth. She had a month to get to Florida before he destroyed the letter and thus her last opportunity to learn about her father.

"Let's all get out of the cold," she called out through the storm, already anticipating the warmth of the Florida sun. "Do you think this hardware store might sell bathing suits?"

Jamie rolled her eyes, clearly thinking her mother had gone nuts.

Meredith laughed as the snow coated her face and hair.

A word about the author...

Julie Howard is the author of the Wild Crime series. She is a former journalist and editor who has covered topics ranging from crime to cowboy poetry. She has also published a number of short stories in several literary journals. She is a member of the Idaho Writers Guild and founder of the Boise chapter of Shut Up & Write. Learn more at juliemhoward.com.

Thank you for purchasing
this publication of The Wild Rose Press, Inc.
For other wonderful stories,
please visit our on-line bookstore at
www.thewildrosepress.com.

For questions or more information
contact us at
info@thewildrosepress.com.

The Wild Rose Press, Inc.
www.thewildrosepress.com

To visit with authors of
The Wild Rose Press, Inc.
join our yahoo loop at
http://groups.yahoo.com/group/thewildrosepress/